THE QUIET ROAD TO DEATH

Also by Sheila Radley

Death in the Morning
The Chief Inspector's Daughter
A Talent for Destruction

THE QUIET ROAD
TO DEATH

SHEILA RADLEY

Charles Scribner's Sons • New York

First United States edition
published by Charles Scribner's Sons 1984

Library of Congress Cataloging in Publication Data

Radley, Sheila.
    The quiet road to death.
    I. Title.
PR6068.A245Q5   1984   823'.914   83-23060
ISBN 0-684-18124-X

Printed in the United States of America.

For my sister Monica

I

14 September; a mellow autumn morning in north Suffolk. Mist hung about the countryside, waiting for the sun to make up its mind whether or not to break through.

Saturday, 6.30 a.m.; few people up, and fewer on the roads. The principal activity in Breckham Market was in the yard behind the main post office where gummy-eyed postmen, up since just after four and at work in the sorting office since five, were loading scarlet Royal Mail vans with the morning's deliveries.

One of the vans also carried a passenger, a recently appointed postman who had been sent out to learn the Ecclesby-Wickford route. Brian Finch was in his thirties: quiet, neatly bearded, his uniform meticulously pressed, shoes polished, cap straight. The warehouse where he had been employed as a dispatch clerk ever since leaving school had closed during the recession, and he had suffered several harrowing months of unemployment. He knew that he was extraordinarily lucky to have been selected from dozens of applicants for the postman's job, and he was nervously eager to learn all he could.

'You'll enjoy being on this route, as long as you're an animal lover,' said the driver of the van, Kenny Warminger, a large mop-haired young man who liked to demonstrate his four years' experience as a postman by no longer bothering to wear his uniform cap at all. Amused by his passenger's earnestness, he was unable to resist the temptation to tease him. 'There aren't more'n half a dozen dogs that'll bite to hurt.'

Finch, who disliked dogs, looked unhappy. He tightened his seat belt.

'The customers are mostly harmless, though,' said Warminger. 'Some'll grumble as though it's your fault when you deliver bills, and one woman'll hold you personally responsible if she doesn't get a letter from her daughter every Tuesday. But the only ones who are likely to make trouble for you are the Arrowsmiths.'

He had driven through the town centre, and out along the Saintsbury road. Now, still within the town boundary, he pulled off to the right and stopped on the recently cemented forecourt of a long two-story eighteenth-century brick building, with small barred windows set at close intervals. From behind the building rose the conical roof of a disused malt kiln. In the forecourt, a large new board displayed the name Arrowsmith MicroElectronics Ltd.

'If everybody had their rights,' said Warminger, 'we shouldn't have to deliver here. It's on one of the town routes. But the owner, Ross Arrowsmith – you know, the man who's made a fortune out of selling calculators and computers by mail order – reckoned he needed an earlier delivery. He made a fuss to the Head Postmaster, so we were lumbered with this stop on our way out to our own delivery area. And the problem is that there are a lot of Arrowsmiths on our route. Ross and his family live in the first village we deliver to, Ecclesby. Then there's an old Mrs Arrowsmith a mile further on, in Upper Wickford, and a Mr and Mrs Arrowsmith across the common from her in Nether Wickford. And it's the devil's own job not to mix all their mail up.'

Warminger took several big bundles of letters from the tray in the back of the van, where he had stacked all the mail in the right sequence for delivery.

'Look, there're at least a hundred letters here for this firm. You get so mesmerised by the name Arrowsmith when you're sorting the incoming mail that it's not surprising if you sometimes slip in a letter for one of the other Arrowsmiths by mistake. And if it's addressed to the woman at Nether Wickford who keeps changing the colour of her hair, you'll be in real trouble when she finds out that you've delivered it here instead. So you'll have to watch it, if you don't want her swearing at you and then ringing up the Head Postmaster to complain.'

Finch promised, apprehensively, that he would watch it.

Warminger fed the mail into the firm's large letter box and drove on, turning out of Breckham Market on a minor road that led towards the village of Ecclesby. After two miles he halted at a crossroads surrounded by misty fields and hedges, and waited for a gap in the light Saturday morning traffic on the A135, one of the main roads leading towards the coastal towns of Lowestoft and Great Yarmouth.

'I always used to think of this as a pleasant sort of road,' he said, sounding idle but spying sideways to see how his new colleague would react to what he was going to say. 'You know, busy in summer with happy holidaymakers. But it was just up there –' he jerked his thumb to the left '– that they found that murdered woman.'

Finch twitched, as Warminger had hoped. 'You mean the one the papers were full of, a few weeks ago?'

'That's right. See the small wood at the top of the rise? The A135 used to run through that wood, until they built the straighter stretch of road beside it. The old road's still there, though. I used to drive a lorry for a Saintsbury firm, and we sometimes pulled off there when we didn't want to get back too early. It makes a hidden layby, handy if you want to stop for a kip, or a leak, or to dump some rubbish. So somebody decided that it'd be a nice quiet place to leave a corpse – all neatly trussed in plastic, but minus her head.'

'So I believe,' said Finch, who had no stomach for such detail.

Warminger let in the clutch and accelerated across the road. 'There were police all over the place for days after the corpse was found,' he remembered. 'Dozens of 'em, searching the layby and stopping every vehicle and asking questions. I was stopped every day for a week.'

'Did they ever find out whose the body was?'

'Not as far as I know, and I've read every mention of it in the local paper. You interested in murder? I am. I've read quite a few books about it. As I see it, this has got to be a crime of passion – some feller doing away with his wife or girl friend. That's why he chopped her head off, 'cause he knew that if the police could identify her, they'd be on to him straight away.'

9

'Do you mind?' said Finch queasily.

Kenny Warminger laughed, and drew up at a flintstone farmhouse, its front garden shaggy with damp autumnal asters. A small black and white terrier, peering through the bars of the garden gate, greeted their arrival with frenzied yaps.

'This is where Ecclesby starts,' Warminger instructed. 'Limekiln Farm – here you are, Brian mate, I'll pass you the letters, you hop out and deliver 'em. Best way to learn the route. Don't worry about the Jack Russell, the worst he'll do is rip your trousers.'

6.55 a.m. In a detached four-bedroomed chalet bungalow displaying the name *Tenerife*, overlooking Wickford common from the Nether Wickford side, the forty-year-old Mrs Arrowsmith who kept changing the colour of her hair lay wide awake, planning her future.

Her only companion, resting with languid elegance beside her on the king-size double bed, was her seal-point Siamese cat. A man had shared the bed for part of the night, an acquaintance so recent that he assumed that Angela Arrowsmith's hair was always dark gold with auburn highlights; but although Angela had, when she arranged his visit, believed that he might play a part in her future, she had taken against him and turned him out just before dawn. Nothing like spending a night with a man for finding out his true character.

She'd thought Len Pratt generous, and found him mean; a pig in bed. But then, so were most men – except Si, of course. A sweeter second husband than young Simon Arrowsmith she couldn't have wished for: loving, admiring, humbly grateful, as big and soft as a teddy bear, and just as boring.

She was fond of him, though. She hadn't wanted to hurt him quite so much yesterday evening, but she'd had to be sufficiently cruel to him to ensure that he'd take himself off to his mother's for the night before his potential replacement arrived. A pity Len hadn't passed the test she'd set him . . .

Not that she'd go to the trouble of taking on a replacement, if it weren't for the problem of money. Simon simply didn't have enough. What she wanted was real money, the kind her husband's half-brother Ross had. She'd put a proposition to Ross some months previously – a purely financial proposition, though with a hint that fringe benefits might be available – but he'd turned her down flat, with such a toffee-nosed look of dislike that she was determined to get even with him as soon as an opportunity arose.

Meanwhile she had other plans, and Simon might still have his uses. He'd be back, of course, shambling and woebegone and begging for forgiveness . . .

'Poor Simple Simon,' she mused aloud, in the diddums-den voice she used when she was tickling her plump and blondly furry husband into total subjugation. 'Poor Big Boy . . .'

She reached across the bed to stroke the cat's cream-and-deep-brown fur. 'But *you're* beautiful, Princess. You're my lovely, lovely friend – we understand each other, don't we? The best of everything, that's what we want for each other, eh, Princess?'

The cat rose to its feet and began to weave round Angela's hand with sinuous grace, the great blue eyes in the delicate wedge-shaped head half closed in ecstasy. 'Oh, your silken fur,' crooned Angela, stroking ceaselessly. 'Silken fur . . . that's what I love, my beautiful, silk and fur, silk and fur – '

But her stroking had aroused it beyond endurance. The highly-bred, highly-strung animal suddenly screamed, turned and lashed out, its slim paw become a vicious weapon. Angela shrieked, flinging the cat from the bed. 'Christ, you spiteful little devil! Look what you've done – '

Three shallow parallel scratches raked the inside of her left forearm. Beads of blood sprang up, conjoined, began to run. Angela scrambled out of bed and hurried to the bathroom, where she put her arm under the cold tap. The cat leaped down the stairs and stretched itself up against the front door, making piercing demands to be let out.

The flow of blood lessened. Angela, in a silk kimono, her arm damp and sore, was on her way downstairs to open the door for the second time within an hour when Gary Hilton, the son of her first marriage and her only child, came shuffling out of his ground-floor bedroom, tall and coathanger-thin inside his pyjamas. His mother appealed to him for sympathy.

'Look what that sodding cat's done to me, Gary! Didn't you hear me scream?'

'No.' Gary, just seventeen, barely awake, his face naked without his glasses, was groping myopically towards the downstairs lavatory.

'Trust you! I could be murdered in my bed, and you wouldn't hear a thing.' She unlocked and unbolted the front door, giving her pet a quick caress before she let it out to show it that she bore no malice. 'There you go, Princess. Mind what you get up to, and don't cross the road.'

By the time she had relocked the door, her son had emerged from the lavatory. 'My arm hurts like anything,' she complained. She attempted a gesture of fondness, reaching up to brush his limp, tangled hair off his forehead with her right hand. 'How about making me a cup of tea, Gary love?'

The boy sidestepped, jerking his head away and lifting his upper lip in a sneer. 'Make it yourself, for once,' he mumbled thickly. He ducked the slap she aimed at his face, and groped back to his room.

Angela scowled after him, and then opened the door of the other ground-floor bedroom. It was occupied, but there was no point in knocking. Harold Wilkes, her brother who lived with them, had been involved some years previously in an accident that had left him totally deaf.

She switched on the light and shook him awake. For a moment, seeing the pallor of exhaustion on the broad face under the close-cropped sandy hair, she felt remorseful; Harold so rarely complained that she forgot he slept badly. But then, with Simon to attend to her wants, there was normally no need for her to wake her brother. It wouldn't hurt him, for once.

She held out her left forearm, and allowed her lower lip to tremble. Harold, struggling to sit up, peered blearily at the scratches.

'That wretched cat again?' he asked in his loud, unmodulated voice. The Princess was accustomed to express displeasure by drawing blood from the nearest human being.

Angela nodded, making her little-sister's-hurt face.

'It's not deep,' said Harold. He'd had less than an hour's sleep that night, and his head was ringing with tinnitus. 'Just bathe it with antiseptic, it'll be all right.'

His sister flinched, as though he'd hit her. 'Oh, Harold . . .'

He sighed, heaved himself out of bed and pulled his dressing gown round his thick-set body. 'All right, I'll do it for you,' he said flatly.

Angela gave him a radiant smile. 'Bless you, love!' Then, 'Cup of tea?' she mouthed at him hopefully.

Harold Wilkes was not an expert lipreader, but some of his sister's requests were uttered so frequently during the course of the day that he had no difficulty in understanding them. With a steam whistle shrieking in his head, and pain stabbing at the back of his eyeballs like forks of lightning, he dragged himself towards the kitchen.

7.20 a.m. Overhead, through brightening mist, the sun's disc was visible, pale as a morning moon. On Wickford common the vapour had begun to lift, leaving the grass white with dew. A man was running along the road that circled the common, and whenever he crossed a grass verge he left a trail of green footsteps behind him.

Ross Arrowsmith, founder, chairman, managing director and technical director of Arrowsmith MicroElectronics Ltd, was out for his morning jog. It was a practice he'd taken up for the sake of his health on his thirtieth birthday, and in nine years he'd rarely missed a day. Like cleaning his teeth, it had become a habit.

But the benefits were not merely physical. An early morning jog, when his mind was at its freshest, gave him a valuable opportunity for uninterrupted thought, and what he usually thought about was micro-electronics. As his wife Jen told him with exasperated affection, he was a workaholic; in or out of his office and design laboratory, he rarely concentrated for long on anything other than silicon wafers, photolithography, binary codes and sequential circuits.

He was always so preoccupied when he went jogging that he

took little notice of his surroundings. They were familiar to him, because he had been born and brought up in Upper Wickford. Occasionally he varied the direction of his run, more in accordance with the season of the year and the taste of the air than with any conscious decision, but usually he ran from his newly built house at Ecclesby up towards Wickford common.

Since his father's death, six months ago, Ross no longer made dutiful calls at the old house overlooking the common, where his widowed stepmother Nellie now lived alone. He was grateful to Nellie for the way she had looked after his father, but he could never think of anything to say to her. He found any kind of purely social conversation difficult. Fortunately Jen made up for this as well as his other social shortcomings, and regularly took the twins to visit Nellie just as she had taken them when their grandfather was alive.

As he jogged past the small house where he had been born, his mind was reviewing the design of his latest microprocessor control system; it would, he hoped, make Arrowsmith as big a name in home computers as Sinclair or Commodore. But despite this preoccupation, he took a moment's conscious pleasure in the evocative smells of the orchard where he had played as a boy, though he noticed how small and scabby the apples on the neglected trees had become.

He turned off the asphalt on to the dirt footpath that connected the villages of Upper and Lower Wickford by a short cut across the common. Mist still lingered in patches, hiding the house three hundred yards away, on the outskirts of Nether Wickford, where his half-brother Simon lived. But the knowledge that the house was there reminded him of Simon and, disagreeably, of Simon's wife Angela.

Ross liked his half-brother well enough, though he found it difficult to remember that they were related by blood. Quite apart from their age difference – Simon was 27 – they had never lived under the same roof. Simon was a computer programmer by profession, and Ross had employed him for five years as a systems programmer. But then, immediately after their father's death, Simon had been taken away from the company, in a fit of pique, by the predatory woman he'd married.

Stupid young fool, to throw away an excellent job. Idiot, to allow a woman like that to capture him. Ross recalled with distaste Angela's hard eyes and thin mouth, her extravagantly long red fingernails, the tarty way she'd half-lowered her metallic-grey eyelids at him when she'd cornered him, after his father's funeral, and asked for a loan to start a beauty salon. It was only the second time they'd met, and the first time they'd exchanged anything more than minimal social courtesies.

He'd refused her the loan, of course. For one thing, most of his money was tied up in Arrowsmith MicroElectronics. He'd only recently moved into the Old Maltings, and buying and renovating the building and equipping it with high-technology laboratories had taken every penny he could raise. Whatever he might be worth on paper, he was in no position to lend anyone ten thousand pounds, just like that, even if he wanted to.

And he didn't want to. He had been shocked that she should ask him for money at that time, not an hour after he'd buried his father . . . and that she should do it so suggestively, hinting that they could discuss it over a meal at a restaurant, just the two of them . . . God, what a bitch of a woman.

The thought of her filled him with disgust; so much so that he couldn't bear to run too near her house. Seeing it ahead, through the evaporating mist, he swerved from the dirt footpath and struck off across the wet white grass, so as to join the road back to Ecclesby about twenty yards from the chalet bungalow that Angela had named *Tenerife*. His thoughts returned with relief to the logic, the purity and the beauty of sub-micron geometry.

7.45 a.m. The sun, now luminous, was rapidly hoovering up the remnants of mist. Cobwebs were draped over every bush, so wet and white that they looked like tatty linen spread out to dry. As he waded across dew-drenched roadside verges to deliver the mail, Brian Finch's shoes lost all their polish and the bottom of his trouser legs became soaked; but he was too anxious about doing his new job properly to mind.

Kenny Warminger had guided him round Ecclesby, pointing out that the house called New Maltings, architect-designed on a large open site, had recently been built for the owner of Arrowsmith MicroElectronics. Now, leaving Ecclesby, the mail van headed for Upper Wickford.

'I generally see Ross Arrowsmith out jogging, somewhere about this time,' said Warminger. 'If I had his money – at least half a million, I've heard – I'd pay somebody to do the jogging for me. Yes, there he is, on the way back home. He usually runs up to Wickford common, though I've sometimes seen him on the other side of Ecclesby, going towards the A135.'

The two postmen watched as the reputed half-millionaire, in running shorts and singlet, all sinewy arms and legs and lank, flopping hair, came padding steadily past. If he noticed the mail van, he gave no sign. Warminger grinned to himself, and then let out a guffaw.

'D'you know what I did? When the police stopped me, after that body was found, they wanted to know what time I crossed the road every day, and what regular road users I saw. I was as helpful as I could be, but when they kept on asking, day after day, I got fed up. So I told 'em about Ross Arrowsmith. Not that I ever actually saw him on the A135, but he certainly does sometimes go in that direction. Let 'em pester him, I thought. It'll serve him right for making us deliver his firm's mail.'

He drove on, into Upper Wickford. 'Here you go, Brian – first delivery, Mill House.'

Brian Finch had looked forward to being on a country route, after spending his first few weeks as a postman doing a cycle delivery on a new town housing estate. The route was, however, much more difficult to learn than he'd anticipated. There were so many detours, to take in all the farms; and then, the complete absence of house numbers was baffling.

But despite that, and the wet feet, there were compensations. The villages were so quiet and civilised, so free from graffiti and the evidence of vandalism. And though the dogs were a worry, there were cats too. Brian Finch loved cats. He understood their timidity with strangers, and whenever he spied one peeping at him round the corner of a house when he went up to the front door, he crouched down and – with one eye on his watch, because he didn't want to get behind schedule – enticed it towards him. Very few cats could resist someone who crouched down and chirruped at them. 'See you again next week,' he whispered hurriedly as they ventured to sniff at his outstretched fingers with their whiskered noses.

He saw yet another cat as soon as he opened the gate of the house called *Tenerife*, on the edge of the Nether Wickford side of the common, where he went to deliver a letter for the Mrs Arrowsmith who, according to Kenny, kept changing the colour of her hair. The cat, a Siamese, was lying on the front doorstep, and it made no attempt to move as he approached. Odd . . . and there was something very strange about the way it was lying . . . about what it was lying in . . .

And then he saw the sticky wetness on the seal-brown paws, the darkly matted cream fur of the coat; saw too the jaggedly severed neck, and the wide pool of blood where the delicate wedge-shaped head should have been.

On the front door of the house, in large red letters, were paint-sprayed the words, YOUR TURN NEXT.

2

'Jealousy,' deduced the detective chief inspector's small plump wife, snatching the butter dish out of her husband's reach and substituting low-fat margarine. When she was dieting, Molly liked to make sure that he suffered too, for his own good. 'It's sheer jealousy, Doug Quantrill, and you needn't try to deny it. You've been as grizzly as a bear ever since you heard that your policewoman friend was going to marry your boss.'

'It's nothing whatever to do with Patsy Hopkins,' growled Quantrill. 'Good grief, woman, I've had a murder investigation on my hands for the past two months. The DCS is coming this morning for a conference about it, and all I can tell him is that I'm making no progress. Do you wonder I'm irritable?'

'You can't be expected to make progress, when someone comes and dumps a headless corpse in your division without so much as a by-your-leave,' said Molly, 'and Chief Superintendent Mancroft knows that just as well as I do.' She unplugged the toaster, to deter her heavyweight husband from putting in another slice of bread. 'Will this be the first time you've seen him since you heard about the engagement, Douggie? Because it really is lovely for him to be getting married again, after being a widower for so long, and you must congratulate him as though you mean it.'

Quantrill muttered into his coffee cup.

'Anyway,' Molly went on slyly, 'it isn't as though you'll be without feminine company at work, now the woman detective sergeant's arrived. What did you say her name is?'

'Lloyd.'

'And about Patsy's age, you said . . . Married, divorced, widowed or single?'

'I really don't know,' he snapped.

He did know, of course, because he'd seen her personal file. Detective Sergeant Hilary Lloyd, formerly a member of the county serious crimes investigation team based at Yarchester, had arrived at Breckham Market two days ago to fill the year-old vacancy left by the promotion of Martin Tait. She was thirty, and unmarried. Feminine, certainly; but she didn't stir the air as she passed him, as Wpc Patsy Hopkins had done.

Which was really just as well, if they were going to achieve a good working relationship.

'All that either of us will be concerned about,' he told his wife sharply, 'is the job in hand. With Patsy it was different – she was in the uniformed branch, so she didn't work with me except on the occasions when I needed a policewoman's help. Yes, all right, I enjoyed her company. But there's been nothing personal in our relationship, and you know it. Dammit, I had no idea she was in the least bit interested in Bill Mancroft, until I heard that they were going to get married.'

'And that's why you're so piqued, isn't it?' said Molly with triumph. 'Not just because she's leaving Breckham, or because she's marrying a man four years older than you, but because you knew her so little that you had no idea she was falling in love underneath your nose! For a detective, Doug Quantrill, you're sometimes hopelessly unobservant.'

He rose with dignity from the kitchen table, and made for the door. 'I don't know when I shall be home,' he said distantly.

'All right, dear. I'll do a cold supper, then. By the way – are Sergeant Lloyd's legs as good as Patsy's?'

'I really haven't noticed,' lied her husband.

The atmosphere in the CID offices at Breckham Market divisional police headquarters was both more concerned and more optimistic than it had been for weeks. At 8.27 a.m. a postman had telephoned from a call box – on behalf of an unnerved colleague – with the news of the finding of a decapitated cat and a threatening message at Nether Wickford, about three miles from the layby where the headless corpse had been found. Detective Sergeant Lloyd, who was on duty when the call came in, had gone out to investigate.

The threat might, of course, have no bearing at all on the headless woman's death – the A135 case, as the police referred to it prosaically, after the route number of the road beside which the body had been found. There were always people who were sufficiently sadistic to try to frighten others into submission by referring to crimes that were currently in the news, just as there were people unstable enough to copy or attempt to copy the crimes themselves.

On the other hand, there could be a link with the A135 case. The police had hoped that the woman's death had been an isolated close-relationship killing, rather than the work of a psychopath, but this morning's threat to the owner of the cat could mean that they were looking for someone who would kill again. The fact that a murderer who had gone to the savage extreme of cutting off his victim's head in order to conceal her – and therefore his own – identity would be crazy to make himself traceable by threatening another woman, merely reinforced the possibility that they were looking for a psychopath.

The Nether Wickford incident could also mean that the murderer might be someone who lived relatively locally. In the absence of any other leads, the death of the cat had at last provided something positive for the CID to work on, and they welcomed it for that reason.

Detective Chief Superintendent Mancroft arrived from Yarchester for the conference full of optimism. He hadn't heard the news but he had other, more personal, causes for satisfaction.

'Good to see you, Doug!'

It was the first time, in the nine years of their acquaintance, that he'd said anything of the kind, thought Quantrill sardonically. Bill Mancroft had always been a spare, morose man, never wasting time on pleasantries, rarely relaxing with his subordinates over a drink, virtually friendless. Seedy, too, since his wife's death; careless about his suits, the trim of his moustache, the encroachment of dandruff. This had been one good reason for Quantrill's total disbelief that the immaculate and long-legged Patsy Hopkins could have looked on the man with favour.

But love had transformed the fifty-two-year-old Chief Superintendent, inspiring him to renew his wardrobe and shave off the moustache. He'd found a new barber, too. His hair was thicker and glossier than Quantrill remembered it, almost as though he'd had it professionally shampooed and blow dried . . .

Swallowing his resentment, Quantrill held out his hand. 'First time I've had the opportunity to say it, Bill – congratulations! I can't pretend we're pleased that you're taking Patsy away from Breckham, but we all think you're a very lucky man.'

'Realise that.' Gruffly embarrassed, Mancroft accepted the handshake. 'Know she'll be sorry to leave, in many ways. She's always spoken of you very warmly, Doug. Sort of father figure in her view, I think – on account of your being a married man, I mean.'

Quantrill wondered what disciplinary action would be taken against a Chief Inspector who spat in a Chief Superintendent's eye. He managed to smile instead, but thinly.

Mancroft clapped him on the shoulder. 'Lucky man yourself, though, eh? There've been some long faces at Yarchester since Hilary Lloyd left, you know. She'll be missed. First-class detective, just the person you need to strengthen your team here. Must get this A135 case cracked – Chief Constable's talking about calling in the regional crime squad, and we don't want that . . . What? New development, eh? Nasty. Potentially very nasty. Interesting, though. Might have no connection, of course, but still . . . Who's investigating? Hilary? Capital, couldn't be better. As I said, you're a lucky man.'

Quantrill hoped the Detective Chief Superintendent's coffee would choke him.

They were joined by Detective Inspector Harry Colman, head of the county serious crimes team and Sergeant Lloyd's former boss. His noble bald forehead, combined with vigorous sidewhiskers and moustache, gave him something of the appearance of Queen Victoria's Consort. Like Prince Albert, he was a devoted husband and father. Much of his working life – he was nearing retirement from the force – had been spent at scenes of squalor and violence, analysing the immediate surroundings of the unnaturally dead, but privately he was a gentle, sensitive man, interested in photography and the cultivation of hybrid tea roses.

He and Quantrill were old friends. He'd hated to lose Hilary Lloyd from his team, he told the Chief Inspector, but at least he had the consolation that he couldn't have lost her to a better man.

'Don't *you* start telling me how lucky I am,' Quantrill grumbled. He jerked a scathing thumb at the door through which the Chief Superintendent had just disappeared, muttering something coy about washing his hands before the conference began; as they both knew, he was really hoping for a glimpse of his fiancée. 'I've had just about enough from the old man. All right, Hilary Lloyd's a good detective. I believe you both. But there's no need to go on as though she's God's gift to Breckham Market. We've managed perfectly well for the past year without a CID sergeant, and I could have waited a bit longer until a man was available.'

'I thought you liked having women in the force?'

'I do. But I don't want a woman as my number two, Harry! I want a sergeant I can be easy with, someone I can swap ideas with at any time of the day or night, in the office or the pub or wherever. It's not a matter of *liking* – you know how I felt about young Martin Tait – but of understanding. I'd spoken briefly with Hilary Lloyd half a dozen times before she was sent here, and I spent most of yesterday working with her, but I don't know any more about her now than I did five minutes after we first met. That lively manner is superficial. She talks fast and laughs easily, but she doesn't relax. She's always self-contained, impersonal. Her smile doesn't seem to get as far as her eyes. God knows what's going on in her head, but I don't feel comfortable in her company.'

Harry Colman's sidewhiskers fluffed out indignantly in his former sergeant's defence. 'Stop treating the girl like a suspect, then! She's every right to clam up if she knows you're trying to probe about in her mind. All I'm prepared to tell you is that she's a career policewoman, determined to make Inspector, at least, but not pushily ambitious like Tait. As far as her private life is concerned, I've always taken the view that it's her own affair. Whatever confidences she's given me, over the years, I'm keeping to myself.'

'Fair enough. But is there a regular boy friend? Tell me that, at least, Harry. I can't have a sergeant whose mind isn't on the job.'

'If there is, she's never yet let him interfere with her work.'

'Hmm,' muttered Quantrill, dissatisfied. He had the old-fashioned masculine suspicion that any young working woman who had a husband or a regular boy friend would be bound to put him first, and would therefore be a nuisance; and that if she had neither, she must have a chip on her shoulder, and would therefore be a problem.

He recalled Hilary Lloyd's features. 'Her scar's a great shame, of course, but it's not in any way disfiguring. No one could call her pretty, but she's not bad-looking.'

'*Not bad-looking?*' Harry Colman, with his photographer's eye, was incredulous and kindly pitying. 'My dear old friend, it's obvious that you don't appreciate good bone structure when you see it! That girl has a splendid profile. And when she does give a wholehearted smile, it's a beauty. I really do hope she's not going to be wasted on you, Doug . . .'

They left the Chief Inspector's office, on their way to the conference room, and met a plain-clothes policewoman with straight dark brown hair. She was almost as tall as Patsy Hopkins, but not, to Quantrill's regret, as shapely. He didn't care for thin women.

From a distance, she seemed to be frowning. Close to, it was apparent that her left eyebrow was puckered by a faint, permanent scar, a memento of her service in uniform. It missed her eye by less than an inch, and left an irregular line above the bridge of her nose, before disappearing under the thick fringe of her hair.

Quantrill, trying to give her features the benefit of the doubt, watched to see whether Hilary Lloyd would bestow an illuminating, whole-hearted smile on her former boss. But all she gave Harry Colman was a passing grin.

Aware of the Chief Inspector's scrutiny – like all detectives, he was an inveterate watcher; a watcher herself, she disliked being watched – she looked him straight in the eye. Her voice, when she spoke, was quick and light, full of enthusiasm for her work but always carefully impersonal.

'Good morning, sir. Do you want to hear about the Nether Wickford incident now, or shall I save it for the conference?'

Quantrill took her back to his office, with Harry Colman following. He wanted to know what cards he would have up his sleeve when the Chief Super started nagging about progress.

Sergeant Lloyd reported briskly what she had been told by the Arrowsmiths: the composition of the household, the fact that Angela had got up at about seven to let the cat out, and had then returned to bed. 'As it's Saturday, they were all sleeping late. The brother's stone deaf, but the other three heard nothing until our motorcycle patrolman arrived to tell them what was on their front doorstep. At least, they all *say* they heard nothing. They also said that none of them had been outside the house, but the bottom of Simon Arrowsmith's trouser legs were dark with damp. They live just across the road from a large common, and the long grass there and on the roadside verges was soaked with dew. I think he had been out, and that he had some reason for lying about it.'

'Is it a domestic dispute? Would he be likely to have killed the cat?'

'I don't see it that way. I'd have thought him too soft-hearted, and too much in love with his wife. It's possible, of course, but there were no obvious signs of bloodstains on him, and if he'd cleaned himself up he'd surely have changed his trousers. What I'm certain of, though, is that whoever decapitated the cat wasn't the same person who decapitated the woman in the A135 case. That was relatively skilful. The job on the cat was botched.'

She was careful not to let her new boss know, by her voice or her expression, how sick she'd felt when she saw it. Her stomach had lurched and she'd wanted to go quietly away, not study what she saw and draw logical conclusions from it.

She always felt sick when she saw the result of death by violence, even after spending two years as a member of Inspector Colman's team and being called to the scene of every murder in Suffolk. The fact that she'd originally trained as a nurse was no help. The sights in the operating theatre could be gory, but the atmosphere there was calm and ordered, the attitude compassionate, the air clinically clean.

It was the smell of murder that got to her as much as anything else. There was always a smell, a compound of corrupted flesh, spilled blood, the victim's lingering terror, and a whiff of evil. It caught her by the throat every time, even when the victim was animal rather than human.

'We found the cat's head under some bushes, just inside the gate,' she went on composedly. 'One side of the head had been crushed by a blow that must have killed it. There was a mess of blood and fur on the ground, so I think that must have been where the head was cut off, out of sight of both the house and the road.'

The Chief Inspector was watching her with eyes as cool as frosted grapes. She knew what he was thinking. After eight years in the force she had learned, reluctantly, to live with the double standards imposed by many – though Harry Colman was a gentle, courteous exception – of her male colleagues. If she showed any emotion in the course of her work, they would despise her for being unprofessional; when she showed none, they thought her unfeminine. It was an outrageously unfair handicap. But then, she had learned that life was unfair before she ever thought of joining the police force.

As long as Chief Inspector Quantrill treated her as a fellow professional, she was indifferent to what he thought of her as a person. She wasn't greatly impressed by him either, except by reputation as a detective. She could see that he was handsome, in a heavy, greying way, but she really couldn't understand why – before Chief Superintendent Mancroft had smartened himself up and indicated that he was interested – Patsy Hopkins had thought Quantrill so unattainably attractive. As far as Hilary was concerned, Patsy was welcome to both of them.

'I've left a small team to make local enquiries, and to start searching for the weapon,' she went on. 'Something with a metal edge, I think, but not a sharp one. Possibly a garden tool.'

'What about the threatening words? Does Mrs Arrowsmith take them seriously?'

'I think so. She seems thoroughly frightened. She couldn't talk rationally, though, because she was very upset about the cat. She was swearing and raving that when she found out who did it, she'd strangle him with her bare hands.' Hilary paused, and gave Inspector Colman another quick grin. 'I believe she'd try it, too. I know her from Yarchester, about five years ago. She was Angela Hilton then, a divorcee with red hair and green fingernails, and she worked in the evenings as a barmaid at the Black Bull. Tough as they come.'

'She'd need to be,' said Harry Colman, 'if she wanted to last longer than a week at the Black Bull in those days. It was one of the Suffolk pubs owned by the Cory brothers,' he told Quantrill, referring to two East London gang leaders who had since been put away for attempted murder.

'It had a bad reputation,' agreed Hilary. 'I was in uniform then, and we were called to the Black Bull several times because of drunken brawling in the bar. To be fair, we had nothing at all against Angela Hilton. She wasn't on the game.

But she was thought to be free with her favours, and she certainly knows – or used to know – some villains. So I was interested to see that she's come up in the world, and is now a respectable housewife with a younger, young-executive-type husband who's obviously devoted to her. She swears that she knows no one who could possibly want to harm her, but she was protesting just a bit too vehemently. I think she's afraid that something – or someone – is about to emerge from her past and destroy her new image. Or perhaps her life.'

3

The CID conference on the A135 case began with a review of the known facts. There was no shortage of them. The problem was that they led nowhere.

Some of the facts had been established by Inspector Colman's serious crimes team at the place where the headless body had been found. Others had been provided by the Home Office pathologist after his post-mortem examination. Some had been reported by the East Midlands forensic science laboratory, to which the dead woman's clothing and plastic shroud had been sent; some had been established through the co-operation of other police forces. The bulk of them had been put together by the detectives of the Breckham Market division, after weeks of dogged enquiry.

The detectives' major problem was their inability either to identify the woman or to establish the precise cause of her death. In the absence of the head this was, as Molly Quantrill had remarked to her husband, not surprising. What puzzled them more was the fact that despite extensive local and national publicity, in the press and on television and radio, no one seemed to know anything about the woman. She had vanished – died – apparently without being missed.

There had of course been plenty of public interest and reaction. Over 500 telephone messages had been received, and more came in daily. Card indexes lengthened, files bulged with statements. But so far, none of this information matched their limited knowledge of the dead woman, any more than their knowledge fitted anyone on either their own missing persons file or the police national computer index.

The body was that of a well-nourished woman aged approximately 32, about five feet four inches tall and three months pregnant, with no distinguishing scars or skin blemishes of any kind. There was no evidence of sexual attack.

She had died two days before the body was found. Immediately before death she had sustained a number of violent blows on her shoulders from a blunt instrument, and it seemed probable that her death had been caused by a similar blow or blows to the head. The severing had been achieved by either an axe or a cleaver, within four to five hours after her death. It had probably been carried out by someone with some knowledge of either anatomy or butchery.

The woman wore a wide, patterned, inexpensive 9-carat-gold wedding ring, of a type manufactured in quantity by a Birmingham firm and retailed by High Street jewellers in all parts of the country over the past seven years. Circular indentations on the second and third fingers of the right hand suggested that she had habitually worn other rings, which had been removed. Her hands were uncared-for. The nails on her left hand were bitten, but inexpertly-applied pink nail varnish suggested that she had made some attempt to smarten herself up.

Her shoes were missing, but otherwise she was fully clothed. Her underwear – tights, bra and pants – had all been identified by Marks and Spencer as steadily-selling current lines, buyable from any branch in the country. Her summer dress, however, was not from Marks and Spencer; the only label it bore was the one with the washing instructions. The material was thirty per cent cotton, seventy per cent polyester, in pink with red and grey vertical stripes.

Extensive enquiries had at length identified it as one of fifty dozen dresses made two years previously by a Leeds clothing manufacturer from material that he had imported from Taiwan. He had sold a quarter of his output to a local wholesaler, who supplied small High Street retailers in the north of England. The remainder went to a firm trading as Jayne Edwards, which had a chain of dress shops in the major Midlands towns. There were no Jayne Edwards shops nearer to East Anglia than Wellingborough.

The dresses had retailed cheaply, at between twelve and fifteen pounds. Any left unsold after the previous summer's end-of-season sales had been bought up by a man who supplied itinerant market traders. The dead woman's dress could have been bought that summer for seven or eight pounds from a market stall almost anywhere in the country.

The plastic in which the body had been wrapped was shaped into a cover such as would fit a double-bed mattress, but it had no distinguishing marks on it. The nylon cord used to truss the plastic-wrapped body was of a type readily obtainable in hardware and Do-It-Yourself shops, and all branches of Woolworths. There had been no sign of a weapon, or any blood, at or near the place where the body was found.

The sinister size and shape of the bundle had been spotted in the undergrowth at the side of the layby by a lorry driver who travelled regularly on the A135. He had seen it on Monday 17 July, and was confident that it had not been there the previous Friday. Although the A135 was busy in the daytime, and particularly so at weekends in the summer holiday season, the traffic flow was always light between midnight and 6 a.m.

The layby was on the east side of the A135, the side of the road used by traffic travelling south in the general direction of London. This suggested that the body had been brought from the direction of Yarchester, twenty miles to the north, or from one of the towns on the coast, Lowestoft or Great Yarmouth. But it could equally well have been brought a comparatively short distance, along one of the many minor roads that joined the A135, by someone local who knew of the existence of the layby.

'We've so far made house-to-house enquiries within a five-mile radius of the scene, in an attempt to establish her identity,' said Quantrill, 'as well as distributing over fifty thousand handbills via newsagents. But this morning's incident at Nether

28

Wickford does of course open up a possible new line of enquiry.'

'Ah, the decapitated cat.' Chief Superintendent Mancroft gave Hilary his new, expansive, about-to-be-remarried smile. 'Very much like to hear your report, Miss Lloyd.'

She began to give it, and those of the assembled detectives who hadn't previously met her seized the opportunity to turn in their chairs and take a good look. Uniformed policewomen had served in the Breckham Market division for years, but a female detective was an intriguing novelty. A female detective sergeant, however, was not entirely welcome. Her new colleagues, conventional to a man, eyed her warily.

What they had dreamed of, when they first heard of her appointment, was someone decorative, under twenty-five, willing, competent, but not too clever; someone who would admire and support them, and be available when required, but make no demands on them either professionally or socially; someone who would ignore the rule book, defend them from the boss, back all their decisions but otherwise keep out of their way.

That was what they wanted. What they expected was a plain-clothes bossyboots, a middle-aged woman with a hair style as rigid as her mind. What they'd got was Hilary Lloyd, and they didn't know what to make of her.

They were not, collectively, much impressed by good bone structure. As far as looks were concerned they preferred Patsy Hopkins, though those with an eye for line and colour were prepared to concede that Hilary Lloyd's casual clothes would do a lot to brighten up Breckham nick. They all noticed that she wore a diamond eternity ring on the third finger of her left hand, and they speculated on its significance.

They were relieved that there was nothing overtly authoritative in her manner. She seemed confident without being assertive; eager to contribute to the discussion, ready to listen to what her colleagues had to say. But they observed, as Quantrill had done, that her eyes kept them at a distance. Like him, they were made uneasy by the fact that however animated she sounded, she always held herself straight-backed and still, graceful but unrelaxed. As CID sergeant, Hilary Lloyd was evidently going to be someone to be reckoned with.

She knew her job, that was obvious. Unlike her predecessor, Martin Tait, a university graduate who had been sent to Breckham Market as a brand new sergeant, straight from police college and still wet behind the ears, she'd had plenty of experience. They'd all heard from Yarchester colleagues about the origin of her scar. Sergeant Lloyd might have a voice almost as classless (and therefore almost as classy) as the former Sergeant Tait, but at least she knew all about the hazards of down-to-earth police work. Her new colleagues were not so rash as to welcome her to Breckham on that account, but they prepared themselves to give her a fair hearing.

What she told them about the former Angela Hilton, the owner of the decapitated cat, made them stir with interest. They quickly compiled a list of the names of known and suspected criminals who were thought to have used the Black Bull at Yarchester during the time when it was owned by the Cory brothers. With luck, they might find a lead on the A135 case. While they waited for the list to be checked and updated on the regional criminal record office computer, most of the detectives began to look at Sergeant Lloyd with reluctant approval.

An exception was Detective Constable Ian Wigby, a beefy blond man in his middle thirties, who was against sergeants on principle. He knew Breckham Market like the palm of his hand, and all the regular villains in the town, and he resented supervision. His superiors sometimes suspected him of knowing some of the villains just a little too well, but they'd never been able to prove anything against him.

Wigby had particularly disliked Sergeant Tait, and had been delighted when Tait was moved to Yarchester on his promotion to Inspector. The sergeantless year at Breckham had suited Wigby very well. But now he had been lumbered with another sergeant, a woman at that, and a woman younger than he was. Wigby seethed.

'Before we get too interested in the Black Bull mob, sir,' he said loudly to Chief Superintendent Mancroft, 'there's another

30

point worth considering. As soon as I heard that this morning's threat had been made to a Mrs Arrowsmith, I remembered that we'd turned up an Arrowsmith in our A135 enquiries. I took particular notice because it was Ross Arrowsmith, the man who's made a fortune with his MicroElectronics firm.'

'Reported as having sometimes been seen jogging in the area of the layby where the headless corpse was found, wasn't he?' said Quantrill, who remembered the name for the same reason.

'That's right. Arrogant, uncooperative bastard. Said he didn't take any notice of either people or vehicles when he was out jogging. He agreed that he occasionally went from Ecclesby towards the main road, but said he hadn't been there for weeks. He claimed that he nearly always went in the other direction, up to Wickford common.'

'Is he related to Angela Arrowsmith's husband?' asked Sergeant Lloyd.

'Yes,' said Wigby. In fact he didn't know, but it seemed a safe bet, and he wanted to appear positive in front of the Chief Superintendent. 'I'm not sure how close the relationship is, but I'll check.'

'Don't bother. I'm going back to see her later this morning, after she's had time to calm down, so I can find out for myself.' She gave the detective constable a nod of appreciation. 'Thanks for the information, though.'

Wigby subsided, glowering.

'Did Mrs Arrowsmith recognise you, Miss Lloyd?' asked the Chief Superintendent. 'Does she know that you've connected her with the Black Bull?'

'I don't think so. She isn't the kind of woman who takes much notice of other women, unless she sees them as rivals. All that would've registered with her in the Black Bull days would have been my uniform. And I thought I wouldn't mention the Bull to her for the moment, because I'd like to know just how much she's trying to hide.'

'Good tactic. Excellent!' Chief Superintendent Mancroft beamed at Hilary with an unqualified approval that indicated to the assembled detectives how lucky he thought they were to have her as their sergeant. The conference broke up.

'You and your wife and daughter will be able to come to the wedding, I hope?' said the Chief Superintendent, as the others disappeared. 'Was going to put you on my guest list, then found that Patsy had put you on hers.'

Quantrill, who hadn't been sure from which side the silver-lettered invitation card had come, felt slightly appeased. 'We're looking forward to it.'

That was true of Molly and Alison, at least. Alison was working in London, but the two of them had discussed clothes over the telephone, with Molly saying loudly when he was in earshot that she knew he wouldn't want her appearance to let him down. This wedding was going to cost him, in more ways than one.

'Would've preferred a quieter affair myself,' confided Bill Mancroft. 'You know, a private visit to the Registry Office, not bells and hymns at St Botolph's followed by a buffet lunch for a hundred and fifty guests at the best hotel in Breckham Market. Still – big day in a girl's life, and of course her parents want to do the right thing. Well-known family in the town, churchgoers too, so it's got to be the lot. Morning dress – ' he added, adjusting an imaginary cravat.

Quantrill looked alarmed.

'Oh, only for myself and Patsy's father and the best man. My brother's going to take care of the ring, and make sure I get to the church on time. Bit nervous, as a matter of fact. Glad when all the fuss is over. Anyway, if I don't see you before then, Doug –' His eyes searched the corridor for his fiancée.

'We'll be in touch, no doubt. The A135 case,' Quantrill reminded him.

'Ah yes! Very interesting development this morning, eh? And now Hilary's working with you – '

'There isn't necessarily a connection between the A135 case and the Arrowsmith incident,' pointed out Quantrill, nettled.

Mancroft looked pained. 'Not *necessarily*, Doug, we all know that. A possibility, that's all. But a new line of enquiry, you said that yourself. Don't know why you're not leaping on to it – you would've done, five years ago.'

'We were both a lot younger then,' said Quantrill sourly.

*   *   *

Hilary Lloyd was waiting for him outside his office. He greeted her without a great deal of enthusiasm, and they spent five impersonal minutes discussing the action they proposed, and allocating areas of responsibility. Hilary rose to go as soon as she could, but turned back at the door.

'I don't *enjoy* being treated as the Chief Super's blue-eyed girl detective, you know,' she said. 'It irritates me just as much as it irritates you. But it's so recent that I'm taking Patsy's advice and making allowances for engagement euphoria.'

Quantrill thawed a little towards her. 'Did you know Patsy before you came here?'

'I met her once or twice, and I'm very sorry that she'll be moving to Yarchester so soon after I've come here. I'd have liked her company. She's been tremendously helpful, though, telling me the best place to have my hair done, and which electrician and plumber to call in an emergency.'

For the first time since her arrival, Quantrill remembered that as a stranger in the town – and a working woman, at that – Hilary Lloyd would have a number of domestic problems to solve. Had she been an unmarried man, he would have thought of it sooner.

'Settling in all right?' he enquired gruffly. 'Where are you living?'

'One of the flats in Riverside Court. Martin Tait used to live there, and he gave me the agent's address.'

'Ah, yes. I'd forgotten that you would know Martin at Yarchester, even though he's in uniform now. Haven't seen him for months. What's he up to, these days?'

A twitch of her scarred eyebrow indicated that she wasn't one of Tait's admirers. 'Beavering his way towards becoming the youngest Chief Constable in the country, I believe.'

'Hah! That follows. It was the youngest *Assistant* Chief Constable when he was CID sergeant here. Still hankering after CID work, though, is he? I know he doesn't find the same scope in Operations.'

'He's away on a CID refresher course at the moment.'

33

'Is he?' said Quantrill, jolted. 'Well, I always thought him a good detective. And as long as he stays in Yarchester – '

Hilary shook her head. 'I heard on the county grapevine before I left that he's been selected for secondment to the regional crime squad. I know he's been longing to sort out the A135 case – he told me how much he envied my posting here. So if the Chief Constable should decide to call in the regional crime squad on the case, Martin's knowledge of the area will make him the natural choice for the job.'

'Reporting directly to the Chief Constable, rather than to me? Over my dead body . . .' snorted Quantrill.

For the first time since he'd met her, Hilary Lloyd gave him something like a real smile. It was partly sympathetic, but it also held more amusement than he cared for.

'I doubt you'll be given that option, sir,' she said.

4

Towards the end of the morning, when the sun had dried the dew from the immaculate lawns of *Tenerife*, the chalet bungalow at Nether Wickford, Angela Arrowsmith's husband gave the remains of her Siamese cat a double inappropriate Christian burial.

The digging of the grave proved an unexpected problem, because the police had removed Simon's garden tools, which he kept in an unlocked shed, for examination. The house was one of an obtrusively modern group of three, standing in isolation from the rest of the village, and Angela was not on sufficiently good terms with either of her neighbours to make it easy to approach them. Eventually Simon, a plump young man with fair bushy hair and a fair bushy beard, went back to Upper Wickford to borrow one of his father's old spades from his mother. Then, extricating his curly-stemmed pipe from the middle of his beard, and grunting with combined emotional stress and exertion, he began to dig a deep hole where his wife had directed, under a silver birch tree.

Angela's son, Gary Hilton, dried the tears he had been shedding noisily over the dead cat, and lent a hand without being asked. His thin stooping shoulders and horn-rimmed spectacles gave him a scholarly, almost middle-aged air, but he was in fact very young for his age, shyly self-conscious of his gawky height, and interested in reading nothing more demanding than space-fiction comics. He liked his stepfather and his deaf Uncle Harold, but usually avoided his mother whenever possible. The shocking events of the morning had however made him more co-operative than usual.

While Gary took over the digging, Harold Wilkes, grey-faced and bloodshot-eyed after a particularly bad night, scrubbed the bloodied front doorstep with a solution of bleach. Simon meanwhile transferred the pitifully limp component parts of the cat into a cardboard box that had once contained a bulk purchase of cans of its favourite food, middle-cut red salmon. With Gary's help, and to the accompaniment of the boy's sniffs and gulps, Simon lowered the box into the hole. Then he returned to the house to wash the blood from his hands, and to put on the brown velvet cord jacket that his wife particularly liked him to wear. When she was ready, he assisted her to the graveside.

Angela's shock and grief were genuine, but her sense of drama had made her demand a proper burial service for her pet, and the attendance of her entire household. Her husband could refuse her nothing, especially after the distress of last night's quarrel. He performed the ceremony with sad reverence, despite being directly under the deadpan scrutiny of a uniformed constable who was standing on the other side of the hedge. As he had already indicated to Harold, Simon was thankful that the police were taking the threat to his wife seriously, and providing protection for her.

Angela wore a black dress for the occasion, and cried a good deal. Afterwards, she felt much better.

The threat, YOUR TURN NEXT, that had been paint-sprayed on the door had at first frightened her badly. She'd been threatened before. Her past – the old days at the Black Bull in Yarchester, and before that at the Goat and Compasses in Lowestoft – had flashed before her and she had caught a vivid glimpse of the face of the Lowestoft seaman who had threatened to carve her up when she'd refused to take him back to her flat. Fortunately, she'd had a protector at the time. She'd been frightened, though, and with good reason; the seaman had been jailed shortly afterwards for using violence against a prostitute.

But that was all a long time ago. The past was over and done with. As soon as she met Simon, four years ago, and saw him as a potential husband, she'd given up work as a barmaid. She hadn't been to either the Goat or the Bull since then.

She'd told Simon about the pubs, though. She'd told him how hard it was to support herself and her son on her pay as a hair stylist, and how she'd been obliged to work in the evenings and at weekends too, getting whatever menial jobs she could and exhausting herself in the process.

Dazzled by her attention, Simon had taken the bait immediately, offering with pride to look after her for the rest of her life. Naturally, she hadn't spelled out to him any of the details of her past, and she didn't want him – or the police – to know about it now. There was no reason why they should know. On reflection, she could see no possible connection between her past life and what had happened this morning.

As for the nasty business of the headless corpse in the layby, she knew nothing whatever about the woman, as she'd already told the police when they went from house to house making enquiries. Angela believed, as most local people wanted to believe, that the body had been brought into the county from a long way away. A murder near home didn't bear thinking about.

The killing of poor Princess was an entirely separate matter. Angela had soon guessed who must have done it: Len Pratt, the man she'd turned out of her bed early in the morning, about half an hour before she first got up, had obviously stayed nearby, hoping for an opportunity to take a cruel revenge. He'd objected to having the cat on the bed, and Princess had scratched him when he tried to throw her off, so no doubt he took great pleasure in attacking the innocent creature when she went out for her morning prowl. He'd then cut off her poor little head and sprayed his message on the door just as a vicious extra.

36

Which only went to show, Angela reflected, that she'd been perfectly right in her assessment of his character. There were better ways of making money than taking a man like that as her third husband.

She didn't think it likely that the police would catch him unaided. Len was too clever. He'd had reasons of his own for approaching the house discreetly, late the previous night, and so she'd told him about the back lane where he could leave his car unobserved, and she'd arranged to flash her bedroom lights to let him know as soon as Simon had gone rushing off to his mother's. Gary always slept like the dead, and Harold knew nothing about anything, so there was no one in the house or the neighbourhood who would be able to point a finger at Len.

It would give her great satisfaction to put the police on to him herself, but there were two good reasons why she didn't intend to. First, Len would make a bad enemy. He was a well-known Yarchester businessman, important in sporting and entertainment circles, and she had no doubt that he would be prepared to employ someone to give her a bad time if she made difficulties for him.

And secondly, there was Simple Simon. She'd kept him in complete ignorance of her brief affair with Len, on the bird-in-the-hand principle, and now she had decided that he might still figure in her plans it was doubly important to assure him of her fidelity, and to be assured of his continuing devotion.

'Oh, Si – '

Leaving Harold and Gary to fill in the cat's grave, she led her husband into the newly built sun lounge, and flung her arms round his neck. She was a petite woman, so slim and so dainty on her feet that from the back, or from a distance, she looked like a girl.

From the front, because of rather than despite her deep suntan, it was immediately obvious that she was no longer young. The tan intensified every line on her face, emphasising her steely eyes and tight lips, but she spoke to her husband like a defenceless child.

'Si, darling – you're so sweet to me. Thank you for helping me through this dreadful morning, after I was so rotten to you last night.' She pressed her face penitently against his shoulder. 'I's sorry we quarrelled. Big Boy forgive Angie?'

Simon groaned with remorse, and hugged her to his barrel chest. He was of medium height but broad frame, and four years of marriage and rich cooking had begun to package his ribs in flesh.

'Darling Angie, the quarrel was all my fault. I was a selfish swine.' He rubbed his bearded face against her hair, and she remembered just in time not to protest that he was spoiling it. 'I'll never forgive myself for rushing off and leaving you alone like that.'

'But you did come back right away when I rang you at your mother's this morning, after the policeman came to tell us about poor little Princess. Thank you for doing as I suggested, Si, and driving up the back lane so that he couldn't see you arriving. I didn't want him to know that we'd quarrelled – he might have started suspecting you!'

'You were a clever girl to think of that.' Simon sat in a cushioned cane armchair, and drew her on to his knee. 'The question is, though, who on earth could have done it? Who could possibly be so cruel to you?' He shuddered, and tightened his arms about her. 'And *why*? For God's sake, why?'

'It doesn't make any sense,' she said dully. She pressed herself against him, hiding her face in his beard. 'Oh, Si, I'm frightened.'

'It's all right, darling, it's all right. I'll look after you.'

She sat up on his knee and fiddled with a curly strand of his hair. 'But how can I rely on you any more?' she asked in a pathetically small voice. 'You'll only go away and leave me all alone again, just as you did last night.'

'I *won't*! Angie, sweetheart, I promise I'll never go away and leave you alone again, ever. As long as you want me, I'll be there. And I'll do anything I can to make up for last night. Anything.'

That was what she wanted to know. She kissed her husband generously.

Then, 'Si – ' she said, stroking his hair with dextrous fingers, 'I've had a marvellous business idea – a real money-spinner. All

38

I need from you, dearest, is a little help to get it off the ground . . .'

5

Three hundred yards away, on the Upper Wickford side of the common, two widows sat sunning themselves outside the back door of a small sixteenth-century timber-framed house, with lichened red pantiles on its roof and yellow washed plaster on its walls. Nellie Arrowsmith and May Cullen, both born and bred in Suffolk, and friends and neighbours for twenty-eight years, were as usual passing the morning in each other's company.

May, white-haired and the elder by fifteen years, lived in a slate-roofed brick doll's house, one up and one down with a lean-to kitchen at the back, which had been slapped up against one end of the old house by a nineteenth-century jerry-builder. May had lived there, as wife and widow, for over fifty years. She and her husband had been childhood friends of Nellie's husband Fred and his first wife. Osteo-arthritis in her hips made it difficult for May to get about now, even with a walking frame, but she could manage the few yards from her own back door to Nellie's.

The friends sat on upright kitchen chairs, which rocked a little on the old, moss-edged, uneven slabs that paved the path. Round them – neglected for years, because it had become too much for Fred Arrowsmith to manage long before he died – two or three acres of garden and orchard rioted to ripeness. The sun, yellow as honey, drew out and mingled the spicy scent of mauve Michaelmas daisies with the fermenting smell of rotten windfall apples; wasps and red admiral butterflies tottered from fruit to flower, drunk on the wing.

The two women were not idle, as they sat easing their bones in the warmth of the day. On a stool between them was a basket heaped with the last of the crop of runner beans that Simon had planted and staked for his mother earlier in the year, and they occupied themselves by slicing the beans into the colanders they held on their aproned laps.

They worked slowly. May's disease had forced her fingers stiffly sideways, at an angle from her swollen knuckles, like clifftop trees permanently bent by gales. Nellie, a buxom woman who wore her greying fair hair in a thick braid round her head, was a comparative youngster at 62, but she had recently come out of hospital after heart surgery and her fingers felt numbed.

Like their work, their conversation was conducted with many pauses.

'It must have been nice for you to have him back in his old bedroom last night, Nellie.'

'Quite like old times. Except that he was so upset. I'd rather know that he was in his own home, and happy.'

As usual, they were talking of Simon. Nellie idolised her only child, but without attempting to possess him. Simon was her pride; her joy lay not in his companionship, much as she valued it, but in the knowledge of his well-being.

She had raised no objection, four years previously, to his proposed marriage at 23 to a divorcee of 29 with a son of 12. Nellie was at that time beginning to worry secretly about her health, and about who would look after Simon if she should die while he still lived at home. She wanted to see him happily married, and was concerned that he was shy and appeared to have no girl friends.

His unexpected – and slightly defensive – announcement that he had found an ideal future wife delighted her. An older woman, Nellie had thought comfortably, would already be an experienced cook and housekeeper; she'd be able to look after Simon far better than some slip of a girl.

Her husband, Fred, had had reservations. He knew that his first wife would have been horrified if their son Ross had made such a marriage. But Simon was Nellie's boy, and Fred had always been too old to be of any consequence in his younger son's upbringing. As long as Nellie and Simon were happy, Fred had minded his own business, and had taken his reservations with him to the grave.

And Simon certainly was happy at first; immensely proud of the smartly dressed, petite young woman who had agreed to be his wife, although he took her home to meet his parents only once before the wedding, and had never taken her to see May Cullen at all. Nellie had been saddened to see so little of her future daughter-in-law, but she accepted Simon's explanation that Angela was too busy to travel out from Yarchester to Wickford. She always accepted without question whatever her son said or did.

May Cullen was more sceptical. For all her age and infirmity, she was the sharper, shrewder of the two. She looked a sweet old lady, her complexion pink and soft, her hair as wispy white as cirrus cloud, but she was nobody's fool. She was very fond of Nellie, who had the kindest heart of anyone she knew, but sometimes she despaired over the younger woman's trusting simplicity.

Simon's failure to bring Angela to meet her, even after the couple came to live just across the common, hurt May very much, but she guessed his reason. She was neither as soft-hearted nor as soft-headed as his mother, and Simon knew it; if he didn't want her to meet Angela, it must be because he realised that he'd picked a wrong 'un.

One look at the wedding photographs – she had been invited to attend, but her infirmity made that impossible – had confirmed May's opinion.

'That woman's no more 29 than I am, Nellie,' she'd protested. 'Why, she looks nearly old enough to be his mother! And where did she get that long blonde hair from? You said it was jet black when he brought her to see you. And as for what she's wearing . . . I'll say nothing about a divorcee getting remarried in church, though I don't hold with it myself. But no woman with a husband living and a son of that age has any business to go to her second wedding in a long white dress, with a veil and all. She ought to be ashamed . . . Oh, Nellie, what has your poor Simon let himself in for?'

'But he loves her,' Nellie had explained. 'And I'm sure Angela loves him. She's all over him when they're together.'

'She would be, wouldn't she?' May had said drily. 'She knows when she's on to a good thing.'

But Simon had made his own choice, and as long as he was happy his mother had no qualms. When he'd told her, after their return from their Canary Island honeymoon, that Angela was not 29 but 36, Nellie didn't even blink. The older the woman, she reasoned, the better Simon would be looked after.

That Angela's idea of looking after Simon did not coincide with her own was a fact that began to dawn on Nellie only gradually, from casual remarks her son made when he called in, alone, to see her. Nellie had absorbed the information and passed it on bit by bit, without comment, to May.

It seemed that Angela wasn't really cut out for domestic work. Her brother Harold had been a chef before his accident; he was better at cooking, and at cleaning and washing and ironing, than his sister, and as he was glad of the opportunity to repay Angela and Simon for providing him with a home, she let him do it. And Simon himself liked to take charge of the household budget, and the joint cheque book, so he made a regular Friday evening visit to the superstore in Breckham Market to buy the week's provisions. He'd told his mother that he preferred to do the shopping on his own, without Angela; it was easier to concentrate, and to keep within his budget.

But Angela wasn't lazy, Nellie had assured her friend. She'd run a business of her own for years, in Yarchester, as a commission agent for some of the big mail-order firms. She had a large number of customers, who chose clothes and household goods from the catalogues she took to their doors and then paid her by instalments. That was why she'd needed a car of her own, after she married Simon and they set up house in Wickford, to keep her business going.

She'd become a representative for Avon cosmetics, too, since her marriage, so she was on the go all the time. It was understandable that she had felt in need of a good holiday, about eighteen months after the wedding, and she'd chosen to go to the Bahamas; not with Simon, but with her twice-divorced sister from Liverpool.

'But only because Simon's too busy to go,' Nellie had told

May, after she and Fred had been on a rare visit for Sunday tea to their son's home. And then, in an unusual outburst of frankness, she had added, 'Angela wouldn't have been *my* choice as a wife for him. Oh, her language . . . I've never heard a man use such words, let alone a woman. And yet she dresses so well, and smells lovely . . . Simon adores her. If she wanted the moon, I think he'd try to find some way of getting it for her.'

Even now, four years after their marriage, when Simon had rushed in distraught the previous night and asked for the use of his old room because he and Angela had quarrelled, Nellie refused to condemn her daughter-in-law. She wanted for Simon only what he had told her he wanted for himself: a reconciliation with the woman he loved.

Nellie had already been round to May's house, immediately after breakfast, to tell her friend about Simon's unexpected overnight stay. Now, as they sliced runner beans for storage in the freezer he had bought his mother, Nellie told May about his return visit to borrow a spade.

'But surely to goodness,' said May, 'the boy's got a spade of his own?'

Nellie looked puzzled. Simon hadn't told her why he wanted to borrow it, and she hadn't thought to ask him.

'Oh yes, he's got a spade,' she said. 'Sure to have.' Then her frown cleared. If Simon wanted to borrow a spade, it was because he wanted to borrow a spade, and that was all that concerned her. Besides, her illness had left her weakened, short of breath and subject to dizziness and blackouts, and she was increasingly conscious of her own mortality. 'But he might as well have his Dad's tools if he wants them. They're doing no good here, and they'll all be his when I'm gone.'

Her friend scolded her.

'Don't you start talking like that, Nellie Arrowsmith! You've got years in you yet, my girl. And just remember that what your husband owned was all earned by the sweat of his brow, and now it's yours you mustn't start giving it away. Fred wouldn't part with it, would he? You told me what he said when Simon tried to persuade him to sell the orchard to a builder, not long before he died. He hardly ever swore, poor old Fred, but when he did he meant it.'

'He wasn't himself, May. All those tablets he had to take upset him.'

'He'd still have refused, even if he'd been well. It would have broken his heart to see his orchard being built over, and Simon must have known it. Oh, not that I'm blaming the boy. I love him as much as if he were my own grandson, you know that. If he'd wanted to borrow the money from the sale for himself, I'd say nothing. But asking to borrow it to set that Angela up in business with a beauty salon . . .'

'She *is* a trained hairdresser, May. Don't you remember, I told you that was how they met, when he went for a haircut in Yarchester one day.'

'And got more than he bargained for, poor boy. His wife's a woman who's never satisfied, I can tell that even though I've never met her. Only four years married, and they've already moved house twice and had two or three different cars. And Simon had a good job in Ross's firm, he was happy and doing well, but Angela pushed him into leaving and setting up on his own, and he's been worried to death ever since. I know, I can see it in his eyes when he calls to ask me how I am. That woman is ruining him, Nellie, and if you give way to her she'll ruin you, too. She'll be after you for everything, land and house and money and all. And your poor Fred didn't work hard all his life to keep her and her first husband's son in luxury and idleness.'

It was a subject on which May Cullen felt strongly. Having lived next door to Fred Arrowsmith, as friend and tenant, for almost the whole of her adult life, she knew far better than Nellie exactly how much sweat and toil had gone into the market garden that had been his livelihood. Fred and his first wife had married with no more than a few pennies between them, but Fred's father-in-law had lent him a little money to put towards the house and land, and they'd borrowed the remainder on a mortgage. For over twenty years they'd both slaved to bring up their family and pay back every penny they owed.

Fred had never stopped working until old age defeated him, but by the time his first wife died, prematurely worn out, when he was in his fifties, he was out of debt. His second wife, Nellie, had always known financial security in her marriage. Unlike her predecessor, she'd never been required to help Fred on the land. But that was no reason, in May's view, for her to give Simon any of his inheritance while she was still alive, and May didn't hesitate to say so.

Nellie looked uneasy, but said nothing. They each sliced up another bean.

'That spade Simon borrowed,' May mused, resting her fiery finger joints again. 'Perhaps he wants to hit Angela over the head with it, and bury her.' She had a dry, earthy sense of humour.

'Oh, really, May, how can you say such a thing?' Nellie had no sense of humour at all. 'Simon would never do that, and you know it.'

But Nellie didn't tell her friend how much her son had shocked and upset her the previous night, when he had knelt with his head on her lap sobbing his heart out over his wife's verbal cruelty. Nor did she say that, lying wakeful and unwell at dawn, she had heard Simon get up and leave the house, and that she had watched him for a short time from her window as he paced the road outside, staring set-faced across the common towards his own home.

He had been back indoors by the time she was up and dressed. But then, just as she was trying to persuade him to eat some breakfast, a telephone call from Angela had sent him dashing off. When he returned, agitated, an hour or two later to borrow the spade, he had begged her not to tell anyone about his quarrel with his wife.

'If anyone should ask you, Mother,' he had said, 'I wasn't here last night. I was at home, with Angela.'

Nellie didn't tell her friend about that, either.

In the sun lounge at *Tenerife*, Angela had just finished outlining her marvellous business idea to her husband. He sat in stunned silence, her tiny weight a millstone on his knees.

'But – but I thought you wanted to open a beauty salon . . .' he croaked eventually.

'Not really, not any more. It's such an ordinary thing to do, and the profit margin's not high enough. But a restaurant will be a goldmine.'

Ever since she had worked as a barmaid at the Black Bull, chatting up the manager and the groups who performed there, as well as the more affluent customers, Angela had dreamed of running a bar of her own. Not a pub, where any roughneck could get in for the price of half a pint of beer, but somewhere more exclusive.

Len Pratt, the man she'd turned out of her bed that morning, had owned just such a place, a restaurant club in Yarchester. She had met him there a few weeks previously, when one of her mail-order customers whose husband was the club bouncer had invited her along one evening for a drink and a giggle. Angela had picked up a lot of information from Len about the running of the business, and it had been her hope, before she took a dislike to the man, that he would be prepared to set her up with a restaurant club of her own.

But Len, the pig, had laughed at her ambitions. He'd thought that it would be enough for her to have the prospect – when they were both divorced – of becoming his wife. He couldn't understand that, much as Angela liked and needed money, she didn't want to be given it at any man's whim. She wanted to make money of her own, to be rich and of consequence in her own right.

Simon wouldn't laugh at that. He wouldn't dare. He'd always been too humbly in love with her, too deeply hooked on the erotic games she'd taught him to risk incurring her displeasure by opposing her in any way. That was why he'd bought her a car, so that she could continue her mail-order business, and why he'd never objected to the amount of time she spent visiting her clients. And now that she'd made him feel so desperately worried and guilty over spending a night away from her, it shouldn't be too difficult to get his support for her new venture.

He was still gaping like a goldfish. 'A restaurant? Angie, sweetheart, you don't even like cooking . . .'

'I don't need to cook. There's a trained chef in the family.'

'But Harold's not a fit man. Has he agreed to this?'

'I haven't told him yet. But he'll do it. He knows that it's been my ambition for years to have a night spot of my own.'

Simon, his mind blowing, clutched at his curly hair as though to hold it on. 'A *night spot*? I thought you said – ?'

'A restaurant club, then. A late-night restaurant, with a bar and a bit of space for dancing.'

He began to sweat. 'Angie, for God's sake be reasonable! A small coffee shop, yes. Even a small daytime restaurant, if Harold's willing and able to work on a regular basis, though I doubt that. But a restaurant club would be a much bigger undertaking, and you know nothing at all about running a place like that.'

'Oh yes I do! I worked in clubs and pubs before we were married, and I know exactly how they should be run. It needs experience and flair, and I've got both. As you well know, Big Boy, don't you? Eh? Don't you, eh?'

He squirmed as her deft fingers worked between the buttons of his shirt and began to tug and tease the curly hairs on his damp chest.

'No, Angie, don't, please . . . you must think seriously about this. I mean, it'll take a lot of money, too. We're already overstretched, with the mortgage, and the hire purchase on your car, and the bank loan we needed to build this sun-lounge extension. You know that Ross won't help, and I can't ask Mother about selling the land, not after Dad was so upset when I asked him last time. So how could we possibly raise the money to start the kind of business you're thinking of?'

She told him. Simon listened appalled, knowing that in any prudent businessman's terms her plan invited financial disaster; knowing, too, that if she'd made up her mind he was not only powerless to stop her, but too much in thrall to deny her the support she demanded.

6

Midday was golden, but the grass on Wickford common was too long to dry out completely. The three or four solitary women who were walking their dogs over the common in the sunshine, along invisible private paths, were all suitably and soberly dressed in green wellington boots and green quilted jackets or jerkins.

'Not what I'd think of as Angela Arrowsmith territory,' said Hilary Lloyd as the Chief Inspector drove her towards Nether Wickford. 'Unless she's changed completely since she was a barmaid at the Black Bull, she must be bored rigid in a quiet place like this.'

'Do we know why she and her husband are living out here?' asked Quantrill. The possible connection with the A135 case had made him anxious to see Angela Arrowsmith for himself, but he had first made a circuit of the common, stopping to hear verbal reports from the search and enquiry teams who had been working through the area all morning. They had paid particular attention to the Arrowsmiths' two neighbours, but had acquired no information of any significance beyond the fact that Angela was regarded with staid disapproval.

'Apparently Simon Arrowsmith's elderly widowed mother lives in Upper Wickford,' said Hilary, 'and he likes to be near enough to keep an eye on her.'

Quantrill grunted, the outward expression of an inward wince.

His own mother had also been left an elderly widow. She would have liked nothing better than for Douglas, her only son, to settle with his family somewhere near her, but despite the fact that he was working in the same county he had declined to do so. And ever since her death, last year, he'd been haunted by guilt.

He'd kept in touch throughout her lifetime, of course. Had a telephone installed for her and paid the bills, travelled the twenty-seven miles to visit her when he could find the time, and always remembered her birthday, which was more than he'd done for his wife. Harassed as he was by the demands of his job and his immediate family, he had thought this enough. But in retrospect how could it have been enough, to visit his ailing mother once every few weeks, tell her warmly to look after herself, and then go off and leave her to the care of the home-help and meals-on-wheels services?

The result was that because he could never think of her without remorse, he had formed the habit of trying to avoid all remembrance of her. And that wasn't right, either. Had there been any way, after her death, in which he could have made up for his neglect and proved his love for her, he would have seized upon it gladly, whatever the cost.

But there was no way of doing that; and so when he met someone like Simon Arrowsmith, who kept a properly filial eye on his elderly parent, Quantrill was predisposed to regard him with a mixture of approval and resentful suspicion. The man might be a good son, but that didn't make him spotless. It certainly didn't mean that he knew nothing at all about this morning's threat to his wife.

It was Simon Arrowsmith who opened the front door to them. He had been expecting the woman detective to return, but not that she would be accompanied by a masculine Chief Inspector. Little of the fair skin of Simon's face was visible, between the tangle of curls on his forehead and the fine fuzz of beard on his cheeks, but what could be seen reddened immediately when Quantrill introduced himself.

Hilary Lloyd had described him to her boss as a chubby, shy, inarticulate man who used his beard as a refuge. He was holding a curly-stemmed pipe in his hand as he opened the door, and having uttered a strangled invitation to come in he thrust the pipe quickly into a recess in his facial hair, and puffed out a smokescreen.

Mumbling at their heels, he manoeuvred them into a room so immaculately furnished that it looked as though it had been ordered in its entirety straight from the display window of a department store. There was no evidence that the room was ever in actual use. Even the books, sharing the shelves of the wall unit with decorative objects in glass and metal, looked as though they might be showroom dummies.

Angela Arrowsmith, her dark gold hair eye-catching above her black dress, was curled small in one corner of a clover-pink velvet chesterfield. She was restlessly buffing her fingernails, colourless but – to Quantrill's eye – almost as long as a Balinese temple dancer's. Though her suntan made it impossible for her to look pale, her smile and her voice were both wan as she invited the detectives to sit down; but her extravagantly made-up eyes immediately fastened on Quantrill. As Hilary had guessed, Mrs Arrowsmith was a woman who had no time for other women when there was a man about.

The Chief Inspector's initial, carefully concealed, reaction was one of surprise at her age. Sergeant Lloyd had reported that Angela Arrowsmith was married to a younger man, but not that he was so very much younger. As he went to stand beside his wife, with every appearance of protective concern, Simon Arrowsmith looked like an overgrown schoolboy wearing a false beard. A rift between such an ill-assorted couple seemed to Quantrill to be natural and inevitable.

'You've had a very unpleasant shock, Mrs Arrowsmith,' he began. 'I'm fond of cats myself – ' he was only moderately fond, and then only of ordinary domestic moggies, but it was one way of encouraging her to talk ' – so I can understand how upset you were. I hope you're feeling better now?'

'A little, thank you. I can't tell you how dreadful it was . . . I shall never get over the shock, never . . .'

The woman was entitled to a bit of exaggeration, Quantrill thought. The shock had been real enough, he could see that in her eyes. But what he couldn't see there was fear.

Sergeant Lloyd had reported, after her visit earlier in the morning, that Angela Arrowsmith seemed thoroughly frightened. It had been one of the reasons why Quantrill had come himself to talk to her. But if she really had been frightened then, she certainly wasn't now; all she seemed concerned about was dramatising her distress over the cat.

Her husband, mumbling round his pipe, tried to dissuade her from crying.

'Here,' he said on inspiration, 'I'll get you another drink.'

He bent to pick up an almost empty glass and a bottle of brandy from the floor beside the chesterfield, where they had been out of view of the visitors. His wife shot him a steely glare, then said in a childish voice, 'Well, perhaps a very tiny one . . .' She turned a brave smile towards Quantrill: 'Would *you* like something to drink?'

The Chief Inspector refused. Angela took his refusal to include his colleague. Whether or not that was what he meant, Hilary Lloyd had no intention of being ignored.

'Thank you,' she said. 'Coffee would be lovely, if it's not too much trouble.'

Angela looked put out. Her husband, handing her the generously refilled brandy glass, raised an uncertain, smoke-wreathed eyebrow at her. 'Go and tell Harold to bring some coffee,' she muttered ungraciously, sending him lumbering from the room. She sipped her drink, leaned back and closed her eyes. 'It was a terrible shock,' she murmured. 'I can't tell you what Princess meant to me – she's irreplaceable . . .'

A scuffling noise came from the sun lounge, which was built as an extension to the sitting room. The rooms were divided by sliding glass doors which were not completely closed. In the sun lounge, a tall bespectacled boy could be seen ducking and peering behind the cane furniture, and making low grabbing motions. His grabs were evidently unsuccessful, because in a moment a leggy seal-point Siamese kitten, hugely eyed and eared but thin as a cardboard cut-out, squeezed through the gap in the doors and erupted into the sitting room.

An unexpected encounter with Quantrill's tweed trouser legs and size twelve leather shoes stopped it short, sideways on, its back and tail defensively arched. It took one brave, stiff-legged bounce forwards, still presenting its maximum profile, and then turned tail and fled, leaping for the long curtain that hung beside the sliding doors.

51

'Sorry, Mum,' gabbled the boy, opening the doors wider and trying to reach for the kitten, which promptly swarmed higher, its great eyes in the triangular head dark with devilment.

'Blast you, Gary,' snapped his mother, abandoning her langour. 'I *told* you to keep her outside. Grab her, quick, before she breaks something – '

Her son pursued the flying, bat-eared kitten round the room, from the curtain pelmet to the shelves of the wall unit. Angela issued shrill instructions and reprimands, pausing only to explain to the detectives that her husband had insisted on going out that morning to buy the kitten for her.

'Simon!' she shrieked, as it made a trapeze-artiste's leap from the highest shelf to the window curtains, and clung there swinging. 'Oh, there you are – always somewhere else when I need you. For God's sake come and get her down – '

Simon, hurrying in, made a nervous, clumsy grab. Evading him, the kitten fell into Gary's hands.

'Gotcha,' the boy chuckled, pressing his cheek for a moment against the palpitating creamy fur. 'I'm glad Mum made you go out and buy her,' he said loudly and clearly to Simon, 'she's nice . . . Sorry about the interruption, Mum.'

He backed quickly into the sun lounge, taking his capture with him. His apology had sounded genuinely contrite, but Quantrill was well acquainted with boys of that age. He had one of his own. Watching Gary's face, he caught a brief glimpse of malicious satisfaction and knew that the boy had quite deliberately let the kitten loose in order to spike his mother's tragic pose.

'Did you buy the kitten in Nether Wickford, Mr Arrowsmith?' asked Hilary. 'We've heard that someone in Mill Road breeds Siamese.'

Simon, busily relighting his pipe, nodded. Angela answered, speaking to Quantrill. 'At least half a dozen people in the village have bought cats from Mrs Bailey, so I'm not the only one who has a Siamese. That's why I think that what happened this morning must have been a mistake. Simon and I have discussed it, and we agree that the message couldn't have been intended for me at all.'

'It wasn't directed to anyone by name,' said Quantrill, 'so that's one of the possibilities we're considering. On the other hand, neither of your neighbours has a cat of any kind, so it couldn't have been meant for them. Possibly it was intended for you, but as nothing more than a piece of immediate unpleasantness. Although the context is alarming, *Your turn next* isn't a specific threat. So tell me: can either of you think of anyone who might want to play a particularly cruel trick on you?'

Simon Arrowsmith, watching his wife, made vigorous noises of dissent from behind an aromatically blue smokescreen.

'Absolutely not,' said Angela, her eyes the colour and strength of gunmetal. 'It could only have been a mistake.'

'You'll be glad to know,' said Hilary, relating some of the findings of the search and enquiry teams, 'that your cat was killed entirely by accident. A regular traveller along this road hit it with his vehicle. It darted out in front of him, across the road towards the common, twenty yards from your gate. He tried to avoid it – there are skid-marks on the road to prove that – but he couldn't help knocking it over. He stopped and went back, but found that it was dead. The man lives in this area – ' he was in fact a baker's roundsman who lived less than half a mile away, but as a matter of policy Hilary concealed his identity '– but he didn't know who the cat belonged to, so he lifted it to the side of the road and drove on.'

A shadow of unaffected sorrow crossed Angela Arrowsmith's face. Hilary recognised it, and spoke with sympathy. 'Your pet wouldn't have suffered. The vehicle must have hit her head, and she'd have died instantly. But the fact is that the person who subsequently found her – or who saw the accident, perhaps – knew where to bring the body. And that really does rule out the possibility that it could have arrived on your doorstep by mistake.'

Simon Arrowsmith, sitting by his wife's side on the pink velvet chesterfield, stared at her unhappily. Angela buffed her fingernails.

'Would you both like to reconsider my question?' asked Quantrill. 'Do you know of anyone who would want to mutilate your cat, and threaten you?'

53

'No,' said Angela.

'Certainly not,' mumbled Simon, puffing hard. His features were almost invisible, his voice wretched.

'I see. Then do you want to make an official complaint about the incident, Mrs Arrowsmith?'

She shrugged. 'What'd be the point? It wouldn't bring Princess back.'

As far as the Chief Inspector was concerned, that clinched it. From her attitude, it was clear that Angela Arrowsmith had decided that the threat wasn't seriously intended. Presumably she knew – or thought she knew – who was responsible for the incident, and had reasons of her own for wanting to protect his identity. Therefore it was, as Quantrill had suspected when he entered the house, what he would class as a domestic dispute; and unless an official complaint was made by the injured or offended party, domestic disputes were no concern of the police.

'Then I don't propose,' he said briskly, 'to waste any more of your time, or my own. Or Sergeant Lloyd's. What happened here this morning was unpleasant, but no crime was committed. We came to see you because of the reference to a murder we're investigating – the A135 murder. I'm quite sure you've heard and read about the decapitated body that was found a few weeks ago beside the main Yarchester road?'

Simon reached protectively for his wife's hand. They both nodded.

'What we need to establish,' Quantrill went on, 'is whether there is any real connection between that murder and this morning's incident. To do that, we must know who was responsible for what happened here. So if either of you knows, or guesses, we need the information. As long as we're satisfied that it was an isolated incident, we can then go away and leave you alone.'

'If the threat was directed at me, as you seem to think,' said Angela sharply, 'there's no way it could possibly be connected with that murder. I told the detectives who came here asking questions a couple of weeks ago that I had no idea who that poor woman was, and I still haven't. I keep on telling you:

what happened this morning wasn't intended for me at all. If you – '

She was interrupted by the arrival of the coffee. It came in a ceramic pot, with matching cups and saucers, wheeled in on a trolley by a pale, heavy-eyed, thick-set man. His cropped sandy hair, closely shaven chin, crisp white shirt, dark trousers, polished shoes and deep, bewildered frown gave him the look of a ship's steward permanently stranded half the world away from his home port.

Like a steward, with no part in the conversation, he began silently and deftly to serve the coffee, without looking at the people he was serving.

'My brother, Harold Wilkes, bless him,' Angela told the Chief Inspector, obviously welcoming the diversion. 'He used to work as a chef on an oil rig off the Norfolk coast, until he lost his hearing in an explosion, poor old boy. But we're very happy to have him as a member of our family, aren't we, Si? We're very fond of our Harold.'

She attracted her brother's attention by catching at his arm as he passed her, and repeated her last remark, mouthing and smiling and nodding at him.

'*We're very fond of you, Harold.* FOND, I said.' She made a kissing mouth at him. 'Bless his heart . . . I know it's a handicap, being deaf, but I sometimes think that the deaf have a lot of advantages over the rest of us. Just imagine all that peacefulness – no aircraft screaming overhead, no telephone bells, no traffic noises . . . They don't know how lucky they are, do they?'

Hilary Lloyd's scarred eyebrow puckered more deeply as she stared at the woman, marvelling at her complacent insensitivity. Harold Wilkes was also staring at his sister. It was impossible to tell how much he could lip-read, but Hilary could see that his eyes were raw with suffering.

She touched his sleeve, lightly and unobtrusively. His blood-shot eyes moved to her face. 'Thank you for the coffee,' she said clearly; and smiled at him.

Seeing her smile, Quantrill realised for the first time why his friend Harry Colman had been so enthusiastic about her appearance. Harry was right. When Hilary Lloyd gave a wholehearted smile, it really was a beauty.

Quantrill's eyes flicked to the deaf man's face, interested to see his reaction. Yes, Wilkes had been bowled over. For a moment the permanent frown had lifted from his forehead as he brightened in response to her smile, irradiated with unexpected joy.

Well, it would be no bad thing to have a member of the CID team who could charm potentially difficult male witnesses. Despite his initial reservations about working with a female sergeant, Quantrill began to think that there were occasions when it might have its advantages.

7

Chief Inspector Quantrill was too old a detective to think in terms of tying up loose ends. Life was too short, and the list of undetected crimes in the division too long, to allow him the luxury of tidying up as he went. He was reconciled to the fact that, in many of the enquiries he conducted, he would never know exactly what had happened. The Nether Wickford incident was a time-waster, but he persisted with it because he had nothing else that looked remotely like a lead in the A135 murder investigation.

The Arrowsmiths were obviously not prepared to talk in front of each other and so he separated them, taking the husband outside. Simon was reluctant to leave his wife with Sergeant Lloyd, and there was no doubt that Angela would have preferred to go with the men; but the Sergeant, with the air of one who had all the time in the world, asked whether she might have another cup of coffee, and so Angela was obliged to stay with her.

Quantrill marched Simon out to the garage, out of earshot of the rest of his family, and spoke to him briskly, man to man. Wives, he said, could sometimes be the very devil: irrational, demanding, ungiving, exasperating. There were times when even the most decent and reasonable husband might be tempted, given the opportunity, to win a bit of peace and quiet for himself by playing some kind of trick on his wife. Was that what Arrowsmith had done?

Simon denied it; and went on denying it. 'I *love* my wife,' he protested.

'That's exactly what another man told me, last year,' said Quantrill. 'He meant it, too. But he's now doing a life sentence for murdering her.'

Simon's eyes popped. 'Who – who's talking about murder?'

'I am. That's all I'm interested in, Mr Arrowsmith, the A135 murder. I'm not concerned with your domestic problems, I just want to know whether I can eliminate this morning's incident from my enquiries. If you weren't responsible for it, who was? Your brother-in-law? The boy? One of your wife's friends?'

Simon Arrowsmith, at bay behind his beard, reaffirmed his earlier statement that he knew no one who could possibly have a grudge against his wife.

At the back of the house, Quantrill found Gary Hilton lying on the lawn like a fallen beanpole, communicating with the Siamese kitten.

He questioned the boy abruptly, getting the same answers that Sergeant Lloyd had been given: Gary had been asleep that morning until he heard his mother having hysterics after the motorcycle patrolman arrived; he didn't know who had paint-sprayed the message on the door, couldn't imagine.

'Do you know anyone who might want to play a nasty trick on your mother?'

The boy, taking a kitten's-eye view of a ladybird that was scaling a stem of grass, muttered an indistinct 'No.'

'How do you get along with her yourself, Gary? Are you on good terms?'

'Yes . . . yes, 'course we are.'

It wasn't true, Quantrill had seen that for himself. On the other hand, how many adolescents were on good terms with their parents? How many parents, come to that, could put their hands on their hearts and say that they actually liked – as distinct from loving – their teenage children? His own son, Peter, frequently infuriated him, and compounded his youthful offences by making it clear that his father's fury was reciprocated.

But Peter had his good points, difficult though it sometimes was to appreciate them, and so no doubt had Gary. The fact that Gary was lying about his relationship with his mother didn't necessarily mean that he had lied in answer to Quantrill's other questions. The boy might well be as ignorant about this morning's incident as he claimed to be.

There was one other member of the family to question, and the Chief Inspector found him in a room at the back of the house. This was a large dining-kitchen, where it seemed that the Arrowsmiths did all their living so that they could keep their main room immaculate. Two-thirds of the kitchen was crammed with dining and television-watching furniture, and the usual untidy bits and pieces of family life. But the cooking area, formed by purpose-built units into a shape as compact as a ship's galley, was evidently run by someone who knew how to combine constant use with orderliness.

Something savoury was simmering in a pan on the ceramic hob of the split-level cooker. A pudding mixture was being whipped up in the bowl of the automatic mixer. Harold Wilkes, made temporarily redundant by kitchen technology, was standing hunched at the sink with his cropped head bowed in an attitude that made Quantrill wonder for a moment whether he might be ill.

Wilkes gave an audible sigh, almost a groan, and turned towards the mixer. It was only then, with a blink of surprise, that he realised that someone was in the room with him.

Not knowing whether the man understood who he was, Quantrill showed him his warrant card. Wilkes glanced at it, his permanent frown deepening.

'I knew you were another detective,' he confirmed in his loud, uneven voice. 'You've come about the cat, haven't you?'

Quantrill opened his mouth to speak, remembered that Wilkes was deaf, and took out his pocket book instead.

The cat was killed accidentally, by a vehicle, he wrote. *But someone found it lying at the side of the road and brought it back here. Was it you?*

Wilkes switched off the mixer and read the words. When he moved his head it was slowly and carefully, like a man with a pounding hangover. 'No,' he said. 'I didn't touch it.'

The men were facing each other across the worktop of the unit that formed one side of the kitchen area. On it, next to the mixer, stood a chopping board, and on the board lay a large, thick-skinned vegetable marrow. The marrow had been cut clean in two. Beside it lay a cook's knife with a broad, rigid, eight-inch carbon steel blade.

Quantrill picked up the knife and balanced it in his hand. It was of French manufacture, high quality, fully-forged, its blade thinned by constant sharpening and cleaning. He raised his eyes from it and gave Harold Wilkes a questioning look.

'I told you, I didn't touch the cat,' said Wilkes. 'I certainly didn't cut it up.'

'I didn't think you did,' said Quantrill, enunciating clearly. 'I'm sure you'd have made a better job of it.'

He put the knife down, and wrote again: *Do you know – have you any idea – who cut off the cat's head and sprayed the message on the door?*

'No,' said Wilkes flatly. He turned to the pan on the hob, stirred and tasted the contents and added a twist of black pepper from the mill. Quantrill, trying to ignore the aroma of chicken with mushrooms, green pepper and tomatoes that was liquefying his mouth, made a final attempt.

Do you know if there's anyone who might have a grudge against your sister?

Wilkes stared at him, his bloodshot eyes ringed with dark, puffy skin, his forehead deeply furrowed. '*If* there's anyone? You must be joking.' He moved away, and busied himself with his cooking.

Quantrill took out one of his personal cards with the address and telephone number of Breckham Market divisional police headquarters, crossed out his own rank and name and substituted that of Detective Sergeant Hilary Lloyd. He touched

Harold Wilkes's arm and gave him the card, indicating that it was Hilary who was in the next room with his sister. Wilkes's frown immediately lightened.

Quantrill gave him a friendly smile. 'Miss Lloyd is a very nice young woman,' he enunciated. It was not a matter on which he had, as yet, formed his own opinion, but other people had said so and he wanted to give Wilkes some encouragement. He pointed to the telephone number. 'If you'd like to talk to her, just ring – '

He stopped, cursing himself for his clumsiness. He'd despised Angela Arrowsmith for her inability to understand her brother's handicap, but now he was being equally inconsiderate. It was so difficult to imagine how comprehensive a disability deafness was, how much of normal everyday life the deaf were cut off from.

He shifted his pointing finger. 'Just call at this address. Or write to her, and she'll come to see you in private.' Both suggestions were unsatisfactory: he didn't know whether Wilkes could drive, and there was no public transport apart from the weekly market-day bus; and members of the public were invariably more reluctant to write to the police than to call at the station or telephone.

But at least Wilkes understood. He nodded, and from the look on his face as he tucked the card carefully into his shirt pocket, it was evident that he'd gladly go out of his way to see Hilary Lloyd again.

Quantrill left the room feeling that although his attempt to obtain information from Simon Arrowsmith and the boy had ended in frustration, something might eventually emerge from a meeting between the deaf man and Sergeant Lloyd. But then it occurred to him that Harold Wilkes's eagerness to keep in touch with the woman detective didn't necessarily mean that he had any information to give her. She would probably spend hours of valuable police time on the man, only to discover that he wanted to see her merely because he found her attractive.

It was, Quantrill thought with gloom, just as he'd first suspected: a female sergeant was bound to be a liability.

A female sergeant was definitely not of the right sex to encourage a man's woman like Angela Arrowsmith to talk. The job had fallen to Hilary only because she had known her in Yarchester. Studying Angela, while Quantrill was still in the room, Hilary had decided that she was so much on the defensive, so suspicious that another woman might be trying to put her down, that the only possible approach to her would be by way of open admiration.

Angela was obviously proud of the décor of her unused room, and the woman detective's comments on it when they were alone together began to disarm her. Hilary went on to compliment her on the cut of her black dress; Angela, who never let slip an opportunity for earning commission, explained that she was a mail-order agent.

'I could find a really smart dress for you,' she said, glancing her disapproval of Hilary's casual clothes. 'I'll show you a catalogue – but it had better be a one-off order, cash down, I can't take on any new credit customers at this stage. I'm planning to give up the mail-order business and open a restaurant, with Harold as chef.'

'That sounds exciting,' said Hilary, who thought it more interesting than exciting; her primary interest was in the fact that Angela had apparently forgotten the morning's unpleasantness completely. 'But is your brother-in-law fit enough for regular work?'

'He's all right, apart from his headaches. It'll do him good to get out of the house more, and I'll take on an assistant to help him. I had a look round a few days ago and found a perfect property I can rent. It used to be a restaurant, but the previous owners had no flair. They didn't make a success of it, and it's been empty for months. It's very dreary inside, it'll have to be completely redecorated and carpeted, and the kitchen needs re-equipping. But it's exactly the size I want. It'll seat over a hundred diners, and still leave room for a bar, and a small stage for the cabaret – '

Angela's eyes were shining with visionary commercial fervour. Incredulous, Hilary managed to force her facial muscles into an angle of approval and applause.

'Really exciting . . . Whereabouts in Yarchester is this?' she asked, knowing that the city was amply provided with restaurants of every size and ethnic variety, as well as hotels, pubs, discos, dance halls and night clubs. An amateur owner with a handicapped chef wouldn't survive for more than a couple of months – unless of course she had some influential backing. Perhaps Angela's old contacts were setting her up in a restaurant to provide them with a front for their activities? But if that were so, she'd hardly tell a policewoman about it . . . unless she'd either forgotten Hilary's job, or didn't realise that her friends from the Black Bull were making use of her.

'It's not in Yarchester,' said Angela, 'there's too much competition, and the rents are too high. The restaurant's in Breckham Market, in Bridge Street. The town's half-dead in the evenings, there's absolutely nowhere for swingers in the twenty-five to forty-five age group to go, and they're the ones with the money. A good restaurant and night spot will be a winner.'

Hilary said nothing. The scheme was so crazy that she couldn't believe that Angela Arrowsmith was being serious.

She had visited Breckham Market on several occasions, though she couldn't as yet claim to know the town well. But what she had learned from Wpc Patsy Hopkins was that, apart from a few well-known layabouts, drunks, vandals and petty villains, the inhabitants of the old town and of the surrounding villages were publicly staid. Suffolk people were not – never had been, even before the expression became outdated – swingers. The Rugby Club dinner and the Civic Ball were the liveliest events in Breckham's social calendar. Anyone who wanted to kick over the traces preferred to go to Yarchester, and do it in anonymity.

The inhabitants of the new town, on the far side of the by-pass, were a good deal less inhibited. They had moved out of London en masse in the nineteen-sixties, lured by new houses and jobs, and they almost certainly thought, as Angela did, that Breckham Market was half-dead. In more affluent times they might have lived up to the image that she still had of them.

But market research – or even an intelligent reading of the

newspapers – was evidently not Angela's strong point. She seemed not to know that money had become short. Many of the factories on the industrial estate had been put out of business in the recession; there was considerable unemployment in the new town, with the threat of more to come. Those who were still lucky enough to be in work were unlikely, Hilary imagined, to become regular customers of a large restaurant club.

'*How* many did you say it will seat?' she asked, so horrified that she forgot, for the moment, the purpose of the interview.

'A hundred and twenty, at least.' Angela noticed Hilary's expression, and laughed. 'Oh, I shan't be relying for custom on passers-by. Publicity and advertising, that's what it's all about. That's how my brother-in-law built up his business – Ross Arrowsmith, you know, the man who's made a fortune out of computers and things. He had a double-page advertising feature in the East Anglian Daily Press at the beginning of this year, when his company moved into the Old Maltings, and that's what I shall have when I open my restaurant. That'll be in November, just in time for the Christmas season. I shall give a pre-opening reception for the press and travel agents and local businessmen, and that'll bring in block bookings for coach parties and office parties . . .'

Angela Arrowsmith was completely, almost alarmingly, obsessed by her scheme; Hilary could see it in her eyes, hear it in her voice. Either the woman was a fantasist, or she had a backer who had reasons of his own for being prepared to invest a considerable sum of money in an overambitious venture that hadn't a hope of commercial success.

'You don't remember me, do you?' the detective sergeant asked suddenly.

Brought back to reality, Angela blinked her enamelled eyelids. 'Should I?'

'The Black Bull, Yarchester, about five years ago. I was in uniform, you were behind the bar. That's why I wondered whether you were going back to Yarchester to open your restaurant. Making use of your old contacts, perhaps?'

Angela Arrowsmith attempted to bayonet her with a look. 'You bitch!' she said furiously. She unleashed the vocabulary

63

that she had been restraining in keeping with her respectably-married image, and told Sergeant Lloyd exactly what she thought of her. Hilary, who felt wryly that she probably deserved the earful, finished her coffee while she waited for the verbal offensive to slacken.

'I've had no connection with anybody from the Bull for years,' Angela asserted eventually. 'I've always been straight, and my restaurant will be strictly legitimate.'

'Of course. You wouldn't have told me about it otherwise, would you? But aren't you taking a terrible risk, in the present state of the economy? It certainly isn't anything I'd want to invest in, even if I had the money.'

'Nobody's asking you to. I'm not a penniless divorcee any more, you know, I own half this house, and a car, and I've got access to other money. And as soon as the restaurant gets started, the takings will roll in.'

'Where's this "other money" coming from?'

'That's none of your business. And don't think you can start raising police objections when I apply for a liquor licence, because you've got absolutely nothing against me.'

'But someone has. A very nasty threat was paint-sprayed on your door this morning,' Hilary reminded her. 'Who did that?'

'How the hell do I know? Isn't that what you're paid for, to find out?'

'I've already found out that you're no longer frightened. You've practically forgotten the incident, haven't you? So I think you know perfectly well who did it. You say it was no one from your past; a member of your family, then?'

Angela denied that vigorously. Having persuaded Simon to help her raise the money to open her restaurant, and intending, as soon as the police went, to talk Harold into working as her chef, she didn't want either of them hassled by further questioning. Above all, she didn't want the police to find out about Len Pratt.

And then Angela had a brilliant idea. Not only would it keep the police away from Simon, Harold and Len; it would also settle more than one old score.

She sighed, as if capitulating out of weariness, and protested that it would be unfair to name someone when she had no proof of his involvement. She could be wrong, and if he found out that she'd accused him falsely . . .

Sergeant Lloyd assured her that the source of the information would not be revealed.

'Well, then – '

Angela hesitated, realising that the false trail wouldn't do more than buy her a little time. The police would probably soon be back. But they were supposed to be overworked, and with the mystery of that headless body in the layby still to solve, they wouldn't want to spend too long over something they'd said they didn't class as a crime.

Meanwhile, she could enjoy the thought that they were questioning that pig of a man who'd looked at her as though she were dirt when she'd suggested a mutually beneficial business discussion over dinner. It would also serve him right for being too mean to give her the financial backing she'd wanted for a beauty salon. And it would pay him back, too, for the trouble and inconvenience she'd been caused by having her mail-order business correspondence so often misdelivered to his offices.

'Well . . . it could be Ross. Ross Arrowsmith, my brother-in-law. He fancies me. He wanted me to go out to dinner with him a few months ago. I wouldn't, of course, and I think he's been trying to find a way of punishing me for it ever since.'

'But where's the connection with what happened this morning?'

'Ross was jogging on the common, just about at that time. I looked out of my bedroom window, on my way back to bed after letting Princess out, and saw him.'

'It was a very misty morning. Are you sure it was him?'

'I couldn't see very well, but I'm almost sure. He jogs round the common most mornings. Not that I'm accusing him, of course. I'm not making a complaint, there's no point. I'm just telling you.'

Hilary thanked her for the information. She half-disbelieved the woman – the Angela she had known in Yarchester would never have turned down any kind of invitation from a wealthy man – but she didn't want to do her an injustice. It wasn't impossible that Angela had changed her habits when she remarried.

It wasn't impossible, either, that her plans for the restaurant were, as she'd protested, strictly legitimate. But if so, she was almost certainly heading for financial trouble.

Hilary had occasionally had to deal with people who had taken to crime – theft or handling or fraud or arson – as a direct result of the failure of injudicious business ventures. She had also seen the broken homes and ruined lives that were all too often the indirect result of business failure. As she rose to go she offered a word of caution, not so much for Angela's own sake – she was a woman who would always look after herself – but for the sake of her hapless family.

'Look,' Hilary said, 'if you're really serious about this restaurant – '

'Of course I'm serious.'

'Then I expect you've already taken professional advice – or you will be taking it, before you commit yourself to anything. It sounds an exciting idea, but if it were mine I'd want to discuss it with a solicitor or an accountant first. There are stories almost every week in the local papers of people who come to grief through starting up in business too hurriedly.'

Angela's thin mouth became lipless. She glared at Sergeant Lloyd. 'You snob!' she said with passion. 'You patronising bloody snob, trying to tell me how to run my life! What do you know about business, *copper?*'

Departing with another earful of invective, Hilary was blundered into on the front doorstep by an anxious Simon Arrowsmith. One hand clutched his pipe, the other clutched heavily at her arm.

'Oh, Miss Lloyd – will you please use your influence with the Chief Inspector? After your first visit this morning you left a policeman outside the house, to protect my wife. Now Mr Quantrill has sent him away, leaving Angela completely unprotected. Can you change his mind, please?'

'Sorry,' said Hilary. 'He carries the rank, so he makes the decisions.'

'But you're a woman. Surely you can persuade him?'

'Sorry,' she repeated. 'I happen to agree with this particular decision, you see. If your wife's no longer worried – and she isn't, you know – there's really no need for you to worry on her behalf. I'm sure she isn't in any danger.'

She could hardly point out to the man that from what she had seen of his relationship with his wife, he was the one who was most in need of protection.

8

1.15 p.m., and the sun was hot on the tables and benches that stood on the gravelled forecourt of the Cross Keys, which overlooked the common from the Upper Wickford side. It wasn't a pub that Quantrill liked. The beer was carbonated, the volume product of a giant brewery combine rather than traditional Suffolk ale, and the old brick building had been prettified inside with fake horse brasses, and outside with windowboxes sprouting plastic roses. If he'd been on his own, Quantrill would have gone elsewhere. But it made a convenient stopping place for a quick lunch, and as the other outside tables were empty he could say what he had to say to his new sergeant without being overheard.

Hoping for granary bread, sharp cheese and crisp pickled onions, he ordered what the blackboard menu described as a Ploughman's Platter. What arrived on the platter was a chunk of steam-baked French loaf, with papery crust and cottonwool crumb, a slice of flabby processed cheese and a spoonful of sweet chutney, the whole decorated with a few bits of limp lettuce and a quarter of underripe tomato. The sight did nothing to improve his humour.

'Well, that's a morning wasted,' he said. 'And right in the middle of a murder enquiry, too.'

He slapped butter on a piece of bread, cheese on the butter and chutney on the soapy cheese. Hilary Lloyd made no move to start her own meal. She sat on the wooden bench with her face turned to the sun, soaking up its warmth and saying nothing. She wanted time to think, to untangle the implications of what she'd heard at Nether Wickford, before coming to any conclusions about it.

'Not that I'm blaming you entirely, Miss Lloyd,' Quantrill went on. 'The incident had to be investigated, once it had been reported, and you were right to take the possibility of a link with the A135 murder seriously. But it looks now as though we can definitely rule that out. I've called off all the enquiry teams, here and in Mrs Arrowsmith's old haunts in Yarchester.'

He paused to drink some beer. His new sergeant's quiet composure irritated him, and irritation made him pompous.

'When a police officer of your rank and experience reports that a witness seems frightened for her life, I don't question the accuracy of your observation. If you say she was frightened when you first interviewed her, I believe you. But what I do suggest is that you misjudged what you saw, and overreacted. Of course Mrs Arrowsmith was frightened. She'd had a very unpleasant shock. But it seems clear to me that her husband had simply seized an unexpected opportunity to try to quieten her for a bit, without intending her any physical harm. She knows – or suspects – that he did it, and has decided to keep it in the family. And that's all there is to it.'

Quantrill was not normally a dogmatic man. The fact was that the company of the woman detective unsettled him. A male sergeant would automatically have gone into the bar to do the ordering and carrying, but although Sergeant Lloyd, politely conscious of her rank, had said, 'Shall I – ?' – though, come to think of it, without actually making a move – he had found himself instinctively getting up and doing the running for her.

But it wasn't merely a question of who fetched the drinks. He fretted at the absence of masculine company. He wanted to talk the enquiry over with a man who had a pint in his fist, a copper he could understand, not with this self-contained young woman who sat with such straight-backed grace on the wooden pub bench, and proposed to lunch off toast, pâté and a glass of white wine. CID work in Breckham Market was never, he realised glumly, going to be the same again.

If Sergeant Lloyd had heard the Chief Inspector's rebuke, let alone taken it to heart, she gave no sign. But he required some response; quiet thinking was evidently not encouraged in this division. She stirred, and began her meal. 'I see . . .' she said with lively interest, breaking up a slice of cold, imitation leather toast. 'But what makes you so sure it was the husband?'

Quantrill explained with confidence. 'It seemed likely, as soon as you told me about the dampness on his trouser legs when you first saw him. When I questioned him about it, he admitted that he did go out this morning, somewhere about eight o'clock. He says he walked across the common to his mother's house to make sure that she was all right, and he didn't think to mention it to you because it's something he does every morning. So he certainly had the opportunity to pick up the dead cat, and I don't think he'd have mourned its death, either. He doesn't like cats. Did you see all the scratches on his hands, and his nervousness when his wife told him to catch the kitten? He took very good care not to get hold of it.'

Hilary had made the same observation, without modifying her original conclusion. 'But if you're right, I don't understand why he should deny it,' she said. 'After all, you'd told him that no crime had been committed. Oh, he'd deny it in front of his wife, of course. But why didn't he admit it when you spoke to him on his own?'

'Ah. Masculine pride,' explained Quantrill, mug in fist. 'I thought we might have difficulty with that, as soon as I saw the age difference between him and his wife. Arrowsmith's denying that he was responsible because he doesn't want to acknowledge that he was a fool ever to marry her. Silly young idiot . . . Any young man tying himself to a middle-aged woman is bound to wake up one day and regret it.'

Hilary winced as her first sip of wine soured her mouth; acid stuff, brewers' plonk, almost as unpalatable as the gritty lump of pâté that accompanied the toast. If this was her new boss's idea of a good pub, the sooner he left her to work on her own, the better.

She very much missed Inspector Harry Colman's company and conversation. Harry was an open-minded man, aware of

69

new ideas and social changes, whereas Douglas Quantrill seemed to be stuck with the attitudes of twenty years ago. It would take a long time to civilise him; and would it be worth going to the trouble?

She couldn't resist a try. If she didn't enjoy a challenge, she would never have joined the police. '*Bound* to regret it . . . ? I wonder what makes you say that?'

'Well, it's obvious.' He lowered his mug. 'Isn't it?'

'I should think that depends on whether you're proposing it as a general rule,' she said pleasantly. 'But then, it would have to apply equally to the sexes, wouldn't it? Oh dear – do you think Patsy Hopkins is a fool to tie herself to a man so much older than she is? Poor Patsy – I do hope she isn't bound to wake up one day and regret it.'

'Ah, that's different.'

She said nothing, but looked at him with composure as she ate a piece of sparingly buttered toast.

Quantrill put his mug on the table. 'Having a go at me, Miss Lloyd?' he demanded.

'Just registering a protest. I don't see why it should be regarded as perfectly natural for a younger woman to be in love with an older man, and to want to marry him, but not the other way round. You seem to think that Simon Arrowsmith must be feeling trapped in his marriage. That he's desperate to get out. But that's not the way it looked to me at all.'

Quantrill flung a handful of breadcrumbs at, rather than for, the sparrows that hopped on the gravelled forecourt near their feet.

'Come off it,' he said. 'If you're trying to persuade me that I've misjudged Angela Arrowsmith, you're wasting your time. The woman's a menace, totally self-centred and demanding. She must make her husband's life hell.'

'I'm afraid she probably does. But it's all down to character and temperament, not to relative ages. He's too weak ever to say "No" to her, and she'd be just as much of a menace if she were married to a man of fifty. But Simon Arrowsmith isn't disenchanted with his wife. Far from it. I'm sure he's genuinely in love with her, and much too soft-hearted to upset her. I don't believe that he was responsible for what happened this morning.'

Quantrill was irked into silence. He'd allowed the woman detective to bait him into making a thoughtless generalisation that, on reflection, was untenable; but that was beside the point. They weren't having a social discussion about what he'd heard his daughter Alison describe darkly as 'sexism'. They were discussing the relationship between the Arrowsmiths and the reason why the husband wouldn't admit to having a domestic dispute – and whatever his new sergeant said, he was still right. Simon Arrowsmith had been a fool to marry the woman, but masculine pride made him unwilling to admit it even to himself.

As to whether the man was in love: yes, Quantrill had to admit that Sergeant Lloyd could be right about that. But that, too, was beside the point. Love didn't preclude domestic disputes, it made them worse, and a police sergeant ought to know enough about human nature to understand that.

He glared sideways at her, resenting the detached air with which she fed not breadcrumbs but pâté to the sparrows. For a moment, he wondered disparagingly whether she knew anything about real life at all. But then he saw the scar on her forehead and remembered that, having had the misfortune to meet one of its more unpleasant manifestations literally head on, she knew quite as much about real life as he did.

'So who do you think was responsible for this morning's incident?' he asked in a more friendly voice. 'You're surely not still maintaining that Mrs Arrowsmith is frightened, are you?'

'No, I agree with you there, sir. But I don't withdraw what I first told you. I'm sure there's someone – or something – in her background that she's extremely anxious to hide. As far as this incident's concerned, though, I've come round to your conclusion that it's almost certainly domestic. Angela thinks she knows who was responsible, and it's someone she isn't afraid of. I've been wondering about her brother – he must be worried sick about the restaurant.'

She saw Quantrill's blank look. 'Didn't either of the men tell you about Angela's scheme?'

They hadn't. Hilary told him. Quantrill boggled.

'The woman must be out of her mind,' he said.

'I think she probably is, on this subject. But I'm sure she intends to go ahead with it.'

'It'd cost no end to set up a place like that. Where's she getting the money from?'

'She refused to say. But she denied all connection with the Black Bull mob.'

'Bridge Street, Breckham Market, eh? I think I know the place she must mean. It was built as a Methodist chapel, but it was disused when I first came to Breckham. Then a local builder bought it, and leased it out for commercial use. First it was a carpet showroom, then a roller-skating rink, then a coffee bar and disco. None of the ventures made any money because the overheads are too high. Last year it was opened as a fried chicken restaurant and take away, but it didn't keep going for more than six months. Only a fool would pour money into commercial premises with that kind of history. Well it's an interesting piece of information. We'll keep an eye on the place. As you say, some villain may be making use of Mrs Arrowsmith's ambitions to provide himself with a cover.'

'And may be putting pressure on her already,' suggested Hilary. 'I know it's an off-chance, but it could account for this morning's threat. Perhaps she was trying to alter our hypothetical villain's plans in some way, and he wanted to keep her in line.'

Quantrill got up from the bench and stretched his legs. 'It's a possibility, yes. But I still think the problem's simpler, and nearer home. The woman's husband is sick with worry and misery. I thought it was hardly surprising, when he was tied to – ' he caught sight of Sergeant Lloyd's quizzical eye ' – married to a wife like that. But with this crazy restaurant scheme of hers, the pressures on the poor devil must be intolerable. And if she's as obsessive as you say, that applies whether her plans are fact or fantasy. Her husband probably took the opportunity to upset her this morning in the hope of frightening her off the idea.'

'The same argument could apply to Harold Wilkes.'

'Yes. Her husband and her brother could be in it together. And there's your explanation as to why Arrowsmith refuses to admit it. The threat didn't work. Mrs Arrowsmith isn't frightened, and from what she told you she's going ahead with her scheme. So if they want to stop her, they'll have to try again.'

Hilary wondered for a moment whether she had been right to conclude that Angela Arrowsmith wasn't in any danger. 'They'll have to try a lot harder, if they want to stop a woman like that.'

'I don't see why you're worrying,' said Quantrill, feeling that honours were at last even. 'If you're prepared to agree with me that we can put this morning's happening down to Simon Arrowsmith, I'll go along with your estimate of his character. If you're right about him, you can be sure that he'll draw the line at cutting up anything other than dead cats.'

They abandoned the remains of their meal to the attendant sparrows, left Wickford and turned their combined attention to the A135 murder.

9

When Angela Arrowsmith had an idea, she wanted to put it into practice immediately. Immature still, at 40, she could never bear to wait.

As soon as the police left the house, she made several telephone calls. Then she changed into a sharply feminine suit, went down to the kitchen, informed her brother that he was going to be the chef in the restaurant she intended to open, and told him not to wait lunch. She went outside, kissed her husband, who was hovering worriedly beside the Austin Princess that he'd just backed out of the garage for her, tugged his beard and told him not to be a silly boy, and drove off to Breckham Market.

The town was busy with Saturday shoppers. Bridge Street

73

was crowded. She drove slowly past a detached grey brick building, in shape like a giant dog kennel, and savoured the handwritten TO LET notice in its wide, modern plate-glass window. The window was topped by a heavy pediment, above which was a stone incised with the words Primitive Methodist Chapel 1863; but all that Angela saw was in her mind's eye, the glitter of a flourishing restaurant club.

There were snags, certainly: no parking space, for one thing. But there was access for delivery vehicles from the rear, and plenty of room for evening off-street parking in the market place, just a few minutes' walk away.

Her eyes reflecting the glitter of her dream, Angela went to make her arrangements with the owner, a local builder. A stranger to the town, she had had great difficulty in finding the address that had been given on the TO LET notice when, earlier in the week, she went to borrow the keys so that she could view the empty property. Even now, having been there once before, she took two wrong turnings before she arrived at the builder's yard down by the river, in a huddled old-town area of dirt roads, dilapidated sheds, makeshift garages and long-dead cars.

At the entrance to the yard was a board with faded lettering: C. Mutimer, Builder and Undertaker, Estimates Free, No Job Too Small. The yard was disorganised, and largely disused. In the centre was what had once been a farmhouse; the great barn still stood beside it, its timbered interior used for storing a small quantity of building material and for making coffins, one of which was propped up just inside the open doors. The house itself, once plastered in traditional Suffolk style, had been weatherproofed with pebble-dashed mortar. The thatched roof was covered with corrugated iron. Its owner, like many old-fashioned small builders, seemed disinclined to spend either time or money on his own property.

Angela parked her car beside C. Mutimer's pick-up truck and went round to the back of the house, having learned on her previous visit that the front door was boarded up. The builder, who had heard her car, was at the back door to greet her. He was a stout man of sixty, give or take a decade, with sparse hair, round, thick-lensed spectacles, and the bland features and lucky-horseshoe smile of a contented baby.

He led her into a silted-up office that smelled of dust and cold bacon fat, cleared a chair of papers, and wiped it over with the free end of the window curtain. Angela sat down, arranging her short but shapely legs at their most flattering angle, and thanked him for having agreed, when she telephoned, to stay at the yard until she arrived.

'My pleasure, Mrs Arrowsmith. Besides, where else could I go? I'm a bachelor, you see . . . I've no Mrs Mutimer to go home to, more's the pity. This is where I work, and this is where I live. Here I am, and here I have to stay.'

Cyril Mutimer forced the corners of his mouth momentarily downwards as he invited his visitor's sympathy. He looked, in his dusty black jacket, tight waistcoat and absurdly formal striped trousers – once his best undertaker's suit, now demoted to working wear – rather like a chubby orphan. The fact that his life style suited him completely, and that his various properties scattered on prime sites throughout the town gave him total assets of several hundred thousand pounds, was nobody's business but his own.

'What a shame,' said Angela. His lenses were too thick for her to see that his eyes were moving with interest from her own hair to the similarly dark gold hair of the girl exposing herself provocatively on the Penthouse calendar that hung on the back of the door.

' – shame,' he echoed sorrowfully, though his mouth had resumed its happy curve. 'Well, now, Mrs Arrowsmith – by the way, if you don't mind my asking: any relation?'

She knew what he meant. It was a question she'd become accustomed to, since her marriage to Simon Arrowsmith. When she answered, 'Sister-in-law', it was with a sense of reflected prestige; and yet she was infuriated, too, that the only Arrowsmith who seemed to count for anything in Breckham Market was Ross. This was one of the things she intended to alter.

Cyril Mutimer looked impressed by the nearness of the relationship. 'A very clever man, Mr Ross Arrowsmith,' he said. 'Thinking of diversifying, is he? A restaurant, I believe you said?'

'It's nothing whatever to do with my brother-in-law,' said Angela sharply. 'Or with my husband, come to that. This is entirely my own project.'

' – own project,' agreed Mutimer immediately. 'Very suitable, for a lady. Morning coffees, light lunches, dainty afternoon teas – '

Angela told him what he could do with dainty afternoon teas. She had at first intended to keep her vocabulary polite, but it seemed that the only way to persuade the builder to treat her as a serious businesswoman was by getting it out of his head that she was a lady. Cyril Mutimer's eyes gleamed behind the lenses as her language ripened, but his smile remained cherubically innocent. He beamed and nodded as she told him her plans, and he agreed with every word she said.

' – big name cabaret acts. Of course. Just what Breckham Market needs. You'll have a gold mine there, Mrs Arrowsmith, a real gold mine. And when were you thinking of taking over the lease?'

'Right away. I want to open in November, and there's a lot to do.'

' – lot to do. Of course. But you know what lawyers are. I don't want to disappoint you, but they could take weeks over drawing up the lease. I wouldn't hold out much hope of a November opening if I were you – unless . . .'

He paused, guileless as a baby who knows perfectly well that he has his mother in his power. Angela, obsessed, urged him on.

'Well . . . I'd be taking a risk. Not that I don't trust you, Mrs Arrowsmith, of course I do, but it isn't good business to give a potential lessee access to a property before the lease is signed. You might back out after a week or two, and then where would I be?'

Angela assured him that she would do no such thing. Cyril Mutimer allowed himself to be persuaded into agreeing to let her have the keys of the property as soon as she paid him the ingoing premium.

'You did realise there'd be a modest premium? Standard business practice, as you know. Let me see – four thousand square feet, and on a prime site . . .' he went through the motions of consulting his account books before mentioning the figure he had already decided on, one that would give him a fat profit without being so high as to deter her. 'Ah yes: five thousand pounds down, and the keys are yours.'

Angela knew nothing about standard business practice, but during the past week she had consulted the Business Premises column of the local newspaper, and she had seen premiums mentioned; in comparison with what was being asked for some considerably smaller retail premises in Yarchester, five thousand sounded reasonable. But she wanted to make it clear to him that she knew what she was doing.

'That's too steep, Mr Mutimer,' she told him. 'For four thousand square feet, in a small town like Breckham Market, I don't expect to pay more than four thousand pounds. After all, my customers will be coming by car, so the site's no advantage. I'm not paying five thousand for the use of a building without a car park.'

Cyril Mutimer's chin quivered with hurt. 'But the potential, Mrs Arrowsmith . . . It's the potential you must look at. And you get the use of all the fixtures and fittings.'

'They're rubbish! I'll have to have them stripped out, and the whole place refitted. I want a quality image.'

' – quality image. Of course. You'll want a lot of work done.' He tugged down the lower edge of his tight waistcoat in an attempt to conceal the shirt that kept making a grubby appearance between it and the waistband of his striped trousers. 'Er – might I ask who you were thinking of employing to do it?'

She smiled magnanimously, sensing victory. 'I did wonder whether you'd be interested, Mr Mutimer. Unless it's too big a job?'

'No, no, no. No job too small, no job too big either. I can use sub-contractors, you see. I'll do it for you with pleasure, Mrs Arrowsmith. Quality work, just as you want it.'

'Four thousand, then?'

He sighed aloud, but went on smiling. With reason: he had

paid under two thousand pounds for the freehold of the disused chapel some ten years previously, and since then had contrived to spend none of his own time or money on it, apart from replacing some roof tiles and renewing the guttering. True, he had gone for long periods without receiving any rent, because none of the tenancies had lasted for more than two years at most, and some had been considerably shorter. But Cyril Mutimer was an optimist, a firm believer that there would be another fool along any minute, eager to part with a sizeable premium for the lease, and then to pay him for redecorating and improving his own property. And all the time its freehold value – at least twenty thousand, at the last estimate – was increasing.

'You strike a hard bargain, Mrs Arrowsmith. Oh, I can see you're a real businesswoman. Four thousand it is, then, for a seven-year lease with a rent review every three years. The rent is a hundred pounds a week, payable monthly in advance. Quite small, when you consider the profit you'll be making, eh?'

Angela did a rapid mental calculation. Yes, once her restaurant club got going, a hundred a week wouldn't really be a lot. Len Pratt made huge profits from his place in Yarchester, if his new Saab saloon and his cigars and champagne were anything to go by, and there was no reason why she shouldn't do the same. But in the weeks before the opening, the rent would be a drain on her borrowed capital.

'I won't pay a hundred a week,' she told him. 'Four hundred per calendar month, that's all I'll go to.'

'Oh, Mrs Arrowsmith,' he beamed sorrowfully, 'I do believe you've a better head for business than most of the men I deal with. The only way I could possibly go as low as that would be by keeping the rent strictly on a cash basis. Not a word to the tax man, eh?' He opened a cupboard and took out a bottle and two smeared glasses. 'We'll drink to our agreement, then, shall we? The keys will be yours just as soon as you bring me the four thousand premium and the first four hundred rent – though how I let you beat me down to that, I shall never understand. But then, being only a bachelor, I suppose I'm an easy victim for a charming young businesswoman.'

His hands, as he passed her a generous slug of neat whisky,

radiated a clammy warmth. Accustomed as she was to her brother's fastidious standard of housekeeping, Angela hesitated slightly before she put the dirty glass to her lips. But she liked whisky, and she was too greatly pleased with herself and her rapidly maturing plans to refuse the drink.

She leaned forward with a smile and patted the baby-faced little old builder on the cheek. 'You're a sweetie, Mr Mutimer,' she told him, wondering how far she could continue to exploit so much good-natured innocence.

When she returned to *Tenerife*, Angela Arrowsmith found a strange Ford Cortina parked in the drive. A clean-shaven young man, in snappily-cut grey suit and striped shirt, was in the immaculate main room with Simon, who was sending up pipe-smoke signals of distress. The visitor leaped to his feet as soon as Angela appeared, holding out his hand and introducing himself.

'Terry Bennett, Oasis Finance Company, Yarchester. Very glad to meet you, Mrs Arrowsmith.' His delivery was quick and confident, his smile as fast as a camera's shutter.

'You didn't waste any time getting here,' Angela complimented him. She enjoyed being looked over by men, and began to preen herself, but his indifferent eyes switched away almost immediately.

'As I told you on the phone,' he said, 'Oasis is on call twenty-four hours a day, three hundred and sixty-five days a year. We're entirely at our clients' service.'

'Hasn't my husband offered you a drink? Typical . . . Get on with it, Simon!'

'Thank you, but I don't drink during working hours. Company policy.' Bennett's lips exposed his teeth for a fraction of a second, and then he sat down and lifted his executive case on to the coffee table in front of him. He was mildly intrigued by the disparity in the Arrowsmiths' ages, but his professional interest was confined to the value of his clients' possessions. He also needed to know, when he was dealing with a couple, which was the dominant partner; there was so little doubt, with the Arrowsmiths, that he addressed himself exclusively to Angela.

79

'You want our help with business finance, I believe? What's the proposition?'

Angela told him, wasting no more charm. 'According to your advertisement,' she added briskly, 'there's no upper limit to the amount you can advance. But I've managed to get the lease of the property for four thousand, much less than the owner asked, so I think an advance of twenty thousand will be enough to start with.'

There was a silence: horrified on Simon's part, quizzical on Bennett's. The wife might be the dominant partner, he thought, but she obviously knew nothing at all about finance.

'Unlimited advances refer only to freehold properties, Mrs Arrowsmith, dependent on their valuation. On a leasehold business, I'm afraid all we can offer you is up to 80% of the purchase price. That'd be £3,200 at maximum, depending on the terms of the lease. Of course, if you can give us some additional security – '

He looked round the expensively furnished room as though seeing it for the first time. In fact he had already mentally inventoried its contents, just as he had assessed the current market value of the house.

'What about this house?' said Angela.

Bennett contrived to give the impression that he had only now noticed its existence. 'Mortgaged?' he asked. 'Could I see the documents, then, please? And also any outstanding hire purchase or loan agreements.'

'Simon – ' commanded Angela.

Shoulders bowed, feet dragging, Simon fetched the papers. Bennett opened his case and took out an Arrowsmith pocket calculator. He skimmed his eye over the mortgage document. 'I see that this property is held in your joint names. Can I take it that you're also applying jointly for an Oasis loan?'

'Yes,' said Angela. Simon put up a troubled smokescreen and hid behind it.

Bennett made some swift calculations. Finally he said, 'Ten thousand. Taking everything into account, that's the absolute maximum I can go to.'

Angela argued. Bennett was adamant: 'Ten thousand, and

that's sticking my neck out on your behalf. You won't get a better deal anywhere else, Mrs Arrowsmith.' He paused, connecting her name with the name on his calculator. 'Of course, if you know anyone – a relative, say – who would be prepared to act as guarantor – ?'

Angela agreed, ungraciously, to accept his offer.

'Right. Good. Wise decision.' Bennett took some forms from his case and began rapidly to fill them in. 'So you are applying to borrow £10,000, repayable over a period of ten years. Your repayments will be only £15.43 per thousand pounds borrowed per month – that's a low true interest rate of 14% – '

Three people listened to the representative of the Oasis Finance Company as he rattled out a confusion of figures. Angela listened pouting with disappointment; Simon listened in fear and despair; and Gary Hilton, listening crouched outside the door, balanced a scribbling pad on his knee and wrote down everything he thought significant, words as well as figures, for the benefit of his uncle.

Harold Wilkes, his head clanging with tinnitus, hovered above the boy and read what he wrote. Once or twice the deaf man softly groaned aloud, and Gary shushed him with an angry grimace.

'And when do I get this measly ten thousand?' the boy heard his mother ask.

'Just as soon as I've completed the paperwork in the office. I can put the cheque in the post on Monday.'

'Don't bother to post it. I'll come to Yarchester on Monday morning to collect it.'

'Just as you like, Mrs Arrowsmith. Any time after eleven. I'll make sure it's ready for you. Now, if you and your husband will both sign the application form, please, here and here – '.

Simon spoke, for the first time. His voice was indistinct, hampered both by the stem of his pipe and by tension.

'Wait a minute. I want to speak to my wife before we sign anything. Would you mind stepping out into the garden, Mr Bennett – here, through the sun lounge. We won't keep you long.'

81

Gary heard the visitor protest that he had another appointment, that funds were limited, that he couldn't promise to keep the offer open for more than twenty-four hours. His sales patter was cut short by the closing of the sliding door. Then Simon spoke again, and although his voice was strained there was an element of hope in it.

'Angie, sweetheart – I realise you're disappointed, but at least you know now what the situation is. Ten thousand's no good to you, is it? I mean, when you think what it cost us to furnish this house . . . you couldn't even begin to equip a big restaurant with what you'd have left after paying for the lease. I know you'd set your heart on it, but it really does look as though you'll have to drop the idea. So there's no point now in borrowing that ten thousand, is there? Let's send the man away, and then go to a travel agent this afternoon and book a holiday for you. What about Florida? Or a Mediterranean cruise?'

'*Drop* the idea? You must be out of your tiny mind, Simon Arrowsmith! You know nothing at all about business, do you? I don't intend to *buy* the furniture and equipment, you idiot, I shall lease it. That's what you told me Ross did when he moved into the Old Maltings, and I shall do the same. I'm going to call my restaurant *Arrowsmith's*, by the way. Sounds good, doesn't it?'

'But sweetheart, Ross didn't move until his business was properly established. He started in a small way, and built it up – '

'. . . So there's hardly anything I need to pay cash for. I'll have to pay old Mutimer the premium and the rent, but he can wait a long time for the money for the alterations and redecoration. In fact I can probably sweet-talk him into doing it for free . . .'

'Couldn't you start small too, Angie? Get yourself established in a nice little coffee shop, and – '

'*A nice little coffee shop?* You're pathetic, do you know that, Simon Arrowsmith? I don't want a frigging *little* anything, I want some excitement. I don't intend to go on spending my evenings sitting here watching video with you and my stupid brother and that boy who's as half-witted as his father, I want to be a Somebody. I mean to think big, and make money fast. As soon as *Arrowsmith's* opens, the profits will roll in.'

'But you said you wanted to open in November. That means it'll be two months before you get any income, and meanwhile you'll have repayments to make, and rent and rates to pay – '

'So I'll open sooner. I'll crack the whip at old Mutimer, and open as soon as possible.'

'But Angie – you still won't have enough money. You've got to be realistic, sweetheart. You can't lease everything you need, you must have some working capital. This ten thousand isn't nearly enough, you know that yourself – '

'Then I'll borrow the rest from somewhere else. Harold can help, for a start. He's always been careful with his money, and they earn a lot on those oil rigs. He must have a few thousand tucked away somewhere, and I've done a lot for him, he owes me. Then there's – well, never mind. But I'll get the extra money, don't worry. Just let's sign for the ten thousand, so that I can make a start.'

'Angie . . . you don't seem to realise what you're letting us in for. If we sign the form, and then can't keep up the repayments, Oasis will take everything we possess that isn't already mortgaged or on hire purchase. We'll be ruined.'

She told him, in words of four letters, what she thought of him. 'God knows why I ever married you, Simon Arrowsmith,' she concluded. 'Well, this is where you make your choice, because if you don't sign I'm off. For good. I'll leave the three of you to your boring existence and go where there's some excitement, Yarchester, London, Tenerife. I mean it, Simon. Sign here and now, or you've lost me.'

Gary, listening angrily behind the door and scribbling notes for his uncle, lifted his head, open-mouthed and bright-eyed with sudden hope. There was nothing he would like better than for his mother to go for good. He mouthed silent, frantic instructions to his stepfather: 'Now's your chance, Si . . . don't sign . . . get rid of her!'

But Simon loved his wife, and so he signed.

10

On the way back from Wickford to Breckham Market, Quantrill made a detour. Instead of crossing straight over the A135 he turned right, northwards, along the main road in the direction of Yarchester.

Ahead, a recently engineered stretch of road went up and over a rise, through a cutting which reduced the gradient. To the right, crowning the rise, was a small wood, its leaves still green except where horse-chestnuts were already yellowing in anticipation of autumn. Quantrill signalled right again, positioned his car on the crown of the road until he could cross the oncoming traffic, and then turned from the main road on to what had been the route of the A135 before the improvements were made.

The old road, curving through the wood for no more than fifty yards before it rejoined the new road, had already been narrowed by an accumulation of dust and leaf debris. In the undergrowth on either side of it, haws and blackberries were beginning to ripen, and dead-nettle and ragged robin were in their second flowering. A bush of honeysuckle bore, simultaneously, buds, small pale flowers, unripe green berries and ripe red ones.

It made an attractive layby, despite the litter that had been tossed from parked vehicles. A family saloon car was there now, with an inflatable dinghy on top and a caravan hitched behind, parked for a break on its return journey from a seaside holiday. The caravan stays had been lowered and a woman was inside, brewing up; her husband had his head under the bonnet of the car, and three children were playing in and out of the undergrowth, all of them evidently oblivious of the fact that they were within a few yards of the place where a headless corpse had lain a few weeks ago.

The car was facing south, the direction from which Quantrill had come. Another car, a hatchback, its rear loaded with small-scale mock-ups of double-glazed windows, was parked lower down, facing in the same direction. The salesman – presumably working on commission and therefore needing to canvass on Saturdays as well as weekdays – sat behind the wheel in a fug of cigarette smoke, reading one of his own leaflets with an expression of profound pessimism.

Quantrill stopped his car beyond the caravan. 'I come back here whenever I run out of ideas on the case,' he told Sergeant Lloyd. 'Sorry to drag you with me, though – I expect you've seen enough of this layby.'

'It's familiar,' she agreed wryly. 'I spent almost a week, with the rest of Mr Colman's team, doing a fingertip search through the undergrowth. We wore masks and overalls and rubber gloves, of course, but it's still revolting to have to search an area that's used as a combined rubbish tip and public lavatory. I don't think any of us would have minded quite so much if it had been the actual scene of the crime, because then we'd have known that sooner or later we'd find something significant. But when the body is plastic-wrapped and has obviously been dumped, there's almost certainly nothing to find and so it's difficult to work with the same enthusiasm.'

It was another reminder, if Quantrill needed one, that for all her graceful composure, Hilary Lloyd was a working detective. Even so –

'Enthusiasm?' he queried.

'Oh yes! It's a fascinating job, searching the scene inch by inch to find the scraps of evidence that'll build up into a case. I'm sorry in a lot of ways to have come off scene-of-crime work. When I leave the force I'll probably take up archaeology as a hobby – going on digs will give me all the interest of scraping and sifting and looking for clues, with the added bonus that nothing I find will squelch or smell.'

Quantrill, who had done plenty of fingertip searches himself, earlier in his career, gave her a grin of acknowledgement. 'I just want to take another look round. Shan't be more than a few minutes.'

85

'I'll come with you. I need to, now that I'm in your investigating team. When I was here before I had to keep my nose to the ground. It's about time I stood up and studied the view.'

They walked slowly, some yards apart and without speaking, to the upper, northern end of the old road. It was from this end that traffic coming from the direction of Yarchester and the coast, travelling on the left-hand side of the road, would enter the layby.

'Is there a parking sign here?' asked Hilary. 'I don't see one.'

'No, there isn't. If you don't know the layby, there's nothing to draw attention to it. We set up an experiment, getting half a dozen policemen from other divisions to drive separately along this road over a distance of twenty miles, looking for a suitable dumping place for an imaginary body they were carrying. Four did their dumping before they reached this spot, two did it afterwards. And of those two, one didn't even realise that this was a layby, and the other realised but not until after he'd overshot the entrance. So we're reasonably certain that the driver knew the road well.

'Alternatively, if he didn't come down the A135, but across country, he must know this particular area. If he knew of the existence of the layby, he might think that by leaving the body here he could persuade us that it had been brought down the main road.'

'But you're satisfied that it wasn't a local murder, sir?'

'I'm satisfied that she wasn't a local woman. But by "local", I mean Breckham Market and the surrounding countryside. She could be from Yarchester or Great Yarmouth or Lowestoft or Ipswich, one of the big East Anglian towns where there's a transient population. But the person who dumped her body here – who wasn't necessarily the murderer, of course – might have more immediate local connections.'

They turned and walked back along the layby, past the parked vehicles. The caravan family were eating a snack lunch. The hatchback car was empty, although the radio was blaring; presumably the double-glazing salesman was behind a bush.

'I've been wondering about the dress the dead woman was wearing,' said Hilary. 'We've been assuming that it was bought

86

for cash, either at one of the Jayne Edwards shops in the Midlands or at a market stall, and that it's therefore untraceable. But a lot of women buy from mail-order firms, either for cash or on credit. Sometimes they buy direct from a catalogue or an advertisement, sometimes through an agent. Angela Arrowsmith told me this morning that she's a mail-order agent – she offered to take me on as a customer. There was a pile of catalogues in her hall, and one of them was a Jayne Edwards. So the firm sells on credit. And that means that they must keep records of their customers.'

'It's an interesting point,' Quantrill acknowledged. 'Certainly worth following up – though it seems too much to hope that the murdered woman would have been one of their credit customers. In fact I'd say it was unlikely, given that she was wearing Marks and Spencer underclothes.'

'Oh yes?' said Hilary, intrigued that he was prepared to pontificate on the subject.

'My wife dragged me round Yarchester Marks and Spencer on my day off last week. First completely free day I'd had since the body was found . . . Anyway, as you know, the firm trades strictly for cash, and they're not cheap. Molly bought a few underclothes, just enough to set her up for the winter, she said. And do you know what she paid for them? Nearly twenty pounds.'

He was silent for a moment, dwelling on the enormity of it. And it wasn't even as though he could accuse Molly of extravagance. No garments could have been of better value and lesser allure than those roomy white cellular cotton panties and stiffly elasticated bras. True, the store did have a much prettier, flimsier, younger range of underwear – the kind of thing the dead woman had been wearing. He had looked it over hopefully, while his wife was trying to decide between ribbon and cotton shoulder straps for her winter vests; but none of it was ever Molly's size.

He pushed from his mind the thought that his own new Marks and Spencer y-fronts had been equally expensive, equally dull. That was different.

'So it seems to me,' he went on, 'that a woman who shops at

M & S can't be short of money. She may take a fancy to a cheap Jayne Edwards summer dress if she sees it in a shop window, but I can't believe that she'd go to the bother of buying it on credit and making fiddling little weekly payments for it.'

'I don't see why not,' said Hilary. 'Mail-order firms give interest-free credit, and that can be very useful. Besides, women who are lonely or housebound may well look forward to having a chat with the agent when she comes to collect their instalments.'

'All right, you've made your point.' Quantrill's new sergeant was clearly a woman who enjoyed arguing. 'As I said, we'll follow it up.'

They had reached the lower end of the layby and were now facing south, the way they had come. Yellow September sunshine dazzled them as they looked down the slope towards the Wickford-Breckham Market crossroads.

'Ross Arrowsmith was mentioned at the conference this morning, wasn't he?' said Hilary. 'He'd sometimes been seen jogging in this direction, though he said that he hadn't been here for weeks. Interestingly, his name came up again when I was talking to Angela about the cat incident.'

She told the Chief Inspector what Angela Arrowsmith had said about her brother-in-law. 'I didn't give much weight to her suggestion that Ross could be responsible for the threat,' she went on, 'because there was an element of spite in her voice. But it's quite true that he was jogging round Wickford common between the time when the cat was killed and the time when the postmen reported finding its body on Angela's doorstep. Both postmen mentioned in their statements that they'd seen Ross Arrowsmith on his way back from the common, and according to the enquiry team he was seen by at least two other local people. I think it might be worth interviewing him again. Because if he was the person who threatened Angela, it's just possible that he could in some way be connected with the murder.'

'Ross Arrowsmith?' scoffed Quantrill. 'Why? Even if the man had enough of a grudge against his sister-in-law to play this morning's nasty trick on her, that's no reason to suspect him of complicity in a murder. What possible grounds for suspicion have you got, beyond the fact that he knows the area?'

'It's a long shot, I agree. But I was thinking of Angela's dreams of making big money, and our suspicion that if she's serious about opening a restaurant, she must have a shady backer. And then I started wondering how Ross began his business, and whether he'd ever had a backer who might still have some hold over him. Enough of a hold, perhaps, to enlist Ross's help in dumping the body?'

Quantrill snorted. 'There's never been a whisper to suggest that Arrowsmith MicroElectronics hasn't been legitimately financed, right from the start. Ross Arrowsmith is a local boy who's made good, and local boys who make good are never popular in small towns. If there'd been any muck to rake over his reputation, it would have been done before now.'

'Even so,' persisted Hilary, 'I'd like to interview him about this morning's incident. If he had nothing to do with it, then I agree, there's nothing at all to connect him with the murder. But if he did threaten Angela – well, it's worth investigating, isn't it? After all, what else do we have to work on, apart from the mail-order angle?'

She was almost as eager with her theories as Martin Tait had been, Quantrill thought sourly. It was a more controlled enthusiasm than Martin's, a search for the truth rather than an ambitious scramble to notch up an arrest, but no more welcome for that. He felt thoroughly middle-aged, dispirited.

And the trouble was that she was right. Right to be eager, right to consider every possible lead. His return visit to the layby had so far given him no new ideas about the murder at all; he was just going through the motions of CID work. So if he had any sense he'd welcome his new sergeant's enthusiasm, instead of being resentful and grouching at her. If the alternatives were to encourage Hilary Lloyd's initiative, while remaining in control of the case, or to have the regional crime squad in the person of Martin Tait sent in over his head, he had no doubt which to opt for.

Hilary was a good deal more decorative than Martin, too. He glanced at her profile, and acknowledged that it was as photogenic as Harry Colman had claimed. Something to do with the height of the cheekbones and the angle of the nose and chin . . . Perhaps, as they'd all told him, he was lucky in more ways than one to have her as his sergeant.

They moved aside as the car and caravan drove past them and out on to the main road, travelling south. The caravan was followed almost immediately by the double-glazing salesman's car, which accelerated past it and roared off as though the driver had just heard a weather forecast on his radio and wanted to clinch as many sales as possible on the strength of a warning of imminent frost.

Quantrill shook off his gloom. 'Right,' he said briskly. 'You'd better talk to Ross Arrowsmith as soon as possible, then. We're only a couple of miles from where he lives, so you might as well go there now. Take my car. I'll stay here and have a quiet think, but I want you back within twenty minutes. We've wasted enough time on the Nether Wickford incident already.'

Hilary went. Quantrill paced the layby, poked about among the undergrowth, stood and thought. There was nothing to disturb his quiet except the hum of insects, and the muffled noise of traffic – chiefly, at this time on a Saturday, holiday-makers going to and from the coast – on the other side of the trees. But hard as he thought, the only fresh ideas in his head were those that had been voiced by Sergeant Lloyd.

II

Saturday afternoon, and in sunshine hot enough for midsummer Ross Arrowsmith's wife and twin son and daughter busied themselves in the grounds of their recently built house at Ecclesby.

In common with most English villages, Ecclesby had no system of numbering for its houses. To the confusion of new postmen, the inhabitants devised their own addresses, factual, topographical, architectural, reminiscent or whimsical: The Old Bakery, Orchard View, White Gables, Marbella, Erzanmyne. Ross Arrowsmith and his wife called their house New Maltings because its brick walls and pantiled roof echoed the eighteenth-century construction of the Breckham Market building that he had made the headquarters of Arrowsmith MicroElectronics.

The house had obviously cost a good deal of money, but it was not built to impress or to be used for formal entertaining. The architect had designed it to be on mannerly terms with the older houses of the village, but primarily to function as a comfortable family home. There was ample evidence, in the guinea-pig hutches that stood against the walls of the garage block in full view of anyone who drove up to the side door, and in the scatter of bicycles, bats and balls in the yard between the house and the garages, that despite their recent acquisition of wealth the Arrowsmiths lived unpretentiously.

Some construction work was still uncompleted. At the back of the house a yellow JCB digger, long-necked and prognathous as a galactic monster, lurked behind a great pile of earth. Beyond the digger, two ponies grazed a paddock. The Arrowsmith children, identical and unisex in tee shirts and jeans, were mucking out the guinea-pigs when Hilary Lloyd arrived; remembering her own childhood obsession with ponies – though there had never been any question of her actually owning one – Hilary guessed that the twin who couldn't bear to be parted from the riding hat was almost certainly a girl.

As she stopped the Chief Inspector's ageing Austin Maxi in the yard and got out, a woman a little older than herself drove across the extensive lawn on a motor mower.

'Hallo,' called Mrs Arrowsmith exuberantly, switching off her engine. She was neatly built and auburn haired and frecklefaced, so like the twins that they might at a distance be taken for triplets. 'I say, these mowers are great fun, aren't they? I've always wanted to ride one, and we've only just acquired it. Have you had a go?'

'Never. In fact it's the first time I've seen one in action, off the television screen.' Hilary walked round the mower. 'Yes, I can see the tempting resemblance to a go-kart. Still, it wouldn't be much use to me – it would never fit my window box.'

Mrs Arrowsmith slid off the machine with a penitent grimace. Like her children, she wore jeans; not designer jeans but a scruffy pair with a chainstore label. 'Sorry . . .' she said. 'You must have thought me ostentatious.'

'Not a bit. With all this grass to cut, only a masochist would do it the hard way. I'm no gardener at all. The summit of my horticultural ambition is to keep my Swiss cheese plant alive – it hasn't taken kindly to the move from Yarchester, and it's going droopy on me. I'm a newcomer to Breckham Market, a policewoman: Hilary Lloyd, detective sergeant. We're making some routine enquiries in this area, and I wondered if your husband could help me.'

'How fascinating!' Mrs Arrowsmith stared at Hilary with frank, bright-brown-eyed curiosity; not about her visitor's purpose, but about her job. 'Well, I've never before seen a woman detective, off the television screen – so that makes us even, doesn't it?'

They exchanged smiles, liking each other. 'My name's Jen,' she continued. 'Ross has just gone indoors to take a telephone call, but he won't be long.'

'I'll wait, then, if you don't mind.' Hilary looked at the mower's controls, giving an appearance of a continuing interest in the machine although she was not at all mechanically minded. What really interested her was that Jen Arrowsmith had expressed no concern, or even surprise, that a police officer wanted to see her husband.

The standard police phraseology, the request for help with routine enquiries, was designed to cause no alarm to the innocent and to suggest no prejudgement to the guilty. But nine wives out of ten, hearing it with reference to their husbands, would be worried or defensive; and the tenth would, at the very least, want to know what it was all about. The fact that Jen Arrowsmith heard it without comment showed admirable discretion, and complete confidence in her husband. Either there were no skeletons in his cupboard, thought Hilary, or his wife had never heard the rattle of their bones.

'Have a ride, if you'd like to,' urged Mrs Arrowsmith hospitably, misinterpreting the attention that Hilary was giving the mower.

'Better not, thanks – my boss would go spare if he saw me on it in working hours. Do you always use the mower yourself, or does your husband hog it when he's at home?'

'He'd better not try! Not that he would, because he gave it to me as a present. It was a sop, really. I didn't want to have such a huge garden, but he insisted – he's a fitness fanatic, you see. He comes home for lunch every day and jogs twice round the garden while I make him a salad. He despises businessmen who snatch sandwiches at their desks and take no exercise at all, and then wonder – if they survive – why they have heart attacks.'

Ross Arrowsmith wouldn't have much time for Douglas Quantrill, then, thought Hilary. She had already noticed that the DCI was addicted to sandwich-snatching, and he certainly wasn't fit.

'I imagine the pressures of building and running a company like Arrowsmith MicroElectronics could be killing,' she said.

'They could be, quite easily, but Ross seems to thrive on work. He's off to Japan tomorrow on a sales trip.'

Astonished, Hilary temporarily forgot why she was there. 'Selling electronics to Japan? You can't be serious?'

'Sounds unlikely, doesn't it?' said Jen proudly. 'But the Japanese are brilliant at developing ideas, and they're always interested in new micro-electronic design. I think Ross's latest home computer is a potential world-beater, at its price – and I used to be a systems analyst, so I have some idea of what's on the market. But then – ' she gave a freckled grin '– perhaps I'm partial.'

'Very probably,' agreed Hilary, returning the grin. 'But then again, you could be right.'

She would have liked to look at her watch. She was enjoying the conversation with Jen Arrowsmith, but she didn't want to keep the Chief Inspector waiting for nothing, and it had begun to seem totally unlikely that a wealthy, confident computer expert who was about to fly off to Japan would have any knowledge of, let alone a hand in, this morning's squalid incident at Nether Wickford.

'Do you go with your husband on any of his sales trips?' she asked.

'No, it's all too rushed. He never stays a minute longer than is necessary, so by the time I've got over my jet-lag he's itching to come back. Anyway, I couldn't leave the twins. They go to school in Breckham Market, and I've no relatives in the area I could park them with.'

'Is there no one on your husband's side of the family who could help? I met your sister-in-law at Nether Wickford this morning.'

For a second or two, Jen Arrowsmith looked blank. Then, 'Oh, you mean Angela,' she said. 'Oddly enough I never think of her as my sister-in-law. Ross and Simon are only half-brothers, you see, they're not like brothers at all. No, I couldn't possibly impose on her . . .'

She paused, lowering her eyes. There was undoubtedly a good deal more that she could have said about Angela Arrowsmith, but she declined to do so.

'Ross has a widowed stepmother living in Upper Wickford,' she went on after a moment. 'Nellie's a dear, but she isn't at all well, I'm afraid. I'm very fond of her, and I tend to think of her as my mother-in-law and the twins' grandmother – but of course, as Ross reminds me sharply, she isn't. His own mother died when he was ten – just the twins' age now. He was taken off immediately by a married sister to live in Cambridge, and he hated being uprooted from the countryside. That's why he wanted to come back and live in this area, so that we could give the twins the country upbringing he'd so much enjoyed.'

'Understandable,' said Hilary. 'And you have a lovely place here.'

'Yes. Yes, we're very lucky.'

The shadow crossed Jen Arrowsmith's face so quickly that Hilary might have thought she'd imagined it, if the voice hadn't been suddenly bleak. Something was wrong, then. Here was a wife who had every material thing she could want; a cheerful, uncomplicated woman who, despite occasional wry shrugs over her husband's foibles, spoke of him with admiration and affection. But something – or someone – was clouding her happiness. Was it Angela Arrowsmith, Hilary wondered? Perhaps after all it would be worth keeping Chief Inspector Quantrill waiting while she tried to find out.

When Ross Arrowsmith emerged from the house, wearing a track suit and training shoes, he chose to ignore the fact that they had a visitor. He jerked out the information that he had revised his travel arrangements to Tokyo and would be leaving that afternoon, and turned back immediately to the house.

He bore no family resemblance to Simon, who took after his sturdy, fair-complexioned mother Nellie. Ross was thin, dark, straight-haired, clean-shaven, with eyes set deep in his narrow face. He had a very high forehead, partly as a result of hair loss. To compensate for this, he grew his hair long on his left temple, parted it two inches above his ear, and brushed it up and over his balding brow. But short of glueing them on, there was no way of keeping the lank strands in place, and they kept slipping forward over his eyes. It was, Hilary thought, an oddly vexatious streak of vanity that impelled a man to keep brushing with his fingers at his flopping hair.

When his wife insisted on introducing Sergeant Lloyd, he acknowledged her with reluctance and undisguised irritation. Hilary briefly explained the reason for her visit, without naming the owner of the dead cat or revealing the wording of the paint-sprayed message. She made no mention of the A135 murder. Even so, Jen Arrowsmith was shocked. Her husband said nothing. Hilary would have preferred to speak to him alone, but she guessed that he would still have said nothing; he was distant, fidgeting, anxious to go.

She put her question to him directly: had he seen anyone or anything unusual while he was out jogging on Wickford common that morning?

Before he could answer, his wife burst into laughter. 'Is *that* why you wanted to talk to Ross?' she asked Hilary. 'I'm afraid you're wasting your time. It's a family joke that if he were to meet any of us unexpectedly, away from home, he'd be so busy thinking about computers that he wouldn't even see us. That's right, isn't it, love?'

Her husband pushed back his hair and muttered something noncommittal.

'Sorry?' said Hilary. 'I didn't quite catch what you said?'

Forced into making a reply he confirmed, grudgingly, what his wife had laughed about. He had noticed nothing that morning, he told Hilary, deepening his voice to make himself heard against the rising sounds of a childish quarrel. The twins were apparently in dispute over the proper care and maintenance of guinea-pigs; shrill assertions and denials were augmented by an unmistakably feminine squeal from the twin in the riding hat. Their mother went to sort them out, and Hilary took advantage of her absence to slip in a loaded question, sympathetically disguised.

'Yes, I do realise that you must have a great deal on your mind, Mr Arrowsmith. Anyway, Wickford common is a large place. Perhaps you didn't go anywhere near the house where the cat's body was left?'

But he was too sharp to be so easily trapped; or else he was telling the truth when, after the pause that usually preceded his words, he said, 'I don't know whether I did or not. I don't know which house you're talking about.'

'Didn't I say? Your brother's house, the one called *Tenerife*.'

'My half-brother,' corrected Ross Arrowsmith distantly. 'Simon's my half-brother.'

His wife, having assisted at the settlement of the twin's dispute, returned in time to hear Hilary's reference to *Tenerife*.

'Do you mean that Angela was the owner of the dead cat? That someone was trying to – '

She bit off the words and glanced uneasily at her husband. Ross frowned and gave an almost imperceptible shake of his head.

'I can't help you,' he said to Sergeant Lloyd. 'I saw nothing this morning. And in fact I made a point of avoiding my half-brother's house.'

'Ah.' Hilary smiled at him pleasantly. 'You can remember doing that?'

96

He shovelled a limp handful of hair off his forehead, and his lips worked with anger as he sought words for his reply. Eventually he said, 'Only because I always make a point of avoiding it. I have no contact with Simon's wife, and I want none. She's just a tart – I haven't seen her for six months, and I have no intention of seeing her ever again if I can help it.' He excused himself curtly and loped back to the house.

Hilary knew that she had outstayed her welcome, and she was sorry; it seemed unlikely that Jen would want to be on friendly terms with someone who had angered her husband. Ross Arrowsmith was obviously a difficult man to live with. In his presence, his wife's cheerful face had become increasingly troubled. Hilary thanked her for her time, and made a tactful retreat towards her borrowed car.

But Jen ran after her. 'Don't think too badly of us for avoiding Angela,' she begged. 'We're not really such snobs as you must think. It's true that we hardly know her – but that's because she's never accepted any of my invitations, or invited us to their home. I hear a lot about her from May Cullen, an old friend of Ross's family who lives next door to Simon's mother, and it's clear that she's not at all a good wife to the poor lad.'

'That was the impression I got when I visited her this morning,' agreed Hilary. What she knew of Angela's past, she kept to herself. 'But what makes your husband dislike her so much?'

Jen grimaced. 'That was because of the way she behaved in February this year. We gave a reception at the Old Maltings to celebrate the company's move. Simon still worked for Ross then, and Angela surprised us by coming with him to the reception. She was abominable – she came overdressed and plastered with make-up; she drank too much, fluttered her false eyelashes at all the men, and tried to give the impression that Simon was Ross's partner. She even managed to be in the centre of the photograph that went into the local paper. We wouldn't have minded so much if her vocabulary hadn't been so obscene . . . Ross was furious.'

'Was that the occasion your husband mentioned, when he said that he last saw her six months ago?'

97

'No, that would have been in March, at his father's funeral. To be fair, Angela behaved perfectly well, and went to a lot of trouble to help Nellie provide us all with tea afterwards. But then she tried to proposition Ross. Do you know whát she wanted from him? A loan of £10,000! It was after that episode that he swore he'd never speak to her again.'

'I don't blame him,' said Hilary. 'I can well believe she'd try a thing like that. From what I saw of her this morning, she's big on ideas but very short on judgement.'

'That's exactly what I've always thought about her, from the moment I first saw her at her wedding.' Jen told Hilary about Angela's virginal dress and veil, and they shared an unkind giggle until Hilary remembered that she'd left the Chief Inspector stranded beside the A135. And all she would be able to tell him was that she'd learned a little more about Angela, but not enough about Ross to know for sure whether she could definitely eliminate him from the Nether Wickford enquiry. Her only achievement seemed to be personal, the striking up of a friendly relationship with Jen.

'I say, do you swim?' said Jen. 'Because that –' she pointed to where the yellow JCB digger loomed over the earth it had excavated at the back of the house ' – is where we're having a pool made. It'll be covered and heated, so we'll be able to use it during the winter. You must come and share it.'

'Thanks, I love swimming. I was wondering where I could find a pool.'

'We go to a country club at the moment, about ten miles away. There are squash courts, too. Do you play? Wonderful – do let me know when you have a day off, and we can go there for a game and a swim.'

Hilary thanked her, and started the car. Jen Arrowsmith had resumed her cheerful look after her husband had disappeared indoors, but now as she bent down to speak to Hilary through the open window her pleasant face was troubled again.

'Look – all those things I've been telling you about Angela, and the way Ross feels about her . . . I hope you don't think that he might have been responsible for what happened this morning. Because Ross wouldn't mutilate anyone's pet, he simply isn't that kind of man. You didn't come here thinking of him as a suspect, did you?'

Hilary gave her a reassuring smile. 'Of course I didn't!' she said warmly. 'Just routine enquiries, that's all.'

This was one of the times when she resented being a detective. It was all wrong when a likely friendship, and the possibility of some kind of social life in Breckham Market, could be founded only on the basis of a lie.

12

Early the following Friday morning, it rained.

The week so far had been dry and sunny, but on Wednesday evening the television weatherman forecast a change. On Thursday afternoon, in a hazy cirrostratus sky, a halo could be seen round the sun. In the evening, the weatherman warned of increasing cloud cover as a frontal depression approached; it brought with it, he said, the probability of rain during the course of the night.

In the event, it came down pouring.

The rain reached Suffolk shortly after midnight, carried on a rising wind that dashed it against the windscreens of vehicles travelling south on the A135. There was very little traffic on the road at that time. Most of the haulage contractors' lorries that carried fruit, vegetables and poultry to the London markets overnight had already left the county, and the remaining traffic was local.

The combination of wind and rain made it difficult for drivers to identify anything – and particularly anything dark – that might be picked out by their headlights as it lay on the wet road ahead. There were always things lying about on country roads: lumps of mud, squashed rabbits and pheasants, sugar beet spilled from farm trailers, branches blown from overhanging trees. There was also, as on any road, the occasional split and crushed carton that had genuinely fallen off the back of a lorry.

And then there were the usual mysterious roadway oddments, oil-stained sheets of canvas and items of clothing that flapped and rolled on the asphalt until they were thwacked flat by the passage of heavy tyres.

It was a local man, a twenty-year-old farm worker returning with his girl friend from a Beccles disco, whose old banger of a car was one of the first to hit the dark bundle that lay at the edge of the southbound carriageway of the A135. The time was approximately twelve-thirty. He saw it – saw something – in his headlights as he came over the brow of the hill on the recently built stretch of road just north of the Breckham Market-Wickford crossroads. It was lying at the entrance to a layby where he'd often pulled in for a quiet cuddle, before its romantic seclusion was ruined by the news of the discovery there of a headless corpse.

What with poor visibility, and the fact that he had just come over the hill, there had been no chance of avoiding the object. He had caught a glimpse in his headlights of a wet bundle of clothes stabbed by rain, and had felt a bump; nothing more.

Of the small number of travellers who passed that way during the course of the night, not all were driving so close to the edge of the road. Not all of them saw the bundle, not all of them hit it; or at least were conscious of hitting it. But towards six-thirty in the morning, when the rain eased and the dawn came up bedraggled, the sodden heap of clothes was flatter than it had been six hours earlier.

Friday 20 September was to be Brian Finch's first solo day as postman on the Ecclesby-Wickford route.

The finding, on the previous Saturday, of the mutilated cat on the doorstep of the Mrs Arrowsmith who kept changing the colour of her hair, had shaken him badly. His wife had suggested that he should ask to be moved to another route, but on reflection Brian knew that he was more afraid of making a fuss than of returning to Nether Wickford. And once he had made the acquaintance of the new Siamese kitten at *Tenerife*, he began to feel a little happier.

As the end of the week approached, he looked forward to

getting rid of his irritatingly joky tutor, Kenny Warminger. He felt sure that he could manage the job perfectly well on his own; it wasn't even as though he had to rely on memorising his delivery route, because while he was under tuition he had carried a notebook with him and had written down everything he needed to know. There was absolutely nothing he needed to worry about, he told his wife as he went to bed at nine-thirty on Thursday night, after polishing his shoes in readiness for the morning and checking that his alarm system was set for four-fifteen.

But – as his wife had cause to know – Brian Finch was a born worrier. To begin with, there was the problem of early rising. It wasn't so much that he minded the prospect of getting up at four-fifteen in the morning, six days a week, for the rest of his working life; what really worried him was the possibility that he might not wake early enough, and that he would be late for work. If he were to be persistently late he would almost certainly be dismissed before the end of his probationary period, and he despaired at the thought of being unemployed again.

Ever since he had started work as a postman, Brian had lain awake at nights worrying that he might oversleep. After the first tormented night, when he had woken in a sweat just after midnight convinced that there had been an electricity failure and that his electric alarm had stopped, he had supplemented it with an old-fashioned clockwork alarm, placed on a tin tray for maximum effect. Even so, he would wake several times each night to reassure himself by peering at the luminous dials on his wrist watch and both of his clocks.

The night before the first solo duty was the worst yet. To his chronic worries about oversleeping were added the problems that he had learned he might expect to encounter during the course of his work. He thought of hostile dogs, and the mistakes he might make as he tried to deliver letters with illegible addresses to houses which displayed neither numbers nor names. He anticipated the complaints that would be made to the Head Postmaster if his anxious guesswork was wrong. Dozing uneasily, he dreamed of letters by the thousand, all of them for one or other of the Arrowsmiths but most of them so bizarrely addressed that he couldn't possibly deliver them, didn't know what to do with them, waded knee deep in them while the Mrs Arrowsmith who kept changing the colour of her hair accused him hysterically of decapitating her cat . . .

Stress went straight to Brian Finch's stomach. He spent most of the next hour in the bathroom, not knowing whether to sit down or stand up, and at three-thirty he decided to cancel the remainder of the night. Drained and shaky, he nevertheless managed to shave round his neat beard and to put on his uniform with his usual care.

His wife made sleepy enquiries from the adjoining bed, but he refused her offer of a cooked breakfast. The thought of food nauseated him, and all he wanted was a sip of water. But he could hear rain beating against the windows of his terraced house, and thinking that he might be glad of a hot drink later in the morning he made himself a flask of coffee. Then he pulled his oilskins over his uniform and set off for the post office through the rain, carrying his flask in a plastic bag slung over the handlebars of his bicycle.

As he stood at his place in front of the sorting-office bench, Brian began to feel slightly better. For one thing, he had plenty of time; for another, it was easier to concentrate without Kenny Warminger's constant chat. He sorted slowly and conscientiously, with frequent reference to his notebook, and by the time he had worked his way through all the incoming mail for Ecclesby and Upper and Nether Wickford, he was confident that he had put it into the correct sequence for delivery. Then, having loaded it into his van just before six-thirty, he allowed himself a short unscheduled break in the washroom; after the bad night he'd had, he needed to fortify himself with hot coffee from his flask before going out to make his deliveries in the rain.

The coffee alone might not have upset his stomach, if it hadn't been for the Arrowsmiths' mail. There had, as usual, been dozens of letters for Arrowsmith MicroElectronics, and he'd sorted through them carefully, twice, before bundling them with elastic bands. When he reached the Old Maltings, in Saintsbury Road, he had been anxious to avoid getting the bundled letters wet, and so he'd pushed them into the firm's letter box without another glance.

But as he drove on, out of Breckham Market on the Ecclesby road, he began to wish that he'd looked through the contents of the bundles again, in the shelter of the van, before delivering them. He ought to have double-checked. Supposing he'd made a slip, become so mesmerised by the name Arrowsmith that he'd included by mistake a letter for the Mrs Arrowsmith at Nether Wickford? What a fool he'd been not to check! He was sure, now, that there had been a letter for her among the others; he could see it, see her address quite clearly, *Mrs Angela Arrowsmith, Tenerife, Nether Wickford* . . . There was no excuse for his mistake, none at all . . .

Anxiety curdled the coffee in his stomach. As he drove up to the crossroads with the A135, he was gripped by a recurrence of the night's pain. He knew that he had to stop the van somewhere, and as soon as possible. But there was nowhere to go, out here in the middle of the countryside, except behind a hedge – and that would mean leaving the scarlet mail van by the roadside, in full view of any passing vehicles. Someone was bound to see it and report him . . .

And then he remembered what Kenny Warminger had told him: that there was a layby on the A135 just a few hundred yards to his left, up among the trees at the top of the hill, on the far side of the road. The fact that a headless corpse had been found there entered Brian's mind for a moment, but the prospect of concealment both for himself and for the mail van was of more immediate concern.

By the time he reached the lower end of the layby, his need was so pressing that he was not deterred by the empty car that was already parked under the trees. Someone with the same problem as himself, perhaps . . . He drove past the car, stopped the van, threw his uniform cap on the seat and stumbled out. Conscious of the need to safeguard the mail, he paused just long enough to lock the van before he tottered, whimpering with misery, into the wet undergrowth.

When he emerged, he was pale and damp and shaken. He leaned for a few minutes against the side of the van, thankful at least for privacy. There was still no sign of the driver of the other vehicle, but Brian was too glad of the fact to be curious about it.

Conscientious though he was, he knew that he couldn't hurry back to his delivery route immediately. He had to steady himself first, to make sure that he didn't need to take to the bushes again before leaving their shelter. His knees were still weak, and to get them going he began to walk slowly up the layby to the northern end.

The rain had stopped, but there was still a lot of water on the surface of the old road. It ran down from the top of the hill in rivulets, channelled and diverted by accumulations of leaf mould that had been formed into miniature mudbanks by the rain. Normally, Brian Finch would have tried to keep his carefully polished shoes out of the water, but they were already so wet that he had ceased to care. He noticed, as he plodded forward, that the rivulets were tinged with pink, but he was too unwell to wonder why.

Nor did he bother to speculate about the drenched and tattered bundle that he could see at the side of the main road, just at the entrance to the layby. He was within a few yards of it before he noticed, lying on its side near the bundle, an empty shoe. He stopped and blinked and looked more closely.

It was only then that he realised that the rags contained a human body; and that what was running pink over his own shoes was rain-diluted blood.

13

'Good to see you again, sir.'

Detective Inspector Martin Tait, recently returned from a CID refresher course and newly seconded to the regional crime squad, was back in Breckham Market. He entered the Chief Inspector's office with consummate self-assurance.

As far as Tait was concerned, this morning's unexplained

road death couldn't have happened at a better moment. Breckham CID were treating it as murder, which meant that they were going to be busy; too busy to continue with their obstinate claims that they were at last making progress towards solving the A135 murder, the case of the headless corpse. The Chief Constable had therefore – and about time too – decided to call in the regional crime squad to take over the earlier case.

It was exactly what Tait had been hoping for. Having previously served for a year in the Breckham Market division as CID sergeant, he was in his own opinion unarguably the best crime-squad detective for the job of sorting out the murder enquiry that had been baffling his old boss for weeks. He'd said as much – though putting it diplomatically – to the assistant regional co-ordinator, when the request for assistance came in this morning; and now here he was, back in his old division, ready to work in co-operation with, but no longer for, Chief Inspector Quantrill. A very satisfactory state of affairs, for an ambitious young police officer.

'And good to see you again, Hilary. Believe it or not, I've missed you.'

He walked round to her side of her desk, which had been moved into the Chief Inspector's office. Like Quantrill she was sitting in brooding silence with a mug of coffee clasped between her hands. When she failed to respond to his greeting, Tait propped his slim behind against the edge of her desk. He folded his arms, crossed his ankles, and looked down at her with a freshly appraising smile. 'Settling in all right? New boss treating you well, is he?'

Martin Tait was 26, four years younger than Sergeant Lloyd. He was confident that by the time he reached her present age he would have been promoted via Chief Inspector to Superintendent, at least. By the time he was 40, to Chief Constable. And after that –

'Do you mind *not* sitting on my desk?' said Sergeant Lloyd.

Undeterred by her lack of welcome Martin Tait continued to smile at her, although he eased himself into a standing position. He was a slight, fair, sharp man, at five feet eight and a half inches only fractionally above the minimum height for members of the county force; not more than two inches taller than Hilary. But he carried himself with an air, confident that he was irresistible to women. His preference was in fact for women who were a little older than himself: young enough to be attractive, sufficiently well established to pay their own share if he took them out, and experienced enough not to become emotionally dependent. Hilary Lloyd fitted his temporary requirements exactly and he fully intended, in such time as he would be able to spare from solving the A135 case, to give her the benefit of his attention.

'You're looking extremely decorative, as always,' he continued. 'Breckham needed an attractive girl in plain clothes. And someone who knows how to make good coffee, too – that is the real thing you're drinking, isn't it, not canteen swill?'

Hilary raised her head. She looked exhausted. 'I'm not here for decorative purposes,' she told him wearily, 'nor yet for making coffee. Dc Wigby is the one who'll be working with you.'

'Ian Wigby?' Tait was no fonder of the detective constable than Wigby was of him. 'That noisy oaf – '

'He's a very experienced detective,' said Quantrill. It was the first time he'd spoken. He looked less distressed than Hilary, but equally sombre. 'And you'll find your office at the end of the corridor.'

'You mean my old office? You shouldn't have turned Hilary out of it – '

'I didn't. Hilary has moved in here because we're agreed it's easiest while we're working on this case. And I don't mean your old office – we've moved things round. You're in what used to be the stationery store.'

Tait felt aggrieved. He hadn't expected the red-carpet treatment, but this antagonism was childish. He was about to say so when he realised that the atmosphere in the room was not in fact antagonistic towards him. Quantrill and Hilary were so intensely, glumly preoccupied that they hardly knew that he was there. Neither of them attempted to drink the mugs of coffee they both held. Quantrill was not, as Tait knew, a man who was easily put off his food, but the plate of sandwiches on his desk was untouched.

'This new murder case you're working on – ?' suggested Tait more sympathetically. 'A nasty one?'

'Very,' said Quantrill. Hilary put her mug on her desk.

'Disguised to look like a road accident, I heard. Multiple injuries?'

'Multiple injuries caused by a number of vehicles over a period of hours,' said Quantrill.

'Very nasty,' Tait agreed.

'A shovel job,' said Quantrill.

Hilary left the room. Quantrill relapsed into brooding silence. Tait retreated to his office and sent Dc Wigby to fetch the files on the A135 murder.

She'd seen worse sights, Hilary reminded herself as she splashed cold water over her face in the women's room. The trouble was that she'd never before felt partially responsible for the victim's death.

Not that she'd known who it was, lying there at the edge of the wet road in a puddle of what looked like Mateus rosé, when she arrived at the scene shortly after seven o'clock that morning. Positive identification was difficult, but the empty car parked in the layby provided a lead. At that stage there was no reason for the patrol-car driver – who had been sent to the scene as the result of a telephone call received from a motorist who had been flagged down by a wild-eyed postman – to suspect murder. It looked to him like a hit-and-run killing. The car's petrol tank was almost empty, and he thought it possible that the driver had been trying to hitch a lift.

He had called out the CID as a matter of routine, to establish the circumstances of the death. But as soon as Sergeant Lloyd learned the ownership of the parked car, she had called out the Chief Inspector as well. The two detectives exchanged guilty looks. Quantrill called out the pathologist, and as a result of his initial examination they had immediately set up a murder enquiry.

It wasn't until mid-afternoon, when they had retreated to divisional headquarters to draw breath, that they had begun to discuss their own part in what had happened. Their discussion had, with reason, plunged them both into gloom. Small wonder, thought Hilary as she redid her face and temporarily shook off her depression, that Inspector Tait had misinterpreted their failure to welcome him.

Hilary had never had occasion to work for Martin Tait, but when they were both at county headquarters she had found his effortless superiority tiresome. The really annoying thing about Tait, though, as everyone at Yarchester admitted, was the fact that he was as good at his job as he imagined himself to be. He would almost certainly solve the A135 case, particularly now they'd made what looked like a breakthrough over the origin of the dress that the headless woman had been wearing.

And that was *her* breakthrough, Hilary remembered. She'd been looking forward to following it up, before this new murder happened. But there was no point in being grudging about it. She decided to give him the information with a good grace, but in front of a witness so that he couldn't afterwards claim the breakthrough as his own.

After consulting the Chief Inspector, she went in search of Tait. Making his presence known at Breckham had evidently been a priority; Dc Wigby, older and beefier and blonder than his former sergeant, was in the process of fixing to a door at the end of the corridor a large notice on which he had been instructed to stencil REGIONAL CRIME SQUAD – INSPECTOR M. G. R. TAIT.

Wigby looked malevolent. 'I'm surprised he didn't tell me to put his bloody university degree as well,' he grunted as Hilary approached.

'Give him time,' she murmured, with nicely judged ambiguity. She knocked, and walked in without waiting to be invited. 'Settling in all right, sir?' she asked briskly. 'Dc Wigby looking after you well, is he?'

As a former stationery store, the room made a perfectly good office. True, the window was frosted, but everyone knew that Tait wasn't a man for wasting his time on looking out. The Inspector had however rearranged the desks and telephones to his liking.

'Sorry Mr Quantrill and I weren't more welcoming when you

arrived,' Hilary went on. 'We'd only just got in after having a bad morning. But I've made some fresh coffee – not because I think it's a woman's job, and I'm the only woman in the department, but simply because I happen to make the best coffee – and you're welcome to join us. The DCI suggests that you may like to bring the file on the A135 case with you. We don't think we're looking for one murderer, but it's possible that there's an indirect link between this morning's death and the headless corpse. We think you should know about our case before you start on yours.'

Tait followed her eagerly to the Chief Inspector's office, his pointed nose scenting not so much coffee as the possibility that he might solve both cases while he was about it.

'Who was it who was killed this morning?' he asked.

Hilary's depression returned, a thick dark cloud that chilled her and shadowed everything within her view.

'A Mrs Angela Arrowsmith,' she said.

14

'So you're off to a flying start with this enquiry,' said Inspector Tait enviously, after Quantrill and Hilary had told him all they knew about Angela Arrowsmith. 'You were in luck, to interview the murder victim just a week before it happened!'

The Chief Inspector and the Sergeant looked at him, sitting there in his pigskin safari jacket, commendably alert, deplorably single-minded.

'That remark,' said Hilary, 'was in very poor taste.'

Quantrill was thunderous. 'For God's sake, man, doesn't it occur to you that we feel indirectly responsible for her death? We knew that she'd been threatened. I ought to have provided her with protection. But I decided not to take the threat seriously – '

'And I agreed with you, sir, once we'd investigated,' Hilary reminded him. 'In fact I told Simon Arrowsmith, when he pleaded with me to protect his wife – ' guilt caught her by the throat as she recalled the desperate look on the young husband's face; she swallowed, and went on '– I told him that he had nothing to worry about, because she wasn't in any danger . . .'

'Oh, come on,' said Tait. 'You've just made it clear that the woman was asking for trouble. From what you've told me, she deserved whatever happened to her.'

'What's that got to do with it?' snapped Quantrill. 'Protecting the public is what we're here for, whether we approve of them or not.'

'Her husband was shattered, when I told him this morning,' Hilary remembered. 'Poor devil . . . he was blubbing like an eight-year-old, and the tears soaked into his beard. You could've wrung it out . . .'

'Now you're being sentimental,' said Tait. 'It was probably the husband who got rid of her, haven't you thought of that?'

Chief Inspector Quantrill gave him an evil scowl. There were times – there always had been times – when the younger man irritated him beyond bearing. 'Of *course* we've thought of it! Simon Arrowsmith has been our prime suspect from the start.' He saw disagreement in Sergeant Lloyd's eye, and amended 'our' to 'my'.

'But as it happens,' Quantrill went on, 'he has an alibi. His elderly mother was rushed to hospital yesterday morning. She wasn't expected to live, and Simon says he spent most of yesterday, and all of last night, at Breckham Market Infirmary with her.'

'You'll check his claim, of course?'

Hilary Lloyd thought for a moment that her new boss would explode as he struggled not to rise to Tait's latest piece of provocation. His face went dark red, his jaw tightened, a vein at his left temple bulged. She intervened before he did himself an injury.

'Mr Quantrill delegates the checking to me, just as he must have delegated it to you when you were his sergeant,' she told the Inspector firmly. 'I shall be seeing the night staff at the Infirmary tonight. But Angela's brother, Harold Wilkes, is more of a problem. He claims to have been at home in bed, and that's always a difficult one to disprove.'

Her intervention had given Quantrill's complexion time to subside to its normal healthy colour. He leaned forward to take the mug that Hilary had just refilled for him from her electric filter coffee-maker, a piece of personal property that she had brought with her from Yarchester, and had warned all thirsty members of the Criminal Investigation Department to keep their thieving hands off. Really, Quantrill would have preferred tea – even canteen tea – at that hour in the afternoon, but he didn't want to offend her. He liked the way she stood no nonsense from young Tait.

'There could have been collusion between the husband and the brother,' he said.

Hilary looked at him with disapproval, withholding the mug of coffee in a way that made the Chief Inspector wonder for a moment whether she intended to stand no nonsense from him either. 'As you know, sir, I don't believe that Simon would harm his wife in any way. Especially as he begged protection for her.'

'Sorry,' said Quantrill, 'but I'm not prepared to rule him out on that account.'

The initial shock of Angela Arrowsmith's death, and his own contributory negligence, had seemed to numb his mind. He'd done a lot of work so far that day, but all of it could equally well have been done by a robotic Detective Chief Inspector programmed to set up a murder enquiry. But now he had begun to think for himself again. His appetite had returned too, and he embarked belatedly on his lunch of ham sandwiches.

'From what Angela's son told us,' he said, swallowing his first mouthful and gesturing with the remainder of the sandwich to emphasise his point, 'she was pushing her husband unmercifully. He couldn't have had far to go to cracking point, and at cracking point the most unlikely person can resort to violence. When he asked you to provide her with protection, it could have been because he was afraid of what he might do if she pushed him too far. Or it could have been a bluff. Perhaps he asked us to protect her, knowing that we wouldn't, in order to avert suspicion from himself.'

'I still don't think that Simon Arrowsmith would be a party to hurting his wife, let alone murdering her,' said Hilary. But she finally gave the Chief Inspector his coffee.

'Have we any proof at this stage that she *was* murdered?' asked Tait.

'We've proof of deliberate intent to cause grievous harm,' said Quantrill. 'I told the pathologist our suspicions when he came out to the scene, and he found fingertip-type bruising on her throat. He says it wasn't the cause of death, but it was certainly an attempt at manual strangulation.'

'And you think that the most likely assailants were her husband and – or – her brother?'

'They're the ones with the motive. Both of them had good reason to want to prevent Angela from going any further with her restaurant project. I happened to see them all in the town on Wednesday evening, as I was walking down Bridge Street. She was giving directions to her husband and her brother while they fixed an advertising banner inside the window of the old chapel. Both men looked worried sick, and no wonder. I sent a photographer down there this morning, so that we could all see what she'd been planning.'

He handed Hilary a blown-up colour print. Tait looked over her shoulder, bending closer than was strictly necessary. Hilary leaned unobtrusively in the opposite direction. They both studied the photograph.

It showed the modern plate-glass window of the former chapel, almost completely filled by a banner that shrieked, in three colours embellished with pink fluorescent stars:

ARROWSMITHS RESTAURANT AND NITE SPOT
* GREAT FOOD * GREAT ENTERTAINMENT *
GALA OPENING OCTOBER IOTH
* ARROWSMITHS OF BRECKHAM * THE INN PLACE *

Tait winced. 'I thought she wanted to open a *restaurant*. All she'd have offered in a tacky place like this would have been scampi and chips and blue jokes.'

'There's nothing wrong with scampi and chips,' said Quantrill. It was what his wife usually chose on the rare occasions when he took her out for a meal at the buttery of the Rights of Man, Breckham's main hotel. 'The point is that this is the wrong town for a night club. She'd have been lucky to have the place half-full for the gala opening, and even if the customers thought she gave value for money they wouldn't consider going back there for at least six months. Commercially, it would have been a disaster. She'd have stood a better chance of making a profit if she'd fed all her money into a one-armed bandit. But of course it wasn't her own money she was gambling with . . .'

Hilary read the advertising banner again. *Arrowsmiths Restaurant and Nite Spot* appealed no more to her than it did to the men; but she knew someone to whom it would appeal even less.

'Ross Arrowsmith must be absolutely furious about the *Arrowsmiths of Breckham* bit. Angela was obviously making a deliberate attempt to associate the place with his company.'

Quantrill looked up quickly. 'Would it have made him furious enough to attack her, do you think?'

'No – o. I can't really see him going to that extreme. Anyway, he flew off to Japan last Saturday. Even if he came back before last night, he probably wouldn't have seen this advertisement.'

'A man of Ross Arrowsmith's calibre,' said Tait authoritatively, 'wouldn't waste his time on such a petty issue. He'd simply instruct his solicitor to issue an injunction restraining Angela from using the name for her commercial venture.'

Quantrill and Hilary, silently deferring to Inspector Tait's claimed knowledge of men of the computer expert's calibre, exchanged glances that were almost, but not quite, grins of fellow-feeling. Tait, his long nose in his coffee mug, failed to notice. When he emerged he said, 'So what led up to Angela Arrowsmith's death? What happened since you saw her last Saturday?'

The detectives' principal informant had been Gary Hilton, Angela's son. It was too difficult to communicate with Harold Wilkes, who had taken their written news of his sister's road death impassively, referring them for any information to her husband. Simon, still at the infirmary with his mother and harrowed by anxiety and sleeplessness, had been reduced by their news to a saturated incoherence; all they could understand from him was that Angela had been a wonderful wife.

But Gary, who had been asleep when they first called, greeted them eagerly when they returned to *Tenerife* from the hospital. His face was still streaked and puffy with tears; much as he had longed to be free of his mother, grief had caught him unawares when his uncle told him of her death. But now there was a brightness about him, a sense of excitement. He wanted some attention, and with his stepfather away and his uncle necessarily uncommunicative, he was glad to talk to anyone who would listen.

He talked freely about his mother, making no attempt to put her words and actions in a good light. It seemed not to occur to him that any suspicion might attach to her death. When Chief Inspector Quantrill said to him, 'What about the threat that was made to your mother last Saturday, Gary? Do you think someone could have planned to kill her?', the boy had shot him a look of alarm. But then he had shaken his head.

'No. As far as I know she didn't upset anybody except Simon and Uncle Harold.' He told the detectives about the conversation he had overheard between his mother and his stepfather when the representative of the finance company had called. 'But however rotten she was to them, neither Si nor Harold would have hurt her. They'd let her get away with anything.'

The sum of the detectives' information was that Angela Arrowsmith had spent most of her time during the preceding week directing alterations at the old chapel in Breckham Market. She had talked about nothing but her restaurant.

Whenever she went to the premises she took with her some – preferably all – of her menfolk. Simon, who worked from home as a freelance computer programmer, could help her only in the evenings; but Gary – who had left school in July and had been unable to find a job – and his uncle were in attendance on Angela for most of the week.

Harold Wilkes had no vehicle of his own. Having given up driving since his accident, he travelled to and from Breckham in Angela's car. He claimed to the police that he had been happy at the prospect of working as his sister's chef, and that he thought the restaurant a good idea. But his real view, according to his nephew, was that the enterprise was bound to fail. Harold had told Gary that Angela had no concept of what running a restaurant involved, and that he himself was too severely handicapped to cope with the work.

There had been several occasions during the week when Angela went to Yarchester on business, but those trips she had made on her own, and always in the daytime. She had told her family nothing of her activities there, apart from throwing them snippets of information about the colour of the wall-to-wall carpeting and the banquette seating she had ordered, and the names of the singer, backing group and entertainer she had booked for the gala opening. Her last visit to Yarchester had been on Wednesday afternoon.

On Thursday, Simon had made his usual early morning visit to his mother Nellie, and had found her unwell. He had called her doctor who, arriving just after Nellie collapsed, diagnosed a heart attack and sent immediately for the ambulance. Simon had followed the ambulance to the infirmary in his own car, first telephoning Angela to tell her what had happened.

Angela was displeased that her husband's attention had been diverted from her. She insisted that Harold went with her to the restaurant, despite the fact that he had a particularly bad headache. Gary usually made his own way to Breckham on his bicycle, but his mother made him go with her and Harold in her car so that he couldn't slip away during the day. She was, said Gary, in a very bad temper. When Simon had telephoned her later in the morning to say that he was going to stay at the hospital with Nellie, she had told him that if he wasn't too busy to spend the day twiddling his thumbs there, he could in future spend more time making himself useful at the restaurant. 'Mum really gave him an earful, poor old Simon,' Gary told the detectives.

During the course of the afternoon, Harold's headache had worsened to such a degree that Angela had finally, crossly, driven him home. While she was away, a fat little man with thick glasses had arrived saying that he was Mr Mutimer, the builder, and that he had come to inspect the work in progress. He waited until Angela returned. She immediately sent Gary into the town to do some shopping for her, and when he brought it, Mr Mutimer had gone.

The carpenters had stayed late, working overtime to finish reconstructing the kitchen area. Angela had loaned them her son as an unpaid mate. By the time the two of them returned to *Tenerife*, it was after nine o'clock.

They were both hungry, and Angela had roused her brother from his bed to cook them some supper. Simon was still at the infirmary. He telephoned Angela at about ten o'clock to tell her that his mother's condition was still critical, and that he proposed to stay there all night. That, Simon told the police, was the last time he had spoken to his wife. Angela, who was tired and already in her silk kimono, her face cleansed of make-up, had snapped at her husband and slammed the receiver down. 'The old woman's still hanging on,' she had told her son. 'If she's going to die I wish she'd get on with it – that'd be the answer to everything.'

In reply to the Chief Inspector, Gary said that he didn't know what his mother had meant by that phrase.

After supper, when Harold and Gary had gone to their respective bedrooms, the telephone had rung again. Angela answered it, as she always did. Gary was watching television on his portable set, and heard nothing of the conversation, but presently his mother came into his room, dressed to go out. She had looked excited.

She said that she was meeting someone, and her son knew better than to ask who or where. She told Gary that she had her latchkey, and that she had stuck a message on the inside of the front door warning Harold, if he should happen to get up, not to bolt it. As she left Gary's room, soon after 11 p.m., she had said to him – as far as he could remember – 'If this works out, I don't mind if the old woman does hang on a bit longer.'

15

'Angela was thinking of money, presumably?' said Tait.

'What else?' said Hilary. 'Her caller must have known that he could tempt her to meet him by offering money. But it would have had to be a big offer – several thousand pounds, at least.'

'Then assuming that the caller was also her attacker, doesn't that rule out Simon Arrowsmith? His wife knew that he had nothing left to offer.'

'Except access to his poor old mother's money,' said Quantrill with disapproval, picking up the last of his sandwiches. 'What Angela said to Gary about the old lady's death being "the answer to everything" suggests that Mrs Nellie Arrowsmith has a sizeable nest-egg to leave to Simon when she dies. Angela must have been confident – with reason – of getting her own hands on it. Knowing that, Simon could have rung his wife to say that even if his mother were to survive the heart attack, he'd make sure that Angela got the money. That'd interest her.'

'Plausible,' said Tait, 'except that I don't see Angela agreeing to go out late at night to discuss it with him.'

'You would, if you'd ever met her. Instant gratification, that was what she demanded. Simon would have known that if he rang her to say that he could get the money she wanted, but that he couldn't talk about it on the telephone, she wouldn't have been able to wait to hear more. And if he'd said he couldn't leave his mother long enough to drive all the way home, Angela would have agreed to meet him half-way.'

'Very plausible,' said Hilary. 'As long as you can believe that Simon Arrowsmith would harm his wife in any way. I can't.'

'So you've told us,' said Quantrill. He nearly added 'several times', but he wasn't so convinced of his own hypothesis that he wanted to squelch her. 'But what about Harold Wilkes? He was at home alone during the early part of yesterday evening. If Simon went home from the infirmary, he and Harold might well have discussed what they were going to do to save themselves from Angela.

'It would obviously have to be something more drastic than the decapitated cat episode. Perhaps they cooked up a plan that involved Simon making the telephone call, and Harold doing the actual meeting. Gary says that his uncle went back to bed after supper, but their bedrooms are both on the ground floor, on opposite sides of the hall. Harold could easily have climbed out of his window later, without Gary's knowledge.'

'Harold hasn't a car,' pointed out Hilary. 'How could he reach the A135?'

'Perhaps Simon rang his wife from a call-box near Wickford,' said Quantrill. 'Then he picked up Harold, drove him to the layby, and left him to deal with Angela. Probably they meant to frighten her badly, rather than to kill her. But the hands on her throat might have alarmed her to such an extent that she ran out on to the road and was knocked down by a hit-and-run driver.'

'And you think Simon would have left her there? Never!'

'Someone did. Someone squeezed her neck, and then left her to be spread over the tarmac. If Simon wasn't involved, who was it? Harold on his own?'

'It wasn't necessarily a member of her family,' Hilary argued. 'We know that she had some very undesirable acquaintances in the past. Perhaps she was trying to raise some money from one of them. Blackmail?'

Quantrill scoffed. 'For the kind of money you yourself said that she needed? No chance. If she'd ever known enough to blackmail a big man in the old Black Bull mob, she'd have been got rid of years ago. Wouldn't she?'

The Chief Inspector and the Sergeant stared at each other crossly. It had been a distressing day, and they were getting nowhere.

'Look, can we forget the speculation for a bit?' interrupted Tait. 'What about forensic evidence?'

Quantrill turned to vent his frustration on the Inspector. '*What* forensic evidence? D'you imagine we'd be sitting here chewing over motive if we had a single scrap of hard evidence to work on? There's been so much rain on that layby that any tyre or footprints must have been washed away hours before we got there.'

'Aren't you still searching?'

'Of *course* we're still searching! Harry Colman's team is still hard at it.' He rubbed his chin despondently. 'I can't say that I'm hopeful, though.'

Hilary was learning to deal with the Chief Inspector's changes of mood. She didn't know what caused his lapses into gloom; respecting his privacy as she wanted him to respect hers, she had no intention of trying to find out. She found his melancholy mood almost endearing, but it was not one that she proposed to encourage. What he needed, she thought, was an injection of optimism. There must be evidence at the scene of the crime, she asserted; and the search team would be sure to find it.

Quantrill brightened immediately.

Not because of what Hilary Lloyd had said. He knew perfectly well how good at their job the searchers were. So why, suddenly, did he feel happier? Puzzled, he began the unfamiliar task of investigating his own emotions and came with pained surprise to the conclusion that it must be because, as she spoke, the girl had smiled at him.

He told himself sharply not to be a fool, but the cheerfulness lingered.

Tait's nose had twitched at the earlier mention of blackmail.

'You mentioned a possible connection with my murder case, Hilary. Do you think Angela Arrowsmith was killed because she guessed the identity of the headless corpse?'

'No,' said Sergeant Lloyd decisively. 'No woman in her right mind would agree to a late-night meeting with someone she wanted to blackmail for murder, particularly at a place where she knew the corpse had been found!'

'Angela wasn't a local woman,' said Quantrill. 'She probably didn't realise the significance of the layby. That would make it an ideal meeting-place from her assailant's point of view, quite apart from its natural seclusion; he could use the story of the headless corpse to terrify her.'

'What makes you so sure it wasn't the A135 murderer having another go?' asked Tait.

'Instinct,' said Quantrill. 'Plus the fact that they used completely different methods. And besides, the A135 murder was committed elsewhere.'

'So where's the connection between your case and mine?'

'Ah – it's only an indirect one, I'm afraid, but you should find it helpful.' Quantrill had finished the last of his sandwiches. Peckish still, having had no time for lunch, he began to tear the packaging from a Lyons blackcurrant and apple pie that his wife, had she known, would never have allowed him to eat. 'Tell Martin what you've been working on, Hilary,' he said.

She told Inspector Tait about the dress the headless woman had been wearing, and about the Jayne Edwards mail-order catalogue. 'I've been in touch with the firm and they've sent me some very interesting information – it arrived only this morning, so I've had no time to follow it up.'

Hilary excavated her in-tray, which had been piled with messages and reports while she was out. 'Yes, here it is: Jayne Edwards advertised that particular dress in their spring catalogue two years ago. I asked for a list of credit customers who bought the dress in the murdered woman's size, 14. I also wanted to know if any of those women had not been heard of by the firm – no new orders put in, or payments made – since the end of June this year. The fact that they've had no recent transactions with Jayne Edwards doesn't mean that any one of them has been murdered, of course, but it's a possible lead. There are thirty of them, nationwide. But what is particularly interesting is that two of them live in Yarchester, and they bought their dresses through Angela Arrowsmith's agency.'

'There you are, then, Martin,' said Quantrill, as proud of his new sergeant as if he'd invented her. 'That gives us the kind of break we've been hoping for. Hilary's done a sound job, and it's a great pity she's too busy to follow it through herself. Still,' he added, preparing to bite with enjoyment into his juicy pie, 'we know you'll be able to wrap it up with your usual efficiency – '

Tait was annoyed. The case of the headless corpse had suddenly lost all interest for him. Following up a list of mail-order agents and interviewing their customers hardly provided a challenge for an inspector from the regional crime squad. It would be much more appropriate if Hilary went round interviewing the women, while he put his mind to the Angela Arrowsmith case. He'd have said so – except that he was no longer a member of Breckham Market CID, and therefore had no say in the matter.

'You've dropped blackcurrant juice on your shirt cuff,' he pointed out unkindly to the Chief Inspector. He was amused to see that Quantrill's instant reaction was to glance in embarrassment at Hilary, before mopping his light checked cuff with his white linen handkerchief. 'Mrs Quantrill won't like that,' Tait added. 'The stains, I mean . . .'

Hilary took a deep interest in her in-tray. Douglas Quantrill glared at the younger man, knowing perfectly well what he meant. Never missed a thing, blast his sharp blue eyes . . .

'Your wife's well, I hope?' continued Tait, his humour restored. 'Do give her my regards. And how's Alison? I hope she's coming up from London for the Chief Super's wedding – please tell her I'm looking forward to seeing her again.'

Quantrill was damned if he'd do anything of the kind. He knew that Martin Tait had, a year ago, been in ardent pursuit of his younger daughter. He had never discovered what had gone on between them, but he was fairly sure that Alison had not welcomed Tait's attentions.

'She may not be able to come,' he said. 'She has a very busy social life in London, you know.' He looked at his watch. 'Just time for a quick one before we go back on the job. Get your coat, Hilary. Inspector Tait is looking forward to buying us both a drink at the Coney.'

16

The Coney and Thistle, an ancient half-timbered building that stood on the corner of Breckham marketplace just opposite the great flint tower of St Botolph's church, was the Chief Inspector's favourite pub. This was Hilary's first visit, and she understood at once why he preferred it.

The Coney was not unlike Quantrill himself, solid, unpretentious, essentially English and not entirely up to date. There was no piped music, no electronic pinging and burbling from space-invader machines. And yet it held some interesting surprises, as Hilary discovered when they went to the bar. The beer was predictably a Suffolk brew, but the lager was best draught Danish, and German and French wines were available by the glass.

When Tait had bought their drinks, Quantrill led the way up two worn stone steps and into the heavily beamed snug. At this time in the evening, it was empty; here, at a table in a corner formed by two high-backed settles, they could talk without being overheard.

They discussed their plans for the evening. Quantrill and Hilary intended first to return to the scene of Angela Arrowsmith's death. They had set up that morning an almost exact reconstruction of the murder enquiry scene in June, with a mobile information room parked in the layby, and road blocks out on the A135. Now they needed to review the situation with the sergeant in charge of the information room, and with Inspector Colman, the scene-of-crime officer.

'I'll come with you,' said Tait. 'My A135 case,' he reminded them when they frowned at him; 'I must examine the place where the headless corpse was found.'

Quantrill and Hilary agreed that after visiting the layby they would return to Angela Arrowsmith's house at Nether Wickford. The news from Breckham Market Infirmary was that Mrs Nellie Arrowsmith was now out of danger, and had been moved from the intensive care unit into one of the wards. Her son, Angela's husband, had returned to *Tenerife*; now that his anxiety over his mother had lessened, the detectives proposed to question him more closely about his wife's death.

'I'll come with you,' said Tait. 'I need to collect Angela's mail-order account books.'

They ignored him. 'I must go to the infirmary, later this evening,' remembered Hilary, 'to check that Simon really was there all last night.'

Quantrill, who had no idea that his sergeant was a former nurse, looked doubtful. 'The infirmary's chronically understaffed and overcrowded. I don't see how the night staff could possibly confirm whether a visitor was there or not.'

'I wouldn't expect them to, in the ordinary course of events,' said Hilary, volunteering no information about her past. 'But if Simon had some nefarious reason for wanting an alibi, he'd have made a point of drawing attention to himself in some way – the old ploy of asking the time, something like that. Not that I think he would have done so – '

'I know,' said Quantrill with good-humoured resignation, 'you're just checking. But don't forget that there's still the possibility of collusion with Harold Wilkes. Come to think of it, the fact that the man hasn't a vehicle of his own isn't really a problem. Young Gary mentioned that he has a bicycle; Wilkes could perfectly well have climbed out of his bedroom window and ridden to the A135 on that.'

He paused to drink some beer. Tait, who had been fidgeting to contribute to the discussion, began to do so. Quick on the swallow, Quantrill interrupted.

'We're going to have a devil of a job piecing together what happened last night, Hilary. But there's a possible short cut. We're assuming that whoever killed Angela was the person who threatened her last weekend, right? So let's tackle the enquiry from that angle, instead.'

'Stage a reconstruction, you mean? Tomorrow morning?'

'Exactly. Saturday, just one week after the incident. The Saturday morning pattern of traffic is quite different from weekdays, much lighter. There's a good chance that our witnesses will be able to recall it.'

'That depends whether we can get hold of them all, at such short notice. For one thing, we don't know whether Ross Arrowsmith is back from Japan yet.'

'Then you'd better find out, right away. There's a telephone in the passage behind the bar.'

Quantrill spoke with deliberate bluntness. He was conscious that Martin Tait, temporarily silenced, was observing everything, and he wanted to indicate that his relationship with his female sergeant was strictly a working one.

Hilary blinked. Her former boss, nice Harry Colman, would have made it a polite request. But remembering her relatively low rank she said, 'Yes, sir,' and went out to find and ring the New Maltings number. She was back within a few minutes, looking as though she hadn't enjoyed the call.

'I spoke to Ross Arrowsmith – he got back yesterday evening. He wasn't best pleased when I asked for his co-operation tomorrow. But he did say, grudgingly, that he'd be jogging at his usual time, and in the Wickford direction.'

'Good. Well, you're the one who knows him, Hilary. Are you going to jog along with him?'

'No,' she said. Besides preferring other forms of exercise, she was anxious not to snarl up her friendship with Jen Arrowsmith by irritating Jen's husband any further. 'Ross has taken a dislike to me, and he's a difficult man to talk to at the best of times.'

'I'll do it, if you like,' offered Tait, eager to make the acquaintance of the micro-electronics expert.

'This is not your case,' Quantrill reminded him, exasperated. 'You get on with your own murder enquiry – when we want your help we'll ask for it.'

'We're looking for someone who's very careful,' said Inspector Colman.

He and Quantrill were sitting in the mobile information

room, where a uniformed sergeant was collating reports as they were brought in by police officers manning the road blocks. It was 6.40 p.m.; still daylight on the A135, but the surrounding trees had brought a premature dusk to the layby. The interior of the police caravan was bright with strip lighting which gleamed on Harry Colman's high, bald forehead. He was tired, after a long day's attention to detail, and his normally vigorous Prince Consort side-whiskers and moustache seemed to droop a little.

'Our man was lucky that it rained heavily, of course,' he went on. 'He couldn't have relied on a downpour that would cover his tracks so completely. But I don't doubt that he went to a lot of trouble to hide his tyre marks and footprints before he left the scene. We haven't found any so far. He did make one big mistake, though – he got into his victim's car.'

'Fingerprints?' asked Quantrill.

'No, he was too careful. He wore gloves, and as if that wasn't enough he cleaned out the inside of the car before he left it. Come and see the evidence of that.'

Refreshed by his brief rest, Harry Colman bustled out of the caravan with Quantrill following. Hilary Lloyd joined them, after pointing out to Martin Tait where the headless corpse had been found. The search team had left when the light deteriorated, and Tait was now standing alone, studying the scene. His colleagues had no doubt, though, that his ears were pinned back to listen to their conversation.

Angela Arrowsmith's car had been taken away for forensic examination, but markers showed where it had stood.

'Look at this,' said Harry Colman, picking up a pale yellow leaf, recently fallen, but torn and bruised. There were a few similar leaves on the ground, lying close together. 'They're from a lime tree, if I'm not mistaken – but limes don't grow in this wood. There's one beside the driveway of Mrs Arrowsmith's house at Nether Wickford, though, and I think that the leaves could well have been walked into her car. And now they're lying level with the driver's door of the car and a couple of feet away, just where you'd expect them to fall if someone stood at the open door and shook the rubber floor mat. I think that's exactly what our man did, on both sides of the car. And he must have done it some time after midnight, when the rain started, because when we examined the car both mats were still slightly damp.'

'It's very helpful of him, to let us know that he was in the car,' said Hilary. 'Dusting the interior and shaking the floor mats may get rid of any obvious traces, but he has no idea what a thorough job forensic does – he hasn't bargained for their vacuum-cleaner technique.'

Inspector Colman nodded and smiled at her. Quantrill was sure that his old friend's whiskers had perked up measurably in Hilary Lloyd's presence.

'True. And I've something else to show you.' With the air of a Victorian uncle presenting a conjuring trick for the delectation and approval of his favourite niece, Colman produced a plastic evidence-bag. It contained a small plug of dried mud.

'Our man wasn't quite as careful as he thought. Although he shook the floor mats, he didn't dislodge this scrape of mud from the mat on the passenger side – it was stuck in the rubber moulding. And it couldn't have been there for more than a few hours before we found it, because although the outside was dry, the inside was still moist. So the chances are that it came from his shoes.'

Quantrill, a countryman by birth and upbringing, regarded mud as his department. He took the envelope into the light of the caravan and identified the stiff blue-grey texture of its contents immediately. 'Clay,' he said. 'Heavy clay. It can't be from anywhere round Breckham, because this is light land. Even deep ploughing doesn't bring clay to the surface round here. Mightn't it have come from Angela Arrowsmith's own shoes, though? We can't be sure that the floor mats weren't switched when he shook them.'

'I'll have her shoes checked,' said Hilary, 'but I don't think the mud came from them. I was the one who picked them up this morning – they'd been torn off by impact as she lay on the road. I didn't look at them particularly closely, but they were flimsy and smooth-soled, and perfectly clean as far as I can remember – apart from rain and road damage, and the blood.'

'Fine,' said Inspector Colman. 'I'll send this mud to the lab for analysis, and with luck they'll be able to tell us something about our man's recent movements.'

Quantrill thanked his colleague. 'Oh, one other thing, Harry: we've been assuming that our man came here by car, but there's now another possibility. When your team starts searching again tomorrow morning, ask them to keep their eyes open for any trace of bicycle tyres, will you?'

At ten-thirty that night, Sergeant Lloyd made a return visit, alone, to Breckham Market Infirmary. She enquired first about Mrs Nellie Arrowsmith, and was told that her condition was satisfactory; her son Simon had spent most of the evening sitting at her bedside.

Hilary then went into the intensive care unit, where Nellie had been treated the previous night. The unit, purpose-built in the new accident and emergency wing of the hospital, had its own small waiting room, an enlarged section of corridor equipped with chairs and ashtrays. This corridor led direct from the reception hall, which was unstaffed at night. Other public areas, including cloakrooms and a large waiting room, also led off the hall. With so many places where he might legitimately have been, there was no chance at all that any one member of the staff would be able to vouch for Simon's continuous presence at the hospital between the hours of eleven the previous night and one o'clock that morning.

But Simon had made his presence known.

'Mrs Arrowsmith's son?' said the staff nurse who spared a few moments to answer Hilary's query. She was West Indian in features and colouring, but second-generation English; and not only English, but Suffolk. Like Quantrill's, her voice was slow and her vowels broad.

'You mean the cuddly one with the beard?' she went on. 'We couldn't get rid of the man! He'd been here all day, and he hung about all night as well. We told him half a dozen times to go home, but he'd disappear for a bit and then sneak back. His brother had more sense.'

'His brother?'

'Yes – you know, the computer man. Ross Arrowsmith. I

recognised him from his photograph in the local paper. Apparently he'd only just got back from abroad and he rushed here in a panic, afraid that he'd be too late to see his mother.'

Hilary saw no point in correcting the staff nurse's minor misapprehension about the Arrowsmith family's relationship. 'What time would that have been?'

'Oh, early. Half past ten-ish, something like that. He hung about for a short time, but when I reassured him that his mother's condition was stable, he had the sense to go home. The cuddly brother disappeared too, for a while, but he was back again before very long.'

'Before how long?'

'Before we wanted him back, that's for sure! Don't ask me to be definite. From eleven o'clock onwards it's usually hectic in this wing, what with the pubs closing and drink-driving accidents – '

'I can remember what it was like. I did an SRN at Addenbrooke's.'

'*Did* you?' The staff nurse, who had been poised to go, relaxed for a few moments. She smiled, her teeth brilliantly white against her dark skin. 'Well, you know all about it, then. Lucky you, to do your training in Cambridge . . . Hey, what happened? Why did you change careers? And how did you get that scar – did an ungrateful patient throw a bed bottle at you?'

Hilary touched her forehead ruefully. 'It was a beer bottle, as a matter of fact. I'd fancied myself more in police uniform than in a cap and apron, until I tried to arrest a man who had a grudge against the police. I've learned to duck, since then. But about Simon Arrowsmith – the one with the beard. It really is important for us to know where he was last night. You can remember having seen him somewhere between ten-thirty and eleven, yes? And after that – ?'

'After that? Let's see . . .' The dark eyes rolled, doing a professional count. 'One cardiac arrest, one young motor cyclist with multiple injuries, one pedestrian with a fractured skull and suspected brain damage after being knocked down by a car. We reversed the cardiac arrest; the pedestrian's still unconscious. The motor cyclist died just before one-thirty this morning. I

went for a break soon after that, and saw the cuddly Arrowsmith brother in the reception hall. He hurried to ask me how
his mother was – he said he'd been asleep in the main waiting
room.'

'How did he look?'

'Pretty good, in comparison with the eighteen-year-old
who'd just died. Sorry, but you know how it is. I didn't take
much notice of him. He'd looked rough all night, as far as I can
remember. I had another go at sending him home but soon
afterwards I saw him sitting in the corridor again. And that's as
much as I can tell you, I'm afraid. As I said, there was a lot
happening between eleven last night and one o'clock this
morning.'

17

21 September; a cool, bright, clear morning. Too clear to stay
dry for long. Rainclouds were already moving in from the west,
but for the moment the rising sun shone brilliantly on the
hedgerows, illuminating the ripening wild fruit: purple clusters
of blackberry and elderberry, scarlet wild rose-hips, and crim-
son hawthorn berries. The air smelled of damp earth, wet grass
and mushrooms.

At 7.07 a.m. Ross Arrowsmith, in singlet and running shorts,
his lank forelock already flopping, padded down the drive of
New Maltings. A tall young man in track suit and training
shoes, who had been brought to Ecclesby by police car a few
minutes earlier, greeted him at the gateway. He was carrying a
small clipboard.

'Good morning, sir. Detective Constable Bedford. Sergeant
Lloyd asks me to thank you for your co-operation.'

Ross Arrowsmith muttered something noncommittal,
turned right and jogged up the road towards Wickford common. James Bedford, a fresh-faced twenty-year-old who,
according to his colleagues, had been promoted to the CID only

because he looked so young in uniform that he destroyed the credibility of the whole county constabulary, eased alongside him and picked up his rhythm.

Bedford had been given the assignment by Sergeant Lloyd because he was a keen young detective who was also known to be a jogger. Fortuitously, he was a computer enthusiast as well; he had taken a part-time course in computer science at Yarchester Technical College, and the computer he owned was an Arrowsmith. He was delighted to have been given the opportunity to meet the micro-electronics expert, and immediately began to ask about the latest Arrowsmith model.

Recognising that the detective's interest was genuine, Ross abandoned some of his normal taciturnity. Without going so far as to enter into a conversation, he consented to give audible replies. And when Dc Bedford, eventually recollecting Sergeant Lloyd's briefing, asked him as a matter of routine how he had spent Thursday night, Ross gave him civil answers.

'Thursday? That was the evening I returned from Japan. My wife told me that my stepmother was critically ill, so I went to the infirmary to see her. My brother? He's not my brother, he's my half-brother. Yes, he was there too. We had a conversation. There was nothing either of us could do, but he insisted that he was going to stay there all night. I left about eleven o'clock.

'After that? The road home passes my office, so I decided to call in and look through my mail. Then I realised how jet-lagged I felt, and decided to stay there the night. No, no, in bed; I have a small private suite there. I often work late, and don't like to disturb my wife by going home in the early hours.'

It was a perfectly reasonable, co-operative reply, and Bedford wondered why Sergeant Lloyd had warned him that he'd be lucky to get a word out of Ross Arrowsmith. Predisposed as he was to like the computer man, Bedford would have accepted his account of his movements without further question. But Sergeant Lloyd had also said that Ross was on the list of possible suspects. Phrasing the question carefully, James Bedford sought for some kind of confirmation of Ross's story.

'Is your office easily accessible at night, sir? I mean, with all the high-tech equipment you must have in the building, I hope you don't leave it unguarded?'

'Good God, no. I employ a security firm, and even I can't get in without being vetted. Quite apart from professional thieves, there are too many people wandering round the town looking for mischief, so I leave nothing to chance. I don't even park my car on the forecourt after dark – I drive it into the yard, and the guards keep the gates locked. And then of course there are electronic alarm devices on all the doors and windows.'

'Glad to hear it, sir. I wish other businessmen were equally security-conscious. Now, if you wouldn't mind thinking back to last Saturday morning . . . If we can piece together what happened then, it may throw some light on Mrs Angela Arrowsmith's death.'

'So I understand.' The exercise was bringing up a light sweat on Ross Arrowsmith's thin face and high forehead, but his movements were easy, his voice almost cheerful. He flicked his dark hair out of his eyes. 'I'll do whatever I can to help, of course. But don't think it odd – still less significant – that I'm not disposed to mourn for Simon's wife. If he had any sense, neither would he. Frankly, he and his brother-in-law are well rid of her.'

At *Tenerife*, Simon was not disposed to consider himself well rid of his wife. Those parts of his face that were visible above his curly beard were blotched with grief; and now that he had been told that the police suspected foul play, he was overcome with indignation and bitterness.

'But you *knew* she was being threatened! I specifically asked you to provide protection for her, and you refused.'

Chief Inspector Quantrill, standing with his hands behind his back and shifting his considerable weight uncomfortably from one foot to another, acknowledged his error. 'I regret that deeply, Mr Arrowsmith. The fact is, though, that your wife herself didn't ask for protection. That was what misled us. If Mrs Arrowsmith had been alarmed, that would have been a different matter.'

Simon blew his nose noisily. 'She was too trusting, that was why. She didn't realise that there are vicious people in the world.'

The Chief Inspector thought of several possible replies, none of them kind. But acknowledging the legal presumption of Simon Arrowsmith's innocence, and consequently the man's right to cherish what illusions he liked, he kept his thoughts to himself.

'Anyway,' said Simon, blowing his nose again, 'I don't see what you expect to find out by coming here at this hour in the morning. I don't see what you want me to do.'

'As I explained last night, sir,' repeated Quantrill patiently, 'we'd like you to repeat your movements of last Saturday morning. Detective Constable Jackson will go with you to ask what you can remember about last week. He's waiting for you now, in the hall.'

Simon tugged wretchedly at his beard. 'How can I go out, when you took away all our shoes last night?'

Quantrill glanced down at the beach sandals the man was wearing. 'I think you'll find that Dc Jackson has brought back one pair of shoes for each of you. The rest will be returned later today. Gary's bicycle may take a little longer, but we'll get it back to him as soon as we can. I'm extremely grateful to the three of you for being so co-operative.'

He looked at his watch. 'Almost eight o'clock. Isn't this about the time you said you went to visit your mother last Saturday morning?'

Simon nodded unhappily. 'Are you leaving now?' he asked.

'No. I need to talk to your brother and your stepson when they get up – at about half past eight, if they follow what they said was last week's pattern. That is of course if I have your permission to stay, Mr Arrowsmith?'

Looking very much as though he would like to refuse it – as though he knew that his co-operation was being assumed to such an extent that as soon as his back was turned the police would examine his car – Simon gave another glum nod. 'What do you want me to do when I get to my mother's house?' he asked hoarsely.

'Just stay as long as you did last Saturday morning, sir. You'll find Sergeant Lloyd there, waiting for you.'

Hilary Lloyd had made a point of arriving early at Mrs Arrowsmith senior's house. She loitered conspicuously in the road, looking at the attractive yellow-plastered house and its small red-brick appendage, and by the time she had wandered up the garden path between overhanging clumps of damp Michaelmas daisies, she found Mrs Arrowsmith's neighbour's back door open.

Hilary introduced herself to the old lady, who stood leaning on her walking frame, and said that she had come by appointment to meet Simon Arrowsmith. Mrs Cullen immediately enquired about Nellie.

'Thank goodness for that,' said May, when Hilary told her that Simon's mother was beginning a slow recovery. 'Will you step inside to wait for him, Miss? There's a cup of tea in the pot. Nellie generally has one with me about this time, we're both early risers.'

The old lady moved with the aid of her frame across the tiny kitchen and into the living room, half of which was now occupied by her bed. She lowered herself painfully into a wooden wheelback armchair from which she had a good view of the road and the common. A tray of tea stood on the table by her elbow, and she reached out to take a second cup and saucer from the sideboard that filled most of the remainder of the room. Hilary, sitting on the only other chair, averted her eyes as Mrs Cullen's cruelly deformed hands attempted to pour the tea into the cup rather than the saucer.

'Ross's wife did pop in yesterday afternoon,' said May, 'to tell me that Nellie had been moved out of the intensive care unit. She's a nice girl, Jen; she knew I'd be anxious about Nellie. I haven't set eyes on Simon since he followed his mother to the infirmary on Thursday morning – but there, he's had other troubles to contend with, poor boy.'

'You know about Simon's wife's death, Mrs Cullen?'

'Jen told me. Well, there . . . I don't wish to speak ill of the dead, but between you and me, Miss, he's far better off without her. What was she doing, out there on the main road at that time of night, that's what I'd like to know?'

The question was rhetorical, indignant. Hilary could see that for all Mrs Cullen's soft complexion and wispy white hair she was a tough-minded old lady. There was no need to wrap sordid facts in gentle phrases for her benefit.

'Apparently Angela went out to meet someone. We think it's likely that he killed her.'

'Oh dear. Oh dear, oh dear, oh dear.' May's facial expression was shocked but her voice was steady. 'Do you know – you may not believe me, but it's as true as I'm sitting here – I thought that's what might have happened. I didn't say so to Jen, and I wouldn't have said so to Nellie, but it's what I said to myself as soon as I heard that she'd been found dead: somebody's done her in.'

'So we're engaged on a murder enquiry,' said Hilary. 'I want to find out all I can about Angela, and I'll be grateful for any help you can give me, Mrs Cullen.'

'There's nothing I could swear to, Miss, because I never met her. All I know about her is what I heard from Nellie. Not that Nellie said anything against her, but I wasn't born yesterday. Angela took advantage of that poor boy's youth and innocence, and she's made his life a misery ever since.'

The old lady told Hilary the unhappy story of Simon's marriage, and Angela's ambitions. 'Oh, she was full of big ideas, that woman, without a penny for her own to pay for them. She came to Nellie's house only last Wednesday morning, cadging money.'

'Did Mrs Arrowsmith let her have any?'

'Oh yes.' May Cullen shook her head over her friend's folly. 'Nellie's soft, you see; that's where Simon gets it from. She lent Angela the money, but she was so worried, when she told me about it afterwards, that I shouldn't be surprised if that was what brought on her heart attack.'

Mrs Cullen paused to drink some tea, raising the cup to her lips by holding it between the fists of both her crippled hands. Her eyes, deeply sunk in her fragile skull, were bright with indignation as she told Sergeant Lloyd how Angela had arrived

134

unexpectedly at Nellie's door and had invited her to go to Breckham Market for a cup of coffee. 'First time she's ever done such a thing. Nellie, bless her heart, thinks how nice Angela is – washes her face and puts on her coat and goes.

'Well, an hour later the car's back. Angela drops Nellie and drives off. Nellie comes straight in here, and she doesn't look at all well. "Oh, May," she says, "I do hope I've done the right thing. Angela was short of money, and she asked me to lend her some, just until her restaurant opens. I couldn't very well refuse, could I? After all, she *is* Simon's wife. So she drove me to the building society and I drew out the money for her." And I said, "Oh, Nellie, you never did! How much?"'

Hilary shared May's despair over Nellie Arrowsmith's gullibility. 'How much, Mrs Cullen?'

The old lady's voice dropped to a horrified whisper: '*Two thousand five hundred pounds*. Nearly all that her husband left her.'

Hilary winced. 'Oh no . . .'

'And that's not the whole story. Angela was a liar, too. She went home and told Simon that his mother had offered to lend her some money, and that it was only a thousand pounds. Simon came to see his mother that night to say that she shouldn't have lent it, and when he heard the truth he was so upset . . . So was Ross's wife when I told her. Well, we all know poor Nellie was silly to do what she did, but Angela was downright wicked. If that was how she treated her own family, how did she treat other people? I'm not surprised that somebody finally stopped her games.'

Hilary was about to question Mrs Cullen further when she saw Simon Arrowsmith, escorted by Dc Jackson, walking across the common on the footpath that led from Nether to Upper Wickford. She explained to the old lady that Simon was reconstructing his movements on the previous Saturday morning.

May Cullen looked puzzled. 'Why is he walking across the common, then?'

'Because that's what he did at about this time last week.'

'No, he didn't. Poor boy, with all the worry and shock, he

must have forgotten. Last Friday evening he had a row with Angela, so he came over and spent the night at his mother's.'

As Simon Arrowsmith and Dc Jackson walked round to the back door of Simon's mother's house, Ross Arrowsmith and Dc Bedford jogged towards it on the road that ran along the Upper Wickford side of the common.

'That car wasn't there last week,' panted Ross, indicating the Metro HLE parked outside the old house.

'No, sir, that's Sergeant Lloyd's. She's having a word with your brother.'

Ross muttered something, and swung off to the left along the path that crossed the common. Bedford consulted his watch and his clipboard.

'There should be a car, any time now, passing from right to left along the road on the Nether Wickford side. A regular traveller, I believe. Do you remember seeing it, last Saturday?'

'Last Saturday was misty. I couldn't even see Simon's house from here.'

'Look, there it goes now. A white Ford Fiesta. Do you remember it?'

'No.'

The car, passing their front 30 yards ahead, suddenly did an emergency stop, its tyres squealing. Dc Bedford looked hard at his companion, who checked his pace and then stood still.

'Yes,' said Ross Arrowsmith thoughtfully. 'That I can re-member – the sound of braking, coming through the mist.' He moved on. 'By that time I'd turned left, off the path and on to the grass – just about here. The mist had begun to lift and I could see the stationary car. I don't remember its make or colour, but I certainly saw a man doing whatever that man's doing now . . . moving to the side of the road . . . going back to the car . . . yes, I remember that. I slowed down, about here, to let him drive away before I reached the road.'

They picked up their jogging pace. 'And is this as near to your half-brother's house as you went, sir?'

'Yes. At this point I heard another vehicle coming from the right, so I stayed where I was on the grass, just at the side of the road. You have to watch the traffic, in misty weather. I stood here looking to the right, waiting for the vehicle to pass.'

They both stood looking to the right. The road was empty, and Bedford had no need to look at his clipboard to know that there was no record, in all the statements that had been taken the previous week, of any vehicle travelling in that direction at that particular time.

'It must have been one we missed,' he said cheerfully, wondering whether Ross Arrowsmith had begun to lie. 'What kind of vehicle was it?'

'I took no notice. I was thinking about my work. But then the mist lifted, and I could see Simon's house quite clearly. A man was standing at the gate.'

'Inside the gate, or outside?'

'I don't know. I formed the impression that it wasn't Simon, and then I looked away almost immediately.'

'Was it his brother-in-law? His stepson?'

'I've no idea. I haven't met either of them.'

The mystery man sounded to Dc Bedford like a fabrication. Unwillingly, he began to regard Ross Arrowsmith as a suspect.

And then a mud-splattered Land Rover came into view, from the right. 'Was this the vehicle you saw?' Bedford asked.

Ross Arrowsmith was tired of being questioned. He shoved his hair out of his eyes. 'God knows,' he said sharply. '*I* don't.'

Dc Bedford made a note of the Land Rover's number.

18

Inspector Tait spent most of Friday night reading through the files on the A135 murder. On Saturday morning he sent Dc Wigby out with a list of the names and addresses of all the women in East Anglia who had bought Jayne Edwards mail-order dresses similar in style, colour and size to the one the headless woman had been wearing. Tait himself went straight to Yarchester, in search of the two women who had bought their dresses through Angela Arrowsmith's agency.

Most of Angela's customers lived in one small area of the city, sloping down from a main thoroughfare, Gold Street, towards the wharves on the riverside. The area had alternated for centuries between prosperity and seediness. Gold Street itself, busy rather than prosperous, contained a variety of small shops, a former cinema that had become a bingo hall, the unisex hairdressing salon where Angela had worked before her marriage to Simon, and the Black Bull pub, now under new ownership and trying to live down its recent disrepute.

Tait's first call was at a block of council flats. His ring at a ground-floor door was answered by a young woman who drooped as though the weight of the entire block was on her shoulders.

'Yes . . . ?' she said.

'Mrs Lynette Willis?'

'Yes . . . ?'

'Detective Inspector Tait, regional crime squad.' He held up his warrant card and she looked at it with puzzled, watery eyes.

'Yes . . . ?' she said.

Normally, he would have asked if he might go in. It was inadvisable – both unsatisfactory and tactless, except when house-to-house enquiries were being made – to interview householders on their doorsteps. But in giving the woman his usual quick once-over glance, he had realised that there was something familiar about the pink, red and grey striped dress she was wearing.

Washed out as it was, the dress was here and not in the forensic science lab; limp as she was, Mrs Willis was alive, not lying headless in the morgue. And that was all he needed to know.

Tait gave her the benefit of his most charming smile. 'Thank you very much,' he said, and went.

His next call was at a small house in an early Victorian terrace. The houses were unappreciatively owner-occupied, their pretty proportions and uniform appearance spoiled by the substitution of a variety of modern doors and windows.

Tait was hoping, in the interests of identifying the headless woman, that he would not find Angela's second customer, Mrs Kath Turner, there. However, she answered his ring: a bustling, forty-ish permed brunette, as much alive as Mrs Willis, only more so. Tait invited himself in, but no further than the narrow hall. Once he had seen the dress, he could go.

But the dress was no longer in Mrs Turner's possession.

'I gave it away. I was tired of it, and it was only a cheapie in the first place. Who to? Some girl – well, girl, I say: round about thirty, a good bit older than her boy friend.'

'What was her name?'

'Now you're asking . . . I only saw her once, and that was months ago. Middle of June, I think, just after we came back from Spain. My Ron was at the pub one evening – the Black Bull, that's his local – and he got playing darts with this young feller he'd never seen before. Well, my Ron! A fool if ever there was one, once he's got three or four pints inside him. Best friends with the nearest stranger. This young feller Mick spun him some hard luck story, so Ron invited him back here for a bacon sandwich, not realising that Mick had got this woman in tow.

'"Who's this?" I said. I was annoyed, I don't mind telling you. "Oh, this is Denise," said Mick, and he took less notice of her after that than if she'd been a dog. Next thing I knew, she was sitting in my kitchen crying her eyes out. Yes, that was her name, Denise.'

'Denise who?' asked Tait. 'Mick who?'

'I've no idea. Ron didn't know and didn't care, and I didn't know and didn't want to know. All I wanted was to get rid of them.'

'But you gave the woman your dress?'

'Ah well, I was sorry for the poor cow. I gave her a cup of tea, and heard more than I wanted to know about her troubles in return. Seems her husband had been in prison for a couple of years, and she'd recently picked up with young Mick. He'd put her in the club. She wanted the baby – wouldn't get rid of it because she'd fallen in love with him. God knows why, he was nothing to look at, all nose and no chin.'

'Why was she crying?' asked Tait. 'Was Mick threatening to ditch her?'

'He was talking about moving on, by himself, at the end of the week. He said it was because he couldn't get a job here, and that as soon as he found one somewhere he'd send for her. Well, that was a load of rubbish. He didn't want her round his neck, and she knew that as well as I did. But what really upset her was that her husband was due out of jail in July. He sounded a thoroughly nasty character – used to beat her up, she said. He'd spent most of their marriage in jail for robbery. They had no children of their own, and she was afraid he'd half-kill her when he found out she was carrying someone else's.'

Tait could feel his scalp bristling with an excitement that he kept well under control. Just one more stroke of luck, and he could wrap up the A135 murder case before lunch.

'Did she mention her husband's name? Or say which prison he was in?'

Kath Turner shook her head firmly. 'No. And I didn't want to know, either. We've never mixed with people like that, and I don't intend to start.'

'Can you tell me anything else about Denise? What did she look like?'

She shrugged. 'Nothing out of the ordinary. Not much over five feet tall . . . short mousy hair . . . round face. I didn't see a lot of her face, she was crying most of the time.'

'Is that why you gave her the dress?'

'Yes – I'd just washed it, and it was hanging in the kitchen to air. I was tired of it anyway, and I could see we were about the same size, so I asked her if she'd like it. Well, she hadn't got much going for her, had she? You should've seen her face light up, poor little cow.'

Recalling the incident, Kath Turner paused. Then, 'Oh yes, there is something else I can tell you about Denise,' she said. 'It was when I gave her the dress. She smiled, and I saw her teeth for the first time. The top two in front were set crooked – there was a gap between them wide enough to push a pencil through.'

140

Inspector Tait went immediately to the Black Bull. At 11.15 on a weekday morning it would have been almost empty, but today the bar was lined with Saturday drinkers. Tait bought a lager from the landlord, a man with a loud, cheery voice and eyes as hard as flint, and showed him his warrant card.

The landlord dropped his jovial act immediately. There was no need for the police to look for troublemakers in his pub, he growled, because he wouldn't give them house-room. He denied having seen, in the summer, the couple Tait described; so did his assistant barman; so did the customers at the bar.

Tait turned his back on them and surveyed the room. The dart board was not in use. A solitary, respectably suited middle-aged man was playing the fruit machine, but Tait decided against interrupting the concentration with which he was feeding it handfuls of silver in return for nothing but ungrateful electronic burps.

Another, scruffier, solitary man sat at a table facing the frosted glass windows. He clutched a half-pint mug of beer as though he cherished it so much that he wanted to keep it intact as long as possible. The back of his head looked uncommunicative, and Tait turned his gaze instead on the five occupants of the adjoining table.

They were merry, so well away that had they been men the landlord would undoubtedly have given them a warning. As they were women, their ages ranging from 60 to 80, he contented himself with giving occasional sour looks in their direction. They were Saturday morning regulars, high not on the small glasses of Guinness they were sipping, but on the pleasures of elderly irresponsibility after a lifetime of being at the beck and call of their husbands and children.

Listening to their cackles of laughter, Tait knew that he wouldn't find it easy to talk to them. He hadn't his colleagues' common touch. He couldn't be as genially patient with them as Quantrill; nor, as Wigby would have done, give them a nudge and a wink and a bit of sauce. On the other hand, he knew that his presence couldn't fail to attract their attention and interest.

'Good morning, ladies,' he said, getting his timing exactly

right and dropping his words into the silence that fell momentarily while they were drinking.

They turned their heads – matt black, grey-blonde, grey, white and mauve – and gazed at him, Guinness in their hands, froth on their upper lips, spectacles gleaming. Tait exercised his charm: 'May I join you?'

Flustered by his approach they twittered and preened themselves, shifting along their perches to accommodate him. Tait made no attempt to introduce himself, but signalled to the barman for another round of Guinness. Questioning the women with idle gallantry, he discovered that they usually called in at the Black Bull while they waited for the bingo hall to open its doors.

'I wonder if you can remember having seen a friend of mine here in the summer – a girl named Denise,' he said loudly. The women were silently attentive, but he wanted to make sure that his words carried to the two solitary men as well. 'I'm worried about her because I haven't seen her for a month or two. Not since early July.'

The women stirred and murmured, their faces blank. The man at the fruit machine was aware of nothing except flashing lights and rolling symbols, but the man with his back to them at the next table held his head still, as though he were listening.

'You'd remember Denise if ever you saw her,' Tait went on. 'She had a gap between her two top front teeth, wide enough to push a pencil through. She was in a bit of trouble, poor girl. She was pregnant by her boy friend, Mick, but she was already married to a man who was due to come out of jail.'

The women clucked with interest and sympathy, but Tait was already sure that they could tell him nothing. He was watching, instead, the man at the next table who suddenly picked up his glass, downed his beer at a gulp and hurried for the door marked Gents. As the man went, he glanced apprehensively over his shoulder. His face was heavy, with the small-eyed shape and the waxy whiteness of a boiled potato.

Tait leaped after him. But he hadn't taken into account the habit of bingo-going pensioners to carry with them capacious holdalls stuffed with spare cardigans, packets of boiled sweets, and batteries of coloured felt-tipped pens. Nor did he expect that the holdalls would be parked beside their owners' chairs. He tripped over one, stumbled, caught his foot in a handle and went sprawling.

By the time he had limped through the door marked Gents, and had found that it led not only to the urinals but also to the back door of the Black Bull, the man with the unmistakable prison pallor had disappeared. And although Tait questioned everyone – the passers-by, the landlord, the barman, every last customer – their replies, true or false, were exactly the same: they had never before set eyes on the man.

19

'So *he* was the one who cut off the cat's head and sprayed the threatening message on Angela's door? But he wouldn't have killed her, surely?'

'It seems unlikely,' agreed Quantrill. 'Not impossible, of course, but improbable.'

'Which means that there's no direct connection between last week's incident and the murder,' said Sergeant Lloyd. 'This reconstruction hasn't really put us any further forward, has it?'

'I wouldn't say that,' the Chief Inspector argued. 'For one thing – '

The detectives were holding an impromptu conference on the back lawn of *Tenerife*, sitting on plastic-coated aluminium chairs designed to look like Edwardian garden furniture. Rainclouds coming in from the west had blotted out the sun, but for the time being they were obligingly withholding their contents.

The reconstruction of the events of the previous Saturday morning had been entirely successful. Dc Bedford had radioed for a computer check on the number of the Land Rover that had passed him and Ross Arrowsmith, and had found that it belonged to a Nether Wickford farmer.

The farmer, when interviewed by Bedford, said that he frequently drove along that stretch of road, but only for about five hundred yards, between the farm and some outlying chicken hatcheries. Yes, he had used the road the previous Saturday – he remembered the morning because of the patchy mist. He knew Ross Arrowsmith – had known him since they were both boys – and knew that he usually jogged along the road at that time, so he had kept a look out for him; didn't want to run him down in the mist.

Yes, he'd seen him standing on the grass at the side of the road. Was glad Ross had his wits about him sufficiently to watch out for traffic when visibility was so dodgy . . . brilliant chap, of course, but he seemed to live in another world most of the time . . .

The man standing by Simon Arrowsmith's gate? Oh yes, the farmer remembered having seen him. Didn't know his name, but knew who he was: tall skinny young chap, son of the woman Simon Arrowsmith had married.

When questioned by the Chief Inspector, Gary had confessed so promptly to decapitating the dead cat and spraying the message on the door that Quantrill, professionally suspicious of confessions, had at first declined to believe him. It wasn't until Gary had shown Dc Bedford where he had hidden the lawn-edger that he had used as a cutting tool, the aerosol canister of red touch-up car body paint, and his blood-spattered sneakers and jeans, that the police were prepared to accept his story.

'All right, son,' Quantrill had said not unkindly; forced to recollect his activities, Gary was near to tears. 'It was a wicked thing to do, and we'll keep an eye on you in future. Try anything of the sort again, and you'll find yourself in trouble. But you haven't broken the law, so I'll let you off this time with a caution. Just tell me why you did it.'

To upset his mother, explained Gary. To pay her back for the way she treated all of them, and especially for the way she treated Simon. To try to frighten her into behaving herself in future, instead of cheating poor old Si.

'Cheating him?'

'Yes.' Gary took off his hornrims and wiped his damp eyes with the sleeve of his sweatshirt. 'Having another man in her bed – in Simon's bed.'

'When was that?'

'Last week. Last Friday night. I thought she was up to something when she picked a quarrel with Si that evening. She often did that, when she wanted something. She'd deliberately start a row, and then she'd cry and say that Simon was being unkind to her. Then he'd apologise, and give her what she wanted. But last Friday she didn't cry. She worked herself up into a rage and finally told him that he could clear off and spend the night at his mother's. Half an hour later, after Uncle Harold and I had gone to our rooms, this man turned up. I heard his voice, and then got a quick look at him when I went to the downstairs bog.'

'Did you know him? Had he been here before?'

'No. I did set eyes on him once, though, about a couple of weeks ago. Mum was with him in his car, in Breckham Market. He was quite old – dark moustache but grey hair – and he was driving a Saab.'

'What was its number?'

'I dunno. Just after they'd passed me, he stopped at a traffic light. That was when I had a chance to look back and see what make the car was. I didn't notice the number, but I did see a sticker in the rear window advertising some place in Yarchester. Something to do with gaslight.'

Quantrill jerked his head at Dc Bedford, who went out to radio an enquiry to the county operations room. There were not many Saabs on the roads of East Anglia, and a list of their owners wouldn't take long to check. Bedford also called Yarchester city police station, confident that their local knowledge would enable them to identify the car sticker.

Within minutes, the county operations room had acquired a computer print-out listing the names and addresses of all East Anglian Saab owners. Shortly afterwards, Bedford heard from the city police. One of the Yarchester night clubs was called *Fanny's by Gaslight*; it was owned by Leonard Arthur Pratt, a local entrepreneur. The fraud squad had their suspicions about some of his business activities, but he was not officially known to the police.

Leonard Arthur Pratt's name appeared on the list of Saab owners. Dc Bedford informed Chief Inspector Quantrill, who asked the city CID for co-operation. A patrol car was sent immediately to pick Pratt up, but his wife said – and his personal secretary confirmed – that he was in the United States. He had flown there on Wednesday, with a group of leisure-industry businessmen, on what was described on his expense account as a fact-finding visit to Palm Springs and Las Vegas.

'This reconstruction hasn't really put us any further forward,' said Hilary Lloyd. She got up and shifted her garden chair to a firmer patch of *Tenerife*'s back lawn. 'Has it?'

'I wouldn't say that,' Quantrill argued. 'For one thing, we now know that Simon Arrowsmith lied to us about where he was a week last Friday night. Since he lied about that, can we believe what he says about spending the whole of last Thursday night at the infirmary?'

'He's still sticking to that story. He says the only reason he lied last week was to protect Angela.'

Quantrill snorted. 'To save his own pride, more like. Where is he now, by the way?'

'At the infirmary, visiting his mother. I must admit that I'm not much happier about his alibi than you are, sir, so I'm going there again tonight to do some more checking.' She looked up as Dc Bedford crossed the grass towards them, still in his track suit. 'Any luck at Ross Arrowsmith's office, James?'

'Yes, Sergeant.' Bedford liked the way she called him by his full, preferred name, rather than arbitrarily abbreviating it – or, worse, calling him Jim-lad or Jimbo, as most of his colleagues did. 'I interviewed the night security guards, at their homes, and they both confirm that Ross Arrowsmith arrived at the Old Maltings at about eleven fifteen on Thursday, and stayed there all night. His car was locked in the yard, and they didn't open the gates again until seven on Friday morning.'

'That eliminates Ross, then,' said Quantrill. 'Look, will you interview Harold Wilkes, Hilary? I'm still betting on collusion between him and Simon. It's high time we got some more information out of him, and you're much more likely to succeed than I am. Pressure him a bit.'

'It's not very easy to pressure someone when you have to communicate in writing,' she pointed out.

'That's no reason for not trying. And while you're doing that, I'm going to have a word with Angela's builder, Cyril Mutimer. He's only an outside chance, but he must have been well aware of her ambitions for the restaurant, and we know that he saw her there on the afternoon before her death. He's a crafty old devil. He always looks pathetic, as innocent as a baby, but that's an act. He owns property all over the town, and it wouldn't surprise me if he allows selected female tenants to pay their rent in kind.'

As Quantrill rose to go, a uniformed constable brought him a message from the civilian scene-of-crime officer at Breckham Market. Angela Arrowsmith's flimsy shoes had been examined and found to be virtually new. Discounting the bloodstains, the saturation by rainwater, and the splashes of mud thrown up by traffic, the smooth leather soles were marked only by scratches and superficial pitting. The wearer had walked for a short distance on a hard surface – paving or flagstones, and probably gravel; demonstrably not on earth or mud.

'So she didn't get out of her car in the layby,' said Hilary slowly. 'That removes the possibility that she ran towards the main road, after having been frightened by the hands on her throat . . .'

'Then she must have been carried,' said Quantrill. 'She was a tiny woman, and her attacker could easily have carried her, semi-conscious, and dumped her in the path of a vehicle coming over the brow of the hill.'

'Risky, for whoever did it – '

'Yes, risky. But it leaves us in no doubt about his intentions, does it? He's ruthless, but at least when we find him he'll have no chance of claiming that it was an accident. This is one murderer who won't get away with a plea of manslaughter.'

'Right,' said Hilary purposefully. 'I'll start by talking to Harold Wilkes.'

'Do that,' said Quantrill. She hurried towards the house, and as an afterthought he beckoned to Dc Bedford.

'Stay with Miss Lloyd, Jim. Don't let her see you, and don't get in her way – but make sure you keep within earshot.'

20

Harold Wilkes looked a little better than when Hilary had first seen him. His skin was still grey, the bags round his eyes dark with sleeplessness, but the eyes themselves were less bloodshot, his manner more relaxed. He was obviously glad to see her. He poured a cup of coffee and handed it to her across the kitchen worktop, together with a scribbling pad and a ballpoint pen.

Hilary smiled her thanks, but wasted no time on attempts at pleasantry. Not knowing whether he was aware of what they had discovered that morning, she wrote, *It was Gary who cut off Angela's cat's head. Did you know that, last week?*

'I guessed,' he said in his loud flat voice, 'when I found traces of blood on the downstairs washbasin, and in his room. He's not a bad lad, though. He'd never hurt a living animal.'

Do you know why he did it? Do you know that Angela had a man here that night?

'Oh yes.' He ran his hands over his cropped hair, his lips working as he selected his words. 'I may be deaf, but I'm not blind and stupid as well. Angela thought I was. She thought I didn't know what was going on. As far as she was concerned I was just a housekeeping machine, with no feelings, no right to any consideration – '

Are you glad she's dead?

He stopped his words and looked at her, his skin darkening. 'I didn't want her dead. Not dead. Just off my back. I couldn't stand the pressures she put on me. As if it wasn't bad enough, to be like this – '

I'm sorry. About your deafness.

'Thank you. Thank you for trying to be considerate. But you

don't understand, you can't, nobody does. People think I'm living in a world of silence. God, if that were all I had to contend with, I'd be lucky. I live in a hell of noise – it's like being on a busy dockyard, with anchor chains rattling and ships' sirens hooting, and it goes on all the time. Sometimes it's not as loud as others, and I feel that perhaps I'm adjusting to it. And then it's as though someone turns the volume up, and up and up again, until I feel that I'm going mad . . . And no one can help. Nothing can be done for it. There isn't a cure for tinnitus.'

He began to pace the kitchen, his lips working silently. Hilary watched him, turning on her high swivel stool, the pen lying useless in her hand. There was nothing she could write, no message of comfort she could give him; particularly as she was in process of interviewing him in connection with a murder.

After a moment she wrote, *Who killed your sister?* But Wilkes was still on the move, talking out loud again.

'Even without the noises, though, total deafness is terrible. It's eerie. You lose your sense of identity. When I'm with a number of people, I feel as though I'm a ghost. I can see them talking and laughing, without any reference to me. It's as if I'm not there. But when I'm with just one person, it's the other way round. When I'm doing the talking, it's the other person who's a ghost.'

He stood still, close to Hilary. 'You, now. I know who you are: Detective Sergeant Hilary Lloyd. You're sitting there looking interested and sympathetic, but are you real or am I dreaming? I can hear nothing from you, not the slightest sound. How can I be sure that I'm not seeing things? – unless I touch you.'

He put his hand on her wrist. It was a square hand, blunt-fingered, pale and immaculately clean, but damp. It trembled with nervous tension.

Hilary looked down at it, willing her own hand not to twitch. Wilkes looked down too, and saw the last note she had written: *Who killed your sister?* His fingers tightened. She felt their moist tips press against her wrist.

Then, abruptly, he released her. 'One of Angela's boy

friends, I suppose,' he said, turning away. 'She had plenty of them, and she gave them enough provocation.'

Do you know who they are? wrote Hilary, hoping that her handwriting didn't look as shaky as she felt.

'No. She didn't bring them here – except the one last week.'

We know about him. Who were the others?

'I don't know. I suppose she met them in Yarchester. I smelled them, though. I used to look after her clothes, and I could smell the different after-shaves, and cigarette and cigar smoke. And then there were the stains, hers and theirs.'

Wilkes's face expressed the distaste he was unable to convey by tone of voice. 'There was one other man who came here to see her, in the summer – but he wasn't a boy friend. He had a big, pale face – straight out of jail, by the look of him. Probably one of the characters she knew when she worked at the Yarchester Black Bull. She brought him in here, and told me to make him a sandwich. While I did that, he was showing her a newspaper cutting. A photograph. I couldn't see what it was, but he seemed to be trying to put some kind of pressure on her.'

Was Angela frightened by him?

'Not her – she was used to working in rough pubs, she knew how to deal with men. She just shook her head at him and laughed. Then she borrowed a fiver from me, and sent him off with it. That was the only time I saw him.'

In the summer? Which month?

'June or early July, as far as I can remember.'

Would you recognise him from a photograph?

'Probably.'

Wilkes could have been making it up, in an attempt to divert her attention away from himself, but his story had to be investigated. Hilary called a patrol car, and took him to county police headquarters to look at the mug book.

Chief Inspector Quantrill found Cyril Mutimer in his Breckham Market builder's yard, down by the river. The yard was still muddy, after Thursday night's deluge, and the assembled rainclouds looked likely to deposit again at any moment. Mutimer was pottering about outside his back door, wearing his tight, soiled black jacket and pinstripe trousers, together with wellington boots.

'Bless my soul – it's Chief Inspector Quantrill, isn't it?' He peered through his pebble glasses, his mouth curved upwards in its habitual smile. 'What can I do for you, sir? A private building job? Nothing in the undertaking line, I trust?'

Quantrill explained that he had come about Mrs Angela Arrowsmith. 'I believe she was a tenant of yours, at the old chapel.'

Mutimer backed metaphorically. '– the old chapel . . . Ah. Yes. Most unfortunate that she should have met her death. Most distressing. Strictly speaking, though, she wasn't yet my tenant. She hadn't actually taken over the lease.'

'But you knew all about her plans for turning the chapel into a night club? A very unsound scheme, in my opinion.'

'*Very* unsound. You've taken the words out of my mouth, Mr Quantrill. Not that the building wouldn't convert ideally, but a big restaurant and night club would never have succeeded in Breckham Market. I told her so myself. I advised her against it. But Mrs Arrowsmith was a very determined lady.'

'So I understand. I suppose you knew that she had nothing like enough money to finance her scheme?'

'– nothing like enough money . . . Well, how could I have known that, Mr Quantrill? The lady didn't take me into her confidence.'

'But you're a shrewd businessman. You knew perfectly well that she hadn't a hope of making enough money to cover her overheads. How did you expect to be paid?'

The infant mouth drooped. 'To be paid? Well, I hardly liked to enquire. After all, she *is* an Arrowsmith, and we all know how successful Mr Ross Arrowsmith is. I assumed that the restaurant was a family enterprise.'

Heavy spots of rain began to fall. Quantrill followed Cyril Mutimer into the shelter of his grimy office. 'You visited Mrs Arrowsmith at the old chapel on Thursday afternoon, I believe, Mr Mutimer?'

'– Thursday afternoon . . . yes. Yes, indeed. I wanted to discuss the conversion work with her.'

'And did you see her again later that night?'

'That night? No, no, certainly not. I always go the Conservative Club on Thursday evenings, to play bridge. I went just after eight, as usual, and stayed there until closing time. Councillor Kenward will be able to confirm that, if you doubt me.'

'It's not that I doubt you, sir. I'm simply collecting information about Mrs Arrowsmith's movements on the night she died. And I do of course want to eliminate innocent witnesses, so if you could tell me what you did after the Club closed – ?'

'After the Club closed . . . I came home. Yes, that was it. With Councillor Kenward, as a matter of fact. He came back with me for a glass of whisky, and we talked into the early hours. Local politics, you know . . .'

It sounded plausible enough. Quantrill turned to go, and found himself face-to-rear with the girl on the Penthouse calendar that hung on the back of the door. He stared, blinked and swallowed. Girlie photographs, however soft in terms of pornography, were bound to put ideas into a man's head. The question was how far Cyril Mutimer – or anyone, come to that – would go in an attempt to put his fantasies into practice.

But at that moment, Mutimer had something else on his mind. He pulled open the door and hurried out into the rain to rescue a pair of black leather shoes. Quantrill had noticed them as he came in, lying on their sides on a wooden box. They were thickly coated with mud, and had evidently been left there to dry out.

'My undertaking shoes!' Mutimer lamented, his chins quivering. 'I had one burial on Thursday, and another yesterday. It's always muddy at a grave-side – bound to be – but yesterday, after all that rain . . . well, you can see for yourself. I knocked a lot of the mud off, but just look at what's left! And now they're wet again. When you think of the cost of a new pair of shoes these days . . .'

Quantrill commiserated with the undertaker, helped himself unobtrusively to a lump of the sodden clay, and hurried through the rain to his car.

Detective Inspector Tait of the regional crime squad despaired over the inefficiency of the criminal records section at Yarchester county headquarters. True, the records of local criminals were kept in order, and regularly and painstakingly updated. The cross-indexing system – names, methods, suspect vehicles, associates, places frequented – was commendably extensive. But it was a steam-age presentation.

The information was typed out on index cards; and the cards, in racks and drawers and on carousels, occupied an office that ran the full width of the building. It was a crazy waste of time and space, thought Tait. It should be computerised, like criminal records at Scotland Yard and the national vehicle licensing centre at Swansea. All he wanted was the name of a villain who had come out of jail in July, having done two years for robbery, and whose home address was in Yarchester. With a computer, the information would be available within minutes. There might be more than one man, but a quick look in their files would reveal which one had a wife named Denise.

Without computerised records, Tait was reduced to looking through the mug book – actually a pile of books – to try to identify the potato-faced villain who had run away from him in the Black Bull. The man had looked too old to be the husband of a thirty-year-old woman, but there was no doubt that he knew something about her.

Tait worked his way methodically through the photographs. He was about to start on the last book when Sergeant Lloyd arrived, on the same errand. They exchanged reasons for being there; Hilary passed on the description that Harold Wilkes had given her of the man who had called in the summer to see his sister.

'Where is Wilkes?' asked Tait, picking up the final book.

'In number three interview room.'

They went together, walking along the corridor side by side, almost but not quite quickening into a run. At the door of the interview room, Hilary removed the book from Tait's hands. She put it in front of Wilkes with an encouraging smile, and they stood watching him anxiously.

Wilkes looked ill again. His forehead was furrowed, his eyes raw. He turned the pages obediently, but Hilary began to wonder whether – always supposing that his story were true – he could concentrate sufficiently to make an identification.

Then, suddenly, he said, 'That's him. That's the man who came to see Angela.'

Hilary spoke her thanks clearly enough for Wilkes to lip-read, and took the book from him. Tait put out his hand for it.

'Sorry,' she told the Inspector, her voice pleasant but firm. 'He's mine – I want to interview him in connection with Angela Arrowsmith's murder.'

'You'd be wasting your time,' said Tait, who had seen enough of the photograph to recognise the man from the Black Bull. 'As far as that murder's concerned, he's just an off-chance. But I have reason to believe that he can identify the headless woman in the A135 case. That's a regional crime squad responsibility, and I have priority.'

He commandeered the book. 'Sorry and all that, Hilary love, but this one's mine.'

21

The ex-prisoner with the boiled-potato face found three detectives awaiting him when he was brought to Yarchester city police station for interview later that afternoon.

To Tait's chagrin, the Chief Inspector had pointed out that the function of regional crime squad officers was to *assist* on particular investigations and to work *with* the detective officers of the force concerned. Accordingly, said Quantrill, he intended to be present while Tait interviewed the man; and as it would be bloody stupid to keep the investigations separate when there were links, however tenuous, between the two crimes, he wanted Sergeant Lloyd to begin the interviewing.

They had all read the man's file and knew his background. Reginald William Pearce, aged 55, had a lengthy record of minor crimes, chiefly thefts of and from motor vehicles. He had also been involved in several burglaries, always acting as driver. His last sentence, served in Yarchester jail, had ended on 20 June. He was unmarried, and lived in the city with his mother.

Pearce was, he told Sergeant Lloyd indignantly, going straight; had been, ever since he'd finished his last stretch. When the coppers had picked him up, just now, he'd been in his bed enjoying a peaceful afternoon kip.

Yes, he did go to Nether Wickford at the end of June, to see Angela Arrowsmith. Nothing wrong with that. No reason why he shouldn't. He'd known her years ago, when she was a barmaid at the Black Bull. He visited her because he'd seen her photograph in the local paper, while he was in jail. She'd obviously done well for herself – there she was, right in the middle of a group photograph taken at the opening of some kind of computer place owned by her brother-in-law. It stood to reason that she must have plenty of money, and Pearce had hoped that she might be prepared to part with a little to help a feller who was down on his luck. Worth a try, anyway.

He'd found Angela's address in the telephone directory. He'd never heard of Nether Wickford, but he asked a lorry driver he knew, and the driver had given him a lift down the A135 and dropped him at a crossroads. He'd walked to Angela's house from there. If he'd known how muckin' far it was, he wouldn't have bothered.

It was a waste of time, anyway. Angela had told him that her husband had left the computer firm, and that they were broke. She was pleasant enough: offered him a beer and a sandwich and a fiver, on condition that he didn't go there again. No, of course he didn't threaten her; what kind of a man did they think he was? No, he didn't nick anything either. Well, all right, he might have accidentally knocked over a table lighter and one or two other bits and pieces, and found later that they'd fallen into his pocket, but the coppers'd have a muckin' hard job to prove it. Then he'd footslogged all the way back to the main road, and hitched a lift to Yarchester. He'd never set eyes on Angela Arrowsmith since.

There seemed no reason to connect him with her murder, and Sergeant Lloyd gave way, reluctantly, to Inspector Tait.

'Why did you run when I started asking questions in the Black Bull this morning?' Tait asked.

'Because I guessed you were a copper.'

'No need to run, unless you're hiding something. What I'm interested in is the murder of the woman whose body was found in a layby on the A135 – the headless woman. You know who she was, don't you? I don't suspect you of being the murderer, but if you're not you'd be wise to talk.'

Pearce talked.

He had been approached one weekend early in July by a man he knew – he refused to give his name, and Tait didn't press for it at that stage – who told him that someone wanted a driving job done. The man gave Pearce a Yarchester telephone number – a call box – and told him to ring at a certain time.

Pearce rang the number, and the man who answered told him to collect a van late that night from a piece of waste ground near the railway station. The van would contain some rubbish that Pearce was to get rid of secretly – somewhere out in the country, at least ten miles from Yarchester. He was then to return the van to the same place. When he did so, he would find a fifty-pound bundle of banknotes hidden under some loose bricks at the foot of an old wall.

Easy money. Pearce had agreed, and picked up the van. He was Yarchester born and bred and didn't know much about the country, but he had been driven down the A135 only a few days previously and so he took that road again. And then he remembered having seen a layby near the Nether Wickford crossroads, one that was surrounded by trees, completely secluded. Ideal for the job.

'Did you know what the rubbish was?' Tait asked.

'No, I didn't, I swear to God. I didn't even look in the back of the van until I reached the layby. I thought it must be a shooter, or some gear that had been worn or used on a job. It didn't worry me, either way. But as soon as I saw the size and shape of this plastic-wrapped bundle – Christ, I panicked, I don't mind telling you. I dragged it out of the van and shoved it into the undergrowth, double-quick. I just hoped it wouldn't be found – and then some muckin' lorry driver had to go and trip over it a couple of days later. I read all about it in the paper. Haven't stopped shaking since.'

'And you knew whose the body was?'

'No!' Pearce hesitated. 'I had a good guess, though. I'd recognised the voice of the feller I spoke to on the phone. We shared a cell in Yarchester four or five years ago – and when you're banged up with a feller for eighteen months, you don't forget his voice. I remembered his missus, too. Saw her sometimes on visiting day. Her name was Denise, and she had a gap between her top front teeth. Once seen, never forgotten. I s'pose that was why he chopped her head off.'

'What was his name?'

Pearce said nothing. His prison-pale face was heavy with worry, and he gnawed at one of his thumbs.

'The man had just come out of jail,' said Tait. 'A few weeks after you. Was he in Yarchester again?'

'No. He had family in London, he often did jobs there. I heard that he was in the Scrubs.'

'What was his name?'

'I can't tell you. If he knew I'd shopped him, he'd be after me.'

'No need to worry about that. He's going to be inside for a very long time. Come on, Reg, who was it? If you tell us, we'll believe that you had no idea what was inside the bundle before you dumped it. If you won't talk, it might look as though you knew all about the – '

Pearce gabbled out the man's name before Tait had time to say 'murder'.

'Big party tonight, Hilary,' said Quantrill with uncharacteristic exuberance as they walked out of Yarchester city police station. 'We usually take over the back room of the Coney and Thistle when we've got something to celebrate.'

'A bit premature for celebration, isn't it, sir? Inspector Tait hasn't picked the suspect up yet.'

'That shouldn't take him long. We know – and so does he – that we did all the hard work and pointed him in the right direction, and that's what we're going to celebrate. Plus the fact it was our new CID sergeant who made the breakthrough. Congratulations!'

Quantrill turned to smile at her. As he did so, his heel slipped off the edge of a low step. He twisted his body to regain his balance and save himself from an ignominious fall, and then clutched at his lower back, grimacing with pain.

He knew exactly what it was: lumbago. It had first smitten him two years ago, when he was doing some furniture-moving at home. He'd thought that he was crippled for life, but the doctor had told him briskly that it was muscular strain caused by lifting heavy objects incorrectly. Quantrill now knew – when he remembered – that he needed to keep his back straight and bend from the knees when he was lifting anything, but his back had become vulnerable. The pain was liable to recur whenever he pulled the same muscles, particularly in cold or damp weather. It would ease magically when Molly rubbed his back with balm, and would disappear completely within a day or two; but meanwhile it would give him gyp. Lumbago made him feel and look ninety. It also *sounded* old.

'My back's gone again,' he said in answer to Hilary's enquiry. 'Disc trouble . . . no, I can manage, thanks.'

'You can't drive like that,' she said. 'Let me have your keys.'

He refused. He didn't know how he was going to operate the foot controls without yelping, but he was damned if he was going to let her do the driving.

Hilary watched him hobble to his car, his hand pressed against his back. She hadn't sweated for three years to gain her SRN without learning that a damaged disc puts pressure on the nerves in the spinal column, producing acute pain in one or other of the legs rather than in the back itself. She suspected lumbago; but she let him cling to his more dramatic diagnosis.

'Very nasty, disc trouble,' she said sympathetically. 'If you try to drive, you might do yourself a permanent injury. I used to be a nurse, so I do know what I'm talking about.'

Hoist by his own lie, but impressed into silence, Quantrill meekly relinquished his keys.

The rain had eased off, earlier in the afternoon, and the roads were rapidly drying out under a brisk south-easterly wind. Quantrill was edgy during the first part of the journey, partly because of discomfort and partly because he had never before been driven in his own car by a woman. But as they left the city, he had to acknowledge that he could find no fault with Hilary Lloyd's driving. Her concentration was good, her gear-work positive, her hands on the wheel light but firm.

He took a surreptitious look at her diamond eternity ring and for the first time allowed himself to wonder about its significance. He would have liked to ask why she had left the nursing profession, in which his elder daughter was perfectly happy, but he was reluctant to betray any curiosity. Besides, he suspected that she would give him a flippant stock answer, and he had no intention of allowing her to fob him off. He turned up the volume of the police radio, and they drove on without speaking.

The main road between Yarchester and Breckham Market, for the most part a wretchedly narrow two-lane highway, was crowded with Saturday afternoon traffic. Tired of travelling behind a touring caravan, Hilary turned off to the left along a pretty, wooded by-road that she knew would join an alternative route to Breckham Market.

The chestnut trees on either side of the empty road had already begun to change colour and lose their leaves. The wind was bringing more large yellow leaves down, bowling them about on the ground. But the movement on the road some thirty yards ahead seemed to be greater than the strength of the wind warranted, and Hilary braked to a gentle stop.

'Oh, look,' she said, delighted. 'Squirrels, playing.'

'They're only grey squirrels,' said Quantrill indifferently. 'Vermin. They do no end of damage to young trees.' But he too was amused by the antics of the lively pair who were chasing and tumbling through the fallen leaves oblivious of the stationary car, their feathery tails whisking. 'Attractive little beggars, though. Better give them a hoot – the button's on the end of the indicator.'

Hilary drove slowly forward, sounding the horn. The squirrels scattered, one to either side of the road, and she picked up speed. One squirrel had already scampered up a tree and she tried to keep an eye on the other, but the leaves were still blowing, distracting her. As she passed the spot, a lithe grey creature with a streaming tail suddenly bounded across in front of her wheels, intent on joining its companion.

'Oh no!' Hilary braked again, this time harder. 'Please God I haven't hit it.'

She stopped, unclipped her seat belt and turned to look anxiously through the rear window. 'Ah, that's all right – I missed it. It's still in the road, playing about as though nothing . . . oh, *no*!'

Her stomach lurched. The squirrel was still alive, still rising and twisting in the leaves, but not this time in play. Sickened and shaken, she turned away from the sight.

Quantrill, moving gingerly, took one look through the window. 'What are you waiting for?' he demanded. 'You can see it's badly injured. Reverse. Kill it.'

His face was a blur, his words incomprehensible. Her gorge rose at the thought of killing a living creature in cold blood.

'Get on with it, woman!' he said angrily. 'For God's sake, you can't leave the animal writhing in agony.' He seized her by the shoulder. 'Oh, come out of the way. Let me do it.'

It was the contempt in his voice that reached her. She swallowed hard, drew a deep breath and found reverse gear. 'You'll have to guide me,' she said. 'I can't look.'

His hand was still on her shoulder, but gripping her more gently. He left it there as, looking back, he gave his instructions: 'Right hand down – a bit more. Now straighten up. Keep it straight . . . more power – ' she felt a tiny bump – 'and now stop. Forward a few yards. Stop again, I'm getting out.'

He released her, climbed painfully out of the car, and went back to assure himself that the squirrel was dead.

It was. And its crushed remains reminded him all too vividly of what had happened to Angela Arrowsmith on the A135. As he stood there, thinking about her death, it came to him that whoever had half-strangled Angela couldn't possibly have risked leaving her semi-conscious at the edge of the road in the hope that she would be killed. Even if her assailant had waited until he heard a vehicle coming, he couldn't be sure that she would be hit, let alone killed outright. So, having carried her to the edge of the road, he would have had to run her over himself. And then he would have had to make sure that she was dead before he left her – just as Quantrill was now doing with the squirrel, though for quite a different reason.

He returned to his car. Hilary was sitting motionless behind the wheel, looking distant and slightly green. He would have liked to touch her shoulder again, in an attempt to convey reassurance and also to show his appreciation of her guts. Most of the women he knew – Molly, of course, and Alison; even Patsy Hopkins – would have been only too glad to relinquish the wheel and the killing to him.

But the occasion for touching her had passed. Instead he said, 'All right,' and lowered himself cautiously into the passenger seat. Hilary unfroze. She bent her head to fit her seat belt into the unfamiliar anchor point on the floor of his car, and as she did so her dark hair fell forward on either side of her face, parting naturally at the nape of her neck.

Quantrill found himself staring at her nape, helplessly fascinated. There was something very attractive about it: something to do with its unblemished skin, its youthful slenderness . . .

'Let's get going,' he said peremptorily. 'We won't bother with a celebration tonight, we'll leave it until we've cracked the Arrowsmith case as well. I'm going to spend this evening quietly at home, and I suggest you do the same.'

His back was playing him up again, twingeing like the devil. His marriage might be dull, the nape of his wife's neck unenticing, but when lumbago struck he found it an undeniable comfort to think in terms of going home to Molly and having his back rubbed.

22

The bells of St Botolph's, the parish church of Breckham Market, were ringing for 9.30 Matins when Sergeant Lloyd drove from her riverside flat to divisional police headquarters. The morning was cool and overcast, the Sunday streets empty.

With the Arrowsmith murder enquiry in progress, the CID offices were busier than usual. Chief Inspector Quantrill was already there, so concentratedly on the trail that he forgot about his back until an injudicious movement made him wince.

'Interesting development, Hilary,' he greeted her. 'We've found the murder weapon.'

She was puzzled. 'I thought Angela was run over?'

'So she was. But not by a passing vehicle. By her own car.'

He explained the conclusion he had come to the previous afternoon, when they had killed the injured squirrel. 'I assumed at first that her attacker must have used his own vehicle. But Simon Arrowsmith was still at the top of my list at that stage, and we've already found that his car is clean. Then I remembered how careful the killer had been to cover the traces of his presence, and I realised that the last thing he'd want would be her blood on his vehicle. So I had a word with forensic yesterday evening. They haven't finished examining her car, but they'd found blood and tissue on one tyre and on the inside of the wheel arch. I've just had confirmation from the path lab that it matches Angela's exactly.'

Hilary sat down, weak at the knees. 'When I think how it felt to run deliberately over a poor wretched squirrel – ' She closed her eyes and shook her head, trying not to imagine what it would be like to steer in cold blood at a human being, to feel the sickening bump as the murder weapon – a ton of metal and glass and rubber – crushed human flesh and bone.

'The point is,' said Quantrill, 'that we now know for sure that her assailant was inside her car. We know that the mud on the floor didn't come from her shoes, so it must have come from his. And forensic say that if the mud originates from anywhere within thirty miles of the scene, it must be subsoil. They tell me it's clay from a deep layer that doesn't come to within more than a few feet of the surface, in this part of Suffolk. That means we're looking for someone who has some occupation or hobby that takes him at least six feet deep – '

Hilary looked up. 'An undertaker? You mean Cyril Mutimer?'

'When I called on him yesterday,' said the Chief Insepctor, 'I nicked some mud from his funeral shoes. It's the same blue clay that Harry Colman found in Angela's car. And when you think about it, Mutimer must be a prime suspect. We know that he went to see her on the afternoon before her death. She probably fluttered her eyelashes at him and gave him a few ideas – not that any *Penthouse* reader is likely to be short of those. Anyway, he'd know how to lure her out to meet him late at night – by promising rent-free occupation of his premises, something like that – in return for sexual favours. But perhaps Angela promised more than she was prepared to perform – '

'Wait a minute,' said Hilary. 'You told me that Mutimer had an alibi for the night of Angela's death.'

'So he said. I've sent young Bedford round to Councillor Kenward's house to hear whether he's prepared to confirm Mutimer's story. Jim should be back by now – the morning's half over.'

Quantrill looked pointedly at his watch. He himself had been in the office since eight. He didn't begrudge the evening off that he'd given Sergeant Lloyd yesterday, but he didn't want her to think that she could take advantage of him. After an early night, nine thirty was much too late to roll into the office when they were working on a murder enquiry.

She took his point, and made one of her own. She told him that she had spent part of the previous evening at the infirmary, making some further checks on Simon Arrowsmith's alibi. It had occurred to her that there might, at visiting time, be someone there who, like Simon, had had a relative in the intensive care unit on Thursday night.

And she had found such a visitor, a man who had been at the infirmary from about 11 p.m. on Thursday until 2 a.m. on Friday. His father had been rushed in with a heart attack. He could remember exchanging a few words with a fellow visitor of Simon's description, and had seen him dozing in a chair in the main waiting room at some stage during the night. Understandably, he was unable to be definite about timing; but he remembered having seen one or two other visitors hanging about the hospital, and Hilary proposed to follow them up.

'We may not need to bother about Simon Arrowsmith, now Mutimer's front runner,' said the Chief Inspector as Dc Bedford appeared at the door of his office. 'What did you find out from Councillor Kenward, Jim?'

'Not a lot,' said Bedford with a fresh-faced grin. 'He's a very worried man – anxious not to let down a friend and supporter, but at the same time determined not to land himself in any trouble. What he finally decided to say was that he can't remember a thing about Thursday night, from the time he left the Conservative Club with Mutimer at eleven until he woke up at home the next morning.'

'A very convenient case of amnesia,' grunted Quantrill. 'So?'

'So I talked to his wife. Mrs Kenward says roundly that her husband arrived home at his usual time, just after eleven, had a large whisky and went straight to bed, as he always does.'

'Mutimer was lying, then. Thanks, Jim.' Quantrill reached for his hat. 'Want to come, both of you? Let's see if we can get this Arrowsmith case wrapped up.'

Cyril Mutimer was not at home. The three detectives were turning away from his back door when they saw his builder's pick-up truck approaching the yard, with a long plank jutting out over the roof of the cab like a pencil stuck behind a carpenter's ear.

Mutimer looked tidier than usual. He wore Sunday and undertaking best, a new black jacket and pinstripe trousers bought large to allow for future waist expansion. His babyish face was a picture of satisfaction and contentment, until he discovered why his visitors had come.

'Last Thursday night – ?' He peered worriedly through his pebble glasses, his mouth drooping. 'Well, perhaps I did make a mistake about Councillor Kenward coming back here with me . . .'

'I think what really happened,' said Quantrill, 'was that when you got home from your club you telephoned Angela Arrow-smith. You persuaded her to meet you at the layby on the A135 – '

Mutimer goggled. 'The A135? I never went near it, Mr Quantrill. And most certainly not to meet Mrs Arrowsmith! No, no. I did go to meet a lady friend, I admit that. I'm not ashamed of it. And I did lie to you about Councillor Kenward. But that was only to protect the lady's good name.'

'Which is?' said Dc Bedford, pocket book and pen ready.

The detectives waited for Mutimer's reply, sceptical partly of his revised story, and partly of the good repute of his lady friend. If she existed at all, they anticipated that they would already be aware of her activities in the town, whether or not she had ever been in breach of the Sexual Offences Act.

After a great deal of hesitation, Mutimer finally blurted out a name. 'It's . . . it's Miss Pringle. She lives at 26 White Hart Street, and that's where I spent Thursday night. Last night as well.'

Quantrill stared at him, faint with incredulity. 'You don't – surely you can't mean the lady who keeps the wool shop?' It was where Molly always bought her knitting wool; had done so for years, ever since their children wore bootees and bonnets. The owner's reputation – like her virtue, Quantrill would have thought – was unassailable. 'Not Miss *Elsie* Pringle?'

'The same,' admitted Cyril Mutimer. He stood his ground with orphan dignity, the shoulders of his jacket so wide that they drooped, the sleeves so long that they hid all but the tips of his fingers. 'Miss Pringle and I were at school together, and we have an Understanding. Her friends and neighbours are aware of it, but I'm glad to say that they have the courtesy not to make it generally known. I visit Miss Pringle regularly, every Monday, Thursday and Saturday – '

The detectives shuffled out of his presence. They checked his story, of course; and found it to be true. Quantrill was tempted to tell Molly and have a chuckle with her about it, but on reflection he had the courtesy not to.

By early afternoon, reports and statements were beginning to pile up in Quantrill's office, on his own desk and on Hilary's. Most of the statements came from drivers who had travelled along the A135 at the critical time on Thursday night, but none of them admitted to using the layby or seeing any other vehicle enter or leave it. Several said that they had glimpsed a bundle lying on the road in the rain. Some said they had hit it, some that they had missed it, or swerved to avoid it; none admitted to having realised that it was a body.

'Lab report on the interior of Angela Arrowsmith's car, Sergeant,' said Dc Bedford, bringing it in. Hilary skimmed through the report and passed it with optimism to the Chief Inspector.

'Take a look at this, sir. Forensic have found some dark blue cotton fibres clinging to the fabric of the driver's seat. They're not from anything Angela was wearing, so with any luck they came from her killer's clothing. And with a bit more luck, there'll have been an interchange. He must have carried her in his arms from her car to the main road, so his clothing might well have picked up some fibres or hairs that are identifiably hers.'

'And where would that get us?' said Quantrill. His back was aching again, making him irritable. 'The old firm of suspects, Simon Arrowsmith and Harold Wilkes, are back at the top of our list. They both have perfectly legitimate reasons for having been in close contact with Angela. Even if we do find something of hers on their clothing – or find that the dark blue fibres match something of theirs – it still won't prove a thing.'

'Pity,' said the Chief Inspector later, reading another report. 'Gary Hilton's bicycle couldn't have been used on Thursday night. There was a lot of road dust on it, so it hadn't been cleaned up to hide evidence of its use. But there were no dried rain splashes on the frame, and the tyres hadn't been through mud, so it couldn't have been out in that downpour.'

'Did you really think that Harold Wilkes might have used it to get to the layby and kill his sister?' said Hilary.

'Why not? We've been assuming that the killer had a motor vehicle, but that's not necessarily so. He could perfectly easily have cycled to meet her. Or walked, as that ex-con did who called on her in the summer. Or jogged, come to that. Ross Arrowsmith isn't the only jogger round here – I've seen people of all ages padding through Breckham, and out into the countryside, at most hours of the day and night. In fact it would have been perfectly easy – '

Quantrill paused, frowning in thought. Then he called for Detective Constable Bedford. 'Ross Arrowsmith, Jim,' he said. 'You checked his alibi for Thursday night, didn't you? The security guards at the Old Maltings told you that his car had been locked in the yard all night – but could he have gone out of the building for an hour or so, on foot, without their knowledge?'

Bedford looked doubtful. 'He told me that they're a very security-conscious firm – even he can't get in at night without being vetted.'

'Damn that for a tale,' said Quantrill vigorously. 'If I were the founder and top brass of a firm, I'd come and go as I pleased. Wouldn't you?'

James Bedford gave a grin that made him look a mature sixteen. 'Yes, come to think of it, sir, I would. Because if I were a micro-electronics wizard, I'd design the alarm system myself. And I'd make sure that my own private door was on a separate circuit.'

The Chief Inspector nodded his approval. 'Go and sus the place out, Jim. See if you can find a back door that Ross could use without being under the eyes of the security guards. And make a few discreet local enquiries about whether he's known to go jogging from his office.'

'Right, sir.' Bedford made for the door, and then hesitated:

'But why Ross Arrowsmith? We know that he disliked Angela, but I don't see what he could possibly gain by killing her.'

'Nor do I,' admitted Quantrill. 'It's a matter of following up all possibilities, whether they're likely or not.'

He reached for his hat. 'I'm off to Nether Wickford,' he told Hilary. 'I want to have another go at the men with the motive. What we need, urgently, is some piece of hard evidence that will connect one or both of them with the killing. I'll find out whether either of them has any dark blue cotton clothing, but what I'd really like to discover at or near their home is a source of blue clay subsoil. I know all their shoes were clean, but Harold Wilkes had had plenty of time to make sure of that. I want to have a good look round their garden – perhaps they've been digging themselves a nuclear fall-out shelter. And while I'm there, Hilary, will you – '

She interrupted him. 'Sorry, sir,' she said, looking at her watch and reaching for the telephone. 'I'd like to take a couple of hours off – to play squash, with a friend.'

23

'I must have been out of my mind, to ask you for a game,' panted Hilary. Her face was pink and streaked with sweat. She peeled off her limp whites, hung them on a locker-room peg, and stepped thankfully under a shower.

'You're out of practice, that's all,' gasped Jen Arrowsmith generously from the adjoining shower cubicle. 'We must do this more often.'

They had spent the previous twenty minutes on an echoing squash court at Jen's country club, their rubber soles slapping and squeaking on the floor as they ran and turned, wristing their rackets to send the ball slamming round the walls. Hilary had been soundly beaten, and not for want of trying; Jen had proved to be fitter and more agile, her freckled face fierce with the aggressiveness a good squash player needs in order to win.

'I'd certainly like a chance to get even,' Hilary said. 'It's fun to play again – I'm so glad you were able to come, at such short notice.'

'It wouldn't usually be possible, on a Saturday or a Sunday. Ross likes weekends to be family times, all of us at home together. But the twins love coming here to swim, and he wanted to catch up with his work after spending most of last week in Japan, so you couldn't have rung at a better time. I'm delighted that you did.'

They emerged from the showers, companionably naked, and began to towel themselves dry. There was no atmosphere, Hilary thought, so conducive to the giving of confidences as a locker room. Other women came and went, changing and showering and chatting, but the club was sufficiently far from Breckham Market and drew its members from a sufficiently wide area to provide anonymity. Here if anywhere, while they were pleasurably tired and relaxed, Hilary hoped to be able to persuade Jen Arrowsmith to talk freely about her husband; and in particular about his relationship with his half-brother's wife, Angela.

Her conscience was not entirely easy about it. She had approached Jen as a friend, and to take advantage of her in this way was arguably unscrupulous.

But murder was unarguably heinous, and a detective remained a detective on duty or off. If Ross Arrowsmith were innocent, no harm would be done by encouraging his wife to talk about him; if not –

If not, thank God that Jen was strong enough to cope with what would necessarily follow. Hilary took a moment's comfort from the thought, until she remembered that her own duty would be the same whether or not Jen – or some future suspect's nearest relative – could cope with the consequences.

This was one of the occasions when she didn't merely resent being a detective, she hated it. But she was a professional, and so she smothered her conscience and got on with the job.

What she learned, rapidly, was that the signs of dissatisfaction and unhappiness she had noticed when she first met Jen were caused by Ross Arrowsmith's belief that his wife ought not to go back to work until their children were at least sixteen.

'He has this fixation about childhood, you see,' sighed Jen as they dressed, sharing her talcum powder. 'His own was idyllic, before his mother died. I don't think he's ever stopped mourning her early death. As a result, he's trying to compensate through our own children. Until he was ten, his mother was always there when he ran home from school – so he wants me to go on being at home, for the twins' benefit. *Well* . . .'

Jen grimaced. 'Don't get me wrong,' she went on. 'I love them dearly, and of course I want to give them a happy childhood. But Ross's mother was always at home because she worked on the family smallholding. Me, I'm a systems analyst. I want to use my skills. I do work, of course, from home – but only as a programmer, and it's not the same. I miss the challenge of my old job, and I miss the daily contact with colleagues and clients. I'm sure you understand that. But my wretched husband either can't or won't see my point of view.'

She paused again. 'No, that's not really fair to Ross. I was the one who chose to have children, and I knew his views right from the start, so I shouldn't complain. I know it grieves him still to remember the hard life his mother had, and he takes pride in having freed me from all financial worry. I ought to be grateful. I *am* grateful. But sometimes I feel so cooped-up and frustrated that – well, do you wonder I play a mean game of squash?'

Hilary sympathised genuinely, and said so. But none of this had any connection with Angela Arrowsmith, and she began to think that her previous suspicions might have been unfounded.

The girl twin, Daisy, came rushing in from the indoor swimming pool, dripping and shivering and gabbling with pleasure, her hair hanging in wet rats' tails round her freckled face. Her mother bundled her under a warm shower.

'What's the latest news about your husband's stepmother?' Hilary asked, tackling her own damp hair with her brush and the club's blow-drier.

'Quite encouraging, thank goodness. She should be out of hospital in a couple of weeks. It's such a relief – we were desperately afraid that she wouldn't recover.'

'You told me how fond of her you all are.'

'I am, certainly, and so are the twins. I can't say the same of

Ross, unfortunately. I suggested to him that we could have Nellie to stay with us for a few weeks, until she's strong enough to go back to her own home. I'd be happy to look after her – I've time enough, goodness knows – but Ross says that any more than ten minutes of her conversation would drive him mad. He offered to pay for her to go to a convalescent home, but Simon insists that he'll take care of her in future, with his brother-in-law's help. Si says he's going to devote himself to his mother, now that Angela's dead . . .'

Hilary passed her the hair drier. 'That must have been a great shock for the whole family. Particularly coming straight after Simon's mother's heart attack.'

'It was shattering to be told that she'd been murdered. God knows what kind of a life Angela led before she met Simon, but I suppose someone from her past finally caught up with her. I won't pretend that Ross and I are grieved, but I do feel sorry for poor Simon. Ross doesn't – he says that Simon is better off without her, and of course that's true in a lot of ways. But I've always felt that their marriage was none of our business. Ross should never have tried to interfere with it.'

'Did he? How?'

'He tried several times to persuade Simon to divorce her. But Simon was too besotted to do any such thing, and I don't blame him. We all know that he was a fool to marry her, but the point is that he loved her. Why should he divorce her, just to please Ross?' She hung up the hair drier. 'Bring me your towel, Daisy, and I'll dry your back.'

Hilary watched, puzzled, as Jen Arrowsmith gave her daugher a brisk towelling. Here was a link between Ross and Angela that she had never suspected. Why should he have been so anxious for Simon to divorce his wife? Because Angela's behaviour might reflect badly on the name of Arrowsmith MicroElectronics? Hardly, when his firm had a national – potentially an international – reputation.

Or were Ross's motives selfless? Did he feel an elder-brother protectiveness towards Simon? The answer to that, in view of his insistence on the fact that they were not brothers, was almost certainly no. Was Ross trying to protect his stepmother, then?

Did he want to remove Angela from the family so that she could make no more raids on Nellie's late husband's life savings? But that incident, according to May Cullen, hadn't taken place until last Wednesday; and according to his wife, Ross wasn't particularly fond of Nellie.

'Are we going to have tea here?' asked Daisy as she wriggled into her jeans.

'I don't see why not,' said her mother. 'Daddy'll be at the office for hours yet. You'll have tea with us, Hilary, won't you?'

But Hilary had just remembered something: a small point, nothing more than a discrepancy between two pieces of information. It was, though, something that she wanted to pass on to Douglas Quantrill as soon as possible.

'Thank you very much, but I can't stay – this isn't my day off, and I have to get back to work.'

'Are you in computers too?' asked Daisy. 'Software or hardware?'

Hilary forced herself to smile and speak lightly. 'Neither. I'm in the police force, as a matter of fact.'

'Wow,' said Daisy.

'So you are,' said Jen to Hilary. 'I'd completely forgotten.' She put a confident arm round her daughter's shoulder and smiled fondly at the child. 'How about that, then? And Hilary's not an ordinary policewoman either, she's a real live detective. We shall have to watch what we say in front of her, or she might start using it as evidence.'

At the CID offices in Breckham Market, a celebration was being planned.

The A135 murder was no longer a mystery. A man with a criminal record, Paul Edward Hanson, had confessed to the unlawful killing of his wife Denise, and was now in custody. He had, he said, wrenched the leg off a broken chair and hit her over the head with it when he discovered that she was pregnant by another man.

Hanson had further admitted to cutting off his wife's head, some hours after she had died from her injuries. He said that he had put the head in a weighted holdall, and had thrown it into the river from Bishop's Bridge in Yarchester. Police frogmen had found the holdall that afternoon. It contained the head of a woman whose skull had been fractured in several places. As soon as word came to Breckham from Yarchester that the woman's top front teeth were widely set apart, Quantrill had authorised the booking of the back room at the Coney and Thistle for a party that evening.

Not that the investigation was over. Hanson might yet retract his confession; the CID was faced with days if not weeks of tracing and checking, until the man's story was proved in every detail. By that time, the detectives' euphoria would have evaporated. But today, at five thirty on Sunday afternoon, 22 September, ten weeks after the discovery of the woman's headless body in the layby, they were high on success and canteen tea.

From the main CID office in Breckham Market, telephone calls were going out to round up as many as possible of the detectives who had worked so hard and so long to trace the identity of the woman. The fact that the final tracing and the subsequent arrest of Hanson had been made by Inspector Tait of the regional crime squad was enough to make the Breckham men spit. But at least they could console themselves with the thought that all the groundwork was theirs; if they hadn't been sidetracked by the Arrowsmith murder, they'd have tied up the A135 case by now themselves.

Besides, Martin Tait had once worked in their division. The older detectives had had to nanny him when he'd first arrived, a big-headed, jumped-up young sergeant who hadn't known enough about the job to keep his feet dry. They reckoned that they'd been the ones who'd cuffed him into shape; if he'd turned into a good detective, a lot of the credit was theirs. And so when he returned that afternoon from Yarchester to share in the celebrations, they patted him on the back with rather more force than was necessary, and assured him patronisingly that they'd always known he would make the grade.

Sergeant Lloyd, when she returned from the country club and heard the reason for the rejoicing, was kinder.

'That didn't take you long, did it? Congratulations, Martin.'

He thanked her with a kiss, partly because he welcomed any opportunity to kiss an attractive woman and partly to score a substantial point against the watching detectives. 'And thank you too, Hilary love, for pointing me in the right direction. I'd have got there without your help, of course, but perhaps not quite so quickly.'

She laughed. 'Your modesty's refreshing, I'll say that for you. How did you persuade Hanson to confess?'

'Skill; how else? He denied it at first. Said he hadn't been to Yarchester or seen his wife since he came out of the Scrubs, and that her boy friend must have done away with her. But I told him that I'd already found out that he'd been seen in July, going in and out of the bed-sit where his wife was living. And that at about the same time, he'd told another neighbour that they were both packing up and moving on. Once I'd shown him that I knew he was lying, the rest wasn't difficult.'

'But you still had no hard evidence to tie the crime to him.'

'Yes, I had. He couldn't know that the pathologist had told us that her head had been cut off by someone with some knowledge of anatomy or butchery. Unluckily for Hanson, I picked him up at his parents' home in north London: a flat over his father's shop. The old man's a butcher by trade, and his son used to work for him. Ironic, isn't it, that by cutting off the woman's head to hide her identity, he gave me enough evidence to charge him with her murder?'

Inspector Tait looked inordinately pleased with himself: another criminal caught, another successful enquiry to his credit – and this one on behalf of the regional crime squad, too. An excellent beginning to this stage of his career.

Hilary Lloyd found his single-minded smugness offensive. '*The woman*, you said. That's all you've called her, either 'his wife' or 'the woman'. Just because she was anonymous for so long, you're talking about her as though she were a butcher's carcase. But we know her name now – she's Denise Hanson. Damn it, Martin, you found that out yourself. She was just as much a person as the other murdered woman, Angela Arrowsmith – except that she was unluckier than Angela in every way, even in her death. Angela didn't know what was coming to her;

she went to meet her murderer eagerly. But Denise Hanson must have spent the last few weeks of her life in terror, half-knowing what her husband would do to her.'

'Then she shouldn't have hung about waiting for him to be released from prison, should she?' said Tait sharply.

'I don't suppose she had anywhere else to go.'

'She could have asked for police protection.'

'Just as Simon Arrowsmith did for his wife? A lot of use we were to her, weren't we?'

Chief Inspector Quantrill, emerging tweed-hatted and purposeful from his office, saw the two of them glaring at each other.

'Surely you're not still feeling guilty about Angela Arrowsmith's death, Hilary?' he said briskly. 'Well, don't. We've already discovered that last week's threat had nothing to do with what happened to her, so stop going on about it. Let's concentrate on finding out who killed her.'

Quantrill was on his way to see Simon Arrowsmith and Harold Wilkes, having been delayed by the news of Hanson's capture and confession. He wanted to get the interviews over, and return to the Coney in time to celebrate the cracking of the A135 case. But when Sergeant Lloyd told him that she had been playing squash with Ross Arrowsmith's wife, and had acquired some interesting information, he returned to his office and tossed his hat on to its usual peg. He felt cheerful. For one thing, his back was very much easier; a couple of drinks that evening and he'd be a new man.

Tait followed Hilary into the Chief Inspector's office. She thought it would be childish to make an issue of his presence, even though what she had to tell the DCI was no concern of the regional crime squad. Quantrill seemed to have forgotten that Tait was no longer a member of his team, and the Inspector decided not to draw immediate attention to himself. He wanted very much to take part in this investigation too.

Hilary repeated what Jen Arrowsmith had told her. Quantrill scratched his chin.

'Young Bedford's been looking round the outside of the Old Maltings, and he says there's a side door that Ross Arrowsmith could have used without being seen by his own security guards. So he certainly had the opportunity, on Thursday night, to slip out and run as far as the A135 and back without denting his alibi. But we still haven't established a motive. Wanting Simon to divorce Angela – for whatever reason – is one thing; killing her is monstrously different.'

'True,' admitted Hilary. 'But there's another thing that Jen told me. Ross doesn't care much for his stepmother, Nellie; he rarely goes to see her – Jen told me that last week – and he isn't prepared to give her house-room for her convalescence. And yet according to the staff nurse I talked to at the infirmary, Ross went there in a panic after he returned from Japan and heard that his stepmother was ill. Nellie was in the intensive care unit, and Ross said to the staff nurse, 'She *mustn't* die. You mustn't let her die!'

'Did he?' said Quantrill slowly. 'Did he? And that was on Thursday evening . . .'

'Yes. And there's just one other thing; I'd forgotten it until this afternoon, when you joked about Simon and Harold digging a nuclear fall-out shelter in their garden. Ross's wife told me last week, when I called at their house, that he often does a short jog round their grounds. Well, they're having a swimming pool dug. There's a JCB behind their house, and a great pile of excavated earth – the hole must be at least twenty feet deep. And if the subsoil that's been dug out is blue clay, I should be very much surprised if Ross hasn't collected some of it on his training shoes.'

'*Very* interesting,' said Quantrill. 'I think it's high time I had a word with Ross Arrowsmith. He's at his office, you said? Right, let's go there. His half-brother and Wilkes can wait a bit longer.'

But Simon Arrowsmith and Harold Wilkes were waiting for no one. As Quantrill – followed by Hilary, Tait and Dc Bedford – crossed the front office, they heard raised voices at the desk. A thickset man with cropped sandy hair was demanding loudly to see Miss Hilary Lloyd, and the desk sergeant was bursting his buttons in an attempt to find out the man's name and business.

Hilary went immediately to Harold Wilkes's rescue, touching his arm to draw his attention. He swung round towards her, his face even paler than usual, his eyes alarmed.

'Oh, Miss Lloyd – ' He seized her hand in both of his, trying to convey his urgency. 'Thank God you're here. Simon and I have been at Angela's restaurant this afternoon, clearing up her things. He suddenly grew very angry – not with me, but about something he'd just thought of. He's usually very patient when he wants to tell me something, and writes it down, but he'd worked himself up into such a rage that he just stood and shouted at me. He's difficult to lip-read, but I'm sure he said Ross's name several times. Then he rushed out, jumped into his car, and drove off.'

'Where?' mouthed Hilary.

'I'm afraid he's gone to have a row with Ross – I think he was saying something about "having things out" with him. Simon's normally a very gentle man, but he can lose his head when he's roused. And the thing is – before he left the restaurant, he went to the cupboard where the carpenters leave their tools. When he ran out, he was carrying a heavy mallet.'

24

The blow had already been struck when the police burst into Ross Arrowsmith's office, closely followed by a scared security guard who kept saying that it wasn't his fault, how was he to know that Simon Arrowsmith wasn't to be admitted? Yes, he'd heard the quarrel, but it was none of his business – a family affair, nothing to do with him.

Detective Constable Bedford pushed him out into the corridor and closed the door on him.

Simon Arrowsmith was standing in the centre of the room, feet planted apart, fists clenched at his side, chest heaving, his eyes as wild as his curly hair. Drops of spittle glistened on his beard. A heavy wooden mallet lay on the carpeted floor.

Ross Arrowsmith was lying sprawled in his chair, his head

flung back. The papers on his desk were spattered with blood. His dark forelock had fallen to one side, revealing his high, balding forehead. His shirt front was soaking red, his face a gory mask.

The detectives stood quite still for a moment, taking in the scene. Then Quantrill stepped forward and put a hand on Simon Arrowsmith's shoulder, moving him aside. Hilary hurried to Ross and gently raised his head.

'Bloody fine mess you've made, haven't you?' the Chief Inspector observed to Simon dispassionately.

Simon shrugged, and loosened his fists. 'Serve him right,' he growled through his beard. 'Serve the bastard right – '

A choking sound came from Ross Arrowsmith's throat. It was followed by a gurgle of protest. Hilary Lloyd, SRN, was raising him to a sitting position, at the same time pinching the soft part of his nose between her forefinger and thumb. 'Breathe through your mouth,' she instructed him. 'Yes, I know your nose hurts – it's bound to, after being thumped. It doesn't feel as though it's broken, though. Yes, I'm sorry, but I must keep on pinching. This is the only way to stop the bleeding – if you put your head back you might inhale blood and asphyxiate yourself. Keep on breathing through your mouth . . . and bend forward. That's right . . . good. Now, prop your elbow on your knee, and do the pinching yourself . . . good . . . never mind the pain, just pinch firmly and the flow of blood will stop . . .'

She stood back, her hands dabbled with blood, and took a critical look at her patient. He was groaning, but doing as he was told. 'Where can I wash?' she asked Simon.

'Private suite,' he muttered, indicating a door at the side of the office. Hilary disappeared through it.

'What was the mallet for?' Tait asked, picking it up from the carpet. The only marks on the heavy head were those of legitimate use.

Simon relaxed his aggressive stance and sucked his fist. 'To break down the door if necessary. I didn't think the murdering devil would have the guts to let me in.'

Ross raised his head and unclamped his nose. 'I've already told you – ' he began, but another flow of blood silenced him.

He gasped and gripped his nose and bent his head forward again. Hilary, returning from his suite, put a damp towel into his free hand, and he wiped the blood away from his mouth.

'We shall want to hear from you later, Mr Arrowsmith,' said Quantrill. 'At the moment we're talking to your brother.'

'He's dot by brother,' Ross mumbled, still pinching his nose. 'He's by half-brother.'

'And *that*'s why you murdered my wife!' Simon's jaw tightened; so did his fists. 'Why don't you admit it? It's perfectly obvious to me, now. It'll be obvious to the police, too, when I tell them.'

He turned to the Chief Inspector. 'I was too upset by Angela's death to think clearly. I couldn't imagine why anyone could possibly hate her enough to kill her. Oh, I knew Ross didn't like her. He's always been an unsympathetic man, and he doesn't consider what a difficult life poor Angie had when she was a single parent. But it never occurred to me that he would harm her – until I remembered, this afternoon, what a fuss he made over my mother when he thought she was dying.

'But Ross doesn't care a rap for my mother. I suppose he resents her, for having taken his own mother's place. He never bothers to go to see her – so why should he worry if she dies? And thinking about it, I realised that it could only be because he knows that I shall inherit her property.'

'The house and land at Upper Wickford?' Quantrill asked.

'Yes. It was just about all that Dad had. He didn't make a will. There was no need, because he knew that the house would automatically go to his widow, and that was what he wanted. Mother's since made a will, and naturally she's left everything to me. Why not? I'm her only child. Even if she hadn't made a will, the house would still come to me because I'm her next-of-kin.'

'That's the law, on intestacy,' agreed Tait. 'My mother's a widow,' he told Quantrill, 'and I read it up when my father died. It can give rise to terrible bitterness when there's a second marriage, because in practice it means that the children of the first marriage inherit nothing.'

Ross Arrowsmith sat up, his nose puffy, his nostrils blood-rimmed. 'For God's sake – ' he said angrily. He shovelled a handful of drooping hair off his forehead. 'Doesn't it occur to any of you that I'm not exactly in need of money? Why on earth should I begrudge Simon his inheritance? He's welcome to it.'

'But Angela wasn't welcome to it, was she?' Simon spat. 'That's why you've been trying to persuade me to divorce her, because you didn't like her and didn't want her to have any share in Dad's property. And when you got home from Japan on Thursday and thought my mother was dying, you decided to take matters into your own hands. You killed Angela, didn't you? Come on, God damn you, admit it or I'll – '

Tait and Bedford seized Simon's arms to prevent him from launching another blow. 'That'll do,' said Tait. 'Cool it.'

'Dc Bedford – take Mr Simon Arrowsmith to another office,' said the Chief Inspector, 'and get a statement about this incident. Inspector Tait will come with you.'

Inspector Tait was displeased. He didn't want to miss a thing. But being given an opportunity to find out more about Simon Arrowsmith, the husband of the murdered woman, was infinitely better than being excluded from the case completely. He went without a murmur.

Ross Arrowsmith stood up, clutching the bloodstained towel, and spoke to the Chief Inspector with complete assurance.

'You do realise,' he said, 'that my half-brother's bluffing? He's trying to blame me to divert your attention from himself. What he says about the Upper Wickford property is perfectly true – it'll go to him when his mother dies. But as I said, I don't really mind. I don't need the house, or the money it would fetch in a sale, either.'

'But the property has a great sentimental value for you, hasn't it, Mr Arrowsmith?' said Hilary. 'I noticed when I fetched the towel that you have a photograph of the house in your private rooms.'

Ross ignored her. 'The old place has very happy associations for me, certainly,' he told Quantrill. 'But that's no problem. The house needs a great deal of money spending on it, and Simon will be only too glad to sell. I decided long ago that I'll buy the property from him as soon as he inherits it. I'll gladly pay full market value, and then restore the house for one or other of my children. So his allegation that I killed his wife to prevent her having the property is a patent lie.

'It's Simon himself who had the urgent motive to kill her. He knew that he was too weak to resist her demands – he's already hopelessly in debt through her folly. When he thought his mother was dying, he realised that Angela would make him sell the property and give her the money for her restaurant . . . in effect, she'd make him throw it away. But his inheritance is the only thing that'll save him from financial ruin, and so he daren't let her get her hands on it. He took the only possible way out, and killed her himself. And now he's staged this little charade, with the help of his brother-in-law, to try to throw the blame on me.'

Quantrill said nothing. He got up and began to wander round the room, his hands in his pockets, looking. Ross followed him warily with his eyes.

'Do you want to prefer any charges against your half-brother?' asked Hilary, diverting his attention. 'The assault,' she reminded him as Quantrill sidestepped, neatly for so big a man, into Ross's suite.

'What? No, I don't want to charge Simon – you're the ones who should be charging him, with murder. I say, do you mind?' He hurried angrily after the Chief Inspector. 'These rooms are private – '

'And very nice too,' said Quantrill. From an entrance lobby, doors opened on to a shower room, a kitchen, and a sitting room with a sofa bed. The rooms were small, but built-in furniture made them seem more spacious. Professing his genuine admiration of the craftsman's fitments, Quantrill opened two cupboard doors before he found the wardrobe he was looking for.

'Ah.' Remembering, for his back's sake, to bend from the knees, he lifted out a pair of training shoes. 'I see you do a bit of jogging from here, as well as from home. And you keep a track suit here, too.' He stood up, took out the garment, looked it over back and front, inspected the maker's label, and nodded his approval.

'Very good exercise, jogging. I sometimes think I ought to take it up myself, but I know my limitations. I'd be on my knees before I'd gone a couple of hundred yards. Whereas you're fit – you can run for miles with no trouble at all, I imagine? From here to the A135 and back would be no problem for you, Mr Arrowsmith, would it?'

Ross pushed aside his flopping hair and dabbed his face gingerly with his stained towel. He said nothing.

'And this is the photograph you mentioned, is it, Hilary?' Moving into the sitting room, Quantrill studied a framed enlargement of a black-and-white snapshot. The photograph was at least thirty years old, to judge by the clothes of the woman and the small boy who stood hand in hand in a summer garden. The house behind them was recognisable as Simon's mother's.

'You and your own mother, Mr Arrowsmith?' Quantrill asked. 'Yes, I can see the resemblance. You must have been – what, five or six at the time? I can remember being that age. I was lucky, like you. I had a very happy country childhood. It gives you a marvellous start, but it does have one big snag: nothing else, in the whole of your life, ever seems to match up to it. It's impossible ever to be quite so happy again. Don't you find that?'

Ross still said nothing. With his towel clutched in his hand, he walked back into his office and stood staring out of the window.

Quantrill followed him. 'I believe your mother died when you were still a boy. That was sad. That makes it much more difficult for you to get over your happy childhood. Because it's only as you grow up that you realise how hard life was for ordinary women of our parents' generation – particularly in the country in those days, with no basic facilities at all, not even water on tap. When you think about it – when you remember it – their lives were drudgery from morning until night. But even so, the best of them managed to keep their families happy – and that's something it's good to be able to repay, as you grow up. I know that's how I've always felt. It gave me a great sense of satisfaction, to be able to do a bit to make my mother's last years as comfortable as possible.'

He brushed aside the guilt that assailed him whenever he thought about the way he'd neglected her, regardless of all that she'd done for him. This was no time for remembering that he rarely managed to put his good intentions into practice.

'But that satisfaction's been denied you, Mr Arrowsmith, hasn't it?' he went on. 'Here you are, having made more money than most of us dream of – and yet you never had a chance to repay your mother for all the love and devotion she gave you. It's hard. It's a hard thing for you to have to live with, especially if you loved her in return. And you did love her, didn't you? I can see that in the photograph.'

He could tell from the rigidity of Ross Arrowsmith's neck and shoulders that he had found the right target. Ross was moved. His childhood memories affected him so deeply that it was all he could do not to weep. Perhaps he was weeping.

'Do you remember washdays?' said Quantrill softly, joining him at the window. Dusk was beginning to blot the light out of the sky; in a thousand labour-saving homes, the inhabitants of latter-day Breckham Market were settling down to an evening of electronic entertainment. 'Do you remember the coal-fired coppers where our mothers boiled all the sheets and towels and shirts? And those wickedly heavy old mangles?'

'Winters were terrible . . .' offered Ross hoarsely, still staring out of the window. 'Oh, not for me. I was loved and protected. But my mother had to work with Dad on his smallholding – both of them needed to labour on it to scrape together enough money to keep us, and to pay the mortgage. My mother had a cruel time every winter. She was out there in the field picking sprouts when the plants were hard with ice. Her fingers were chapped to the bone, but she never complained. And then she'd come back and do the washing, just as you said. But our copper fire would never burn properly. I've seen her on her hands and knees in the bitterly cold wash-house, the brick floor wet with soapsuds and coal dust, blowing her lungs out to try to keep the fire going . . . I've seen her weeping over that bloody copper fire . . . And when she'd finally hauled the wet clothes out of the copper into the tub, she'd rub to get them clean until her fingers bled. Then she'd tie strips of rag round her fingers before she did the mangling and hung the linen out, so as to keep the blood off the clean sheets . . .'

'I remember,' Quantrill agreed quietly. 'All that work, all that hardship, all that scrimping and saving to pay off the mortgage: no holidays, always second-hand clothes . . . but unlike my mother, yours didn't live long enough to benefit from owning the family home.

'All the benefit of ownership would have gone to Angela instead, wouldn't it? What a marvellous time she'd have had, spending the money from the sale of the property! Clothes, drink, cars, holidays in the Caribbean – not to mention flaunting herself at her night club. Was that what your poor mother worked her fingers to the bone for? So that a bitch like Angela could have a good time? My God, it's enough to make any son bitter!'

Ross Arrowsmith was too choked to speak. He pressed the towel against his nose, although the bleeding had stopped.

'But then, I don't suppose your mother ever expected any benefit,' Quantrill went on, 'apart from the satisfaction of giving you a good start in life. I'm sure she'd have been tremendously proud of what you've achieved. But look at it this way, Ross. Would she still be proud of you, if she knew what you did last Thursday night? Would she be proud to know that you were so resentful on her behalf that you'd do anything – anything at all – to prevent Angela from getting her hands on the property? Would your mother really have wanted you to commit murder for her sake?'

Ross Arrowsmith let his towel fall. 'You bastard . . .' he said slowly. He turned to the Chief Inspector. The lower half of his face was blotched with dried blood, his eyes were red-rimmed. 'You bastard, trying to trick me with your sympathy! Well, you've guessed wrong. You're quite right about my reason for wanting Simon to divorce the woman, but you've taken your theory one giant step too far. You can't adduce resentment as a motive for murder!'

'Why not?' said Quantrill. 'Resentment and nostalgia make a potent combination.'

'It's the most far-fetched allegation I've ever heard,' said Ross disdainfully. 'Would I – a man in my position, with a happy family of my own – risk everything for a reason like that?'

'Yes,' said Quantrill. 'Because you're a clever man, and you were sure you could get away with it. You knew that Angela had already been threatened by someone else. So you assumed that you'd never be suspected, as long as you covered your tracks thoroughly and set up a convincing alibi. But you weren't quite as thorough as you imagined – you left some evidence at the scene of the crime. Sergeant Lloyd?'

She produced the plastic bags into which she had put the clothing that Quantrill had taken from Ross's wardrobe.

'One pair of training shoes,' she said briskly, 'with dried blue clay on the welt; a lump of dried blue clay was found in Angela Arrowsmith's car. And one dark blue track suit, according to the label 80% cotton; similar dark blue fibres were also found in Angela's car. Both the shoes and the track suit are still slightly damp. On the night of Angela's murder, it poured with rain.'

'You call that evidence?' scoffed Ross. 'There was rain yesterday evening too, you know. And there's nothing exclusive about my track suit – as you've seen from the label, I bought this one at Marks and Spencer. Thousands of people wear them. As for the mud: everyone who lives in Suffolk has mud on their shoes.'

'This evidence will do, to begin with,' said Quantrill. 'And the other interesting item from Mr Arrowsmith's private room, Sergeant Lloyd?'

She placed on the desk a framed copy of a poem by A. E. Housman. It had hung beside the photograph of the boy Ross and his mother.

Into my heart an air that kills
From yon far country blows:
What are those blue remembered hills,
What spires, what farms are those?

That is the land of lost content,
I see it shining plain,

185

The happy highways where I went
And cannot come again.

Ross protested. A copy of a poem couldn't possibly be used against him. The phrase 'an air that kills' was just a figure of speech – the poet hadn't intended it literally. And no, he himself hadn't taken it literally. Of course not. The police had no grounds whatsoever for accusing him of murder.

But they had. There was still a great deal of work to be done on the case, but the Chief Inspector already had sufficient hard evidence to make an arrest.

Quantrill had been lucky. He had found, on Ross Arrowsmith's track suit, exactly what he had hoped for: two long golden hairs. They were clinging to the fabric of the upper arm, where Angela's head would have rested as her murderer carried her semi-conscious body from her car to the edge of the A135 before running her over.

Hairs, unlike fingerprints, are not positively identifiable. No expert witness can say that they belong without doubt to any particular person. But frequent chemical treatment can make them sufficiently distinctive to enable an expert witness for the prosecution to satisfy a jury as to their origin: and Angela Arrowsmith was a woman who for years had kept changing the colour of her hair.

25

28 September; 11.15 on a radiant Saturday morning, and the bells of St Botolph's church were pealing in celebration of the marriage of Woman Police Constable Patricia Anne Hopkins and Detective Chief Superintendent William George Mancroft.

The one hundred and fifty adult guests, with a small vocal accompaniment of toddlers, streamed out through the south porch to wait in their finery among the lichened gravestones for the bridal party to emerge. Among those present, Mrs Douglas

Quantrill and her younger daughter Alison, both becomingly dressed and hatted, edged their way to a position from which they would have an uninterrupted view as the photographs were taken.

'Thank goodness your father's back's better,' said Molly, 'or he wouldn't have been able to help.'

'Poor Dad,' said Alison. 'I bet he'd prefer lumbago.'

'Of course he wouldn't! I'm sure he's only too glad to give the Chief Superintendent some support. Look, that must be Mr Mancroft's brother, with his ankle in plaster – such a shame that he should have fractured it, and only the day before the wedding, too. What a piece of luck that he's a big man, and your father could wear the morning suit he'd hired . . . Oh, here they come!'

Glowing with excitement, and slightly unsteady on her un-accustomedly high heels, Molly watched eagerly as the bridal party moved from the shade of the porch into the sunlight. The elegant bride wore a long dress of oyster-coloured Thai silk with a matching hat, and carried a bouquet of rosebuds, freesias and stephanotis; but Molly, usually avid for such details, could spare her only a glance.

'Doesn't your father look handsome?' she sighed, her eyes on the substitute best man. 'I always knew that a tail coat and top hat would suit him . . .' She blinked away a prickle of tears as she thought of her own makeshift wedding, a hurriedly arranged formality held in a registry office because she was pregnant and Douggie, a national service aircraftsman in the RAF, was about to be posted to Germany.

At the time, she'd been too greatly relieved that he was marrying her at all to mind that her girlish dreams of a proper white wedding in church had been shattered. It was only later, and particularly when she attended other weddings, that she had come to feel a sense of loss. But at least she could compensate through her own daughters: Jennifer and Alison would have weddings every bit as elaborate as Patsy's, and Douggie would wear morning dress whether he liked it or not. Having done so for Patsy's wedding, he could hardly refuse when he became the father of the bride.

Molly glanced speculatively at her daughter. She wondered whether Alison's eagerness to attend this wedding had anything to do with the fact that Martin Tait would be a fellow guest. True, Alison had seemed completely indifferent to the overtures he had made to her eighteen months ago; but they were both still unattached, as far as Molly knew, and in her opinion they would make an ideal couple.

'Have you seen Martin yet, dear?' she said, trying to sound casual. But Alison's immediate concern was for her father. Though he was smiling for the photographer he looked uneasy.

'Poor old Dad,' said Alison. 'He must be dreading the prospect of making a speech at the reception.'

'It won't hurt him,' said Molly. She spoke without vindictiveness, but her pleasure at seeing her husband in morning dress was spiced by her knowledge of what he must be feeling. She wasn't as unaware of his emotions as he liked to think – she'd known for years that he had an eye for Patsy Hopkins. Bad enough for him, then, that the shapely policewoman would be moving to Yarchester immediately after her wedding, and taking her long legs with her; but being asked at short notice to play a part in the ceremony of marrying her to his boss was bound to cause him additional vexation, and Molly intended to enjoy his discomfort to the full.

Meanwhile, there was something of more positive importance to be pursued. 'Have you seen Martin Tait yet, dear?' she repeated.

'He's over there,' said Alison, in a carefully neutral voice. 'On the other side of the path, just behind the dark girl in the coral outfit. I heard someone saying that she's Dad's new detective sergeant.'

'Which one? Where?' demanded Molly, standing precariously on tiptoe. She hadn't yet met Hilary Lloyd. Douggie had said very little about her, and Molly couldn't decide whether or not the omission was significant. She stared challengingly at the female detective, trying to see her through her husband's eyes; and in doing so, she gradually relaxed.

Sergeant Lloyd was not particularly attractive. Her dress and hat were stylish, but she had what seemed to be a permanent frown. She was too thin, and her legs were not as long as Patsy's. Foolishly susceptible though Douggie could be, there was nothing about his new sergeant that was likely to turn his head.

That was all right, then, thought Molly comfortably.

Hilary was looking with admiration at the bride's dress. She turned to share her pleasure with Martin Tait, by way of apology for having snubbed him when they were last together. He had tried to persuade her to have supper with him, on that euphoric evening when they'd helped to crack both the A135 and the Arrowsmith murders; but the venue he'd suggested was her flat, and Hilary preferred to issue her own invitations.

'Doesn't she look lovely, Martin?' she said of the bride.

'Yes,' mumbled Tait, with a humility that took him entirely by surprise. He wasn't looking at Patsy, nor yet at Hilary; one glimpse of Alison Quantrill, more confident and even prettier than she'd been last year, and he'd lost all interest in older women.

1.15 p.m., and in the Rights of Man, Breckham Market's leading hotel, the wedding breakfast had been eaten, the speeches made, the toasts drunk and the cake cut. Formalities over, the bride and bridegroom began to circulate among their guests. The best man, looking slightly sheepish, rejoined his wife; Martin Tait and Alison Quantrill gravitated towards each other, and Harry Colman, his Prince Consort whiskers perky with pleasure, sought out Hilary Lloyd.

He greeted her with a kiss on the cheek, a compliment on her dress, and congratulations on the excellent start she had made in the Breckham Market division.

'Thank you, Harry. Yes, I'm very pleased with the way those two enquiries went.'

She pushed from her mind the persistently recurring image of Jen Arrowsmith, unaware that she had already been persuaded to betray her husband, joking to her daughter that they would in future have to watch what they were saying in front of their friend Hilary. So much for the value of a police officer's friendship; so much for a police officer's chances of making friends at all, outside the force.

Harry Colman observed the bleakness of her expression, and misinterpreted it. 'I hope your new boss isn't cramping your initiative?'

'What?' Then her face cleared: 'Oh, no. No, we seem to have set up quite a reasonable working relationship.'

Douglas Quantrill had just moved through the crowds into Harry's view, looking for someone; his wife, who had been close behind him, paused to take an opportunity to speak to the bride. Drawing Hilary's attention to Quantrill, Harry said, 'That was a very neat speech that Doug made, wasn't it?'

'Very,' she agreed. 'Though I wasn't surprised, after hearing him talk Ross Arrowsmith to the brink of making a confession. I wish you'd heard him. It was an impressive performance.'

Harry chuckled. 'I can believe it. A good detective – and Doug *is* good – needs to be able to rise to an occasion. And how do you think he looks, in morning dress?'

Hilary glanced at Quantrill again, her scar puckering her forehead into what could be mistaken for a frown. 'I think,' she said, 'that he looks really rather distinguished.'

Then she turned back to Harry Colman. 'Oh, it's good to see you again! I've missed you, you know – ' She gave him one of her rare, warm, wholehearted smiles.

'*Doesn't* she look lovely?' said Molly Quantrill, returning to her husband's side and unkindly directing his attention to the new and completely unattainable Mrs Mancroft. She glanced up at Douglas – who, as she knew, hated to be called Douggie – and tried to interpret his expression: slightly bemused, she thought, but definitely hankering.

Exasperated, Molly pinched his arm. With a Japanese smile on her face for the benefit of the assembly, she hissed at him out of the corner of her mouth, 'Pull yourself together, Doug Quantrill, for goodness sake! It's no use your mooning after her like that, she's married now – '

But Quantrill hadn't hankered after Patsy Hopkins for a week or more.